'The Ottoman Motel is a novel about fear and loss, and human fallibility. With this assured, emotionally sophisticated debut, Christopher Currie proves himself to be one of the brightest young novelists in Australia.'

South East Advertiser

'Aussie newcomer Currie unveils a splendid mystery.'

Weekend Gold Coast Bulletin

'This debut novel evokes small-town Australia perfectly with that curious mixture of oddballs and distrust . . . Currie effortlessly inhabits a child's mind and while The Ottoman Motel is an intriguing mystery, it also stands out as a moving study of childhood fear and loss. I look forward to more from this author.'

Sunday Star Times

Scottish Borders Library Service

3 4144 0091 3437 6

'Vividly and engagingly written, THE OTTOMAN
MOTEL speeds the reader through a plot full of suprising
twists and turns. Small-town Australia at its most sinister.'
Jane Rogers, author of The Testament of Jessie Lamb
Shortlisted, Commonwealth Book Prize, 2012
Shortlisted, Queensland Literary Awards, 2012

'Currie, reaching into the dark corners of the human
psyche, has produced a disturbing and exhilarating thriller. The novel plays with the genre, flitting from small-
town mystery to an authentic and moving exposition
on the loss of childhood innocence. His depiction of the
moment when childhood wonder collides with the brutal
and careless banality of the adult world is beautifully ren-
dered, as is his uncanny ability to inhabit a child's mind.
Read it before your next excursion into the Australian
countryside. You won't view our myriad of little towns
and hamlets quite the same way again. A bold, assured
and exciting debut.'
Matt Condon, author of The Motorcycle Café,
Lime Bar, Mulligan: on being a hack golfer

'Currie gets the blurring of the creepy-friendly small town just right: as if an eleven-year-old boy walked into his own Wake In Fright.'

Malcolm Knox, author of
Fierce Focus and The Captains

'The Ottoman Motel is an assured debut.'

Canberra Times

'Chris Currie has written an excellent first novel in The Ottoman Motel, part thriller, part crime story and part analysis of the meaning of loss, all told through the eyes of a small boy.'

Otago Daily Times

'The debut novel is one the 28-year-old author should be proud of, with its vivid descriptions, excellent character development and knack of getting the reader turning the pages faster, trying to find out what happens next.'

Hobart Mercury & Sunday Herald

'. . . an engrossing and deeply creepy read.'

Age

THE OTTOMAN MOTEL

Christopher Currie

SCOTTISH BORDER COUNCIL LIBRARY INFORMATION SERVICES	
ACCESSION NO.	CLASS NO.
3414400 9134376	AF

SANDSTONEPRESS
HIGHLAND | SCOTLAND

First published in Great Britain by
Sandstone Press Ltd
One High Street
Dingwall
Ross-shire
IV15 9WJ
Scotland.

www.sandstonepress.com

All rights reserved.
No part of this publication may be reproduced,
stored or transmitted in any form without the express
written permission of the publisher.

© Christopher Currie 2013

The moral right of Christopher Currie to be recognised as
the author of this work has been asserted in accordance with the
Copyright, Design and Patent Act, 1988.

The publisher acknowledges subsidy from
Creative Scotland towards publication of this volume.

ISBN: 978-1-908737-19-9
ISBN e: 978-1-908737-20-5

Cover design by Guilherme Gustavo Condeixa
Typeset by Iolaire Typesetting, Newtonmore
Printed and bound by TOTEM, Poland

SCOTTISH BORDERS COUNCIL
LIBRARY &
INFORMATION SERVICES

❧

Simon's cheek stung. The winter sun had followed him all morning, baking his idle passenger skin, giving him slow seatbelt burns through his T-shirt. He slipped lower in his seat, adjusting his head below the window until the land disappeared. He watched power lines snaking black against the sky, their tension changing, forking and converging. He counted the thick tick of power poles, each one noted by pressing his tongue against the roof of his mouth.

The car passed some trees and Simon closed his eyes to let a projector-flicker of sun and shadow stutter his vision. He smelled, suddenly, the tang of new leather. His mother's voice floated from the front seat. He peered through his eyelashes.

'Can you sit up, Simon?'

He didn't move. It was painful, the seatbelt buckle digging at his waist, but he waited.

'Sweetie?'

Simon's mother turned around and placed a hand on his knee. Simon felt one of the scars on his leg begin to buzz. That strange feeling, where the skin was numb, but itchy. He heaved himself up, making a show of vast effort, letting his head swing alarmingly on his shoulders. His mother stared past him, out the back window. 'Can't have the police pull us over, can we?' she said, already turning back to her seat. Simon leant his head against the

1

window. He peered at the small sliver of his father's face visible between the headrests, the portion of skin between temple and beard that was white like milk.

A flat voice slid into the silence: Turn left in five. Hundred. Metres.

Simon's mother sighed.

'You want me to turn it off?' said Simon's father.

'No.' Simon's mother plucked a loose thread from her sleeve with a violent tug.

'I just thought, with the sighing—'

'No, it's just—do we need it on?'

'How else am I supposed to find this place?'

'Seriously, Bill? This place?' She made quote marks in the air. 'Just leave it on, I don't care.'

'Well, Louise, clearly—' Simon's father lifted his left hand. 'Forget it.'

Simon turned away, back to the window, allowing his eyes to slip from focus. He let the road's bumps and dips turn to wavering lines, made fences and reflector posts become repeating patterns. The sky and grass and hills melted into easy flowing colours. Simon liked how things became simpler when you sped them up, when you just let them go by.

The trip. His parents had talked—and actively avoided talking—about nothing else all week. Arguments about departure dates and stopovers and work schedules, hardly mentioning why they were actually going. It had been Simon who'd taken the call in the first place. In their new house, with the answering machine not yet connected. The phone's clammy electronic bell going on and on, bouncing off the bare walls. The voice, at first, he didn't even recognise. It's Iris, Simon. It's Grandma.

Late afternoon now, the sun drawing lower, inescapable. Simon picked crumbs from between the creases in his shorts. Stale cake from a roadhouse they'd stopped at earlier, where he'd drunk a cup of weak tea, suffered a series of family photos in the parking lot. The rest of the day a procession of cluster-housed coastal towns summed up by their billboards: Welcome flashing past and Thanks for Visiting disappearing behind.

'Can we get some lunch soon?' Simon asked.

His father huffed and cleared his throat. 'We'll have something when we get there.'

'Won't be long now sweetie.' His mother had an open magazine in her lap. She tore open a perfume sample, sniffed at it. 'Well,' she said. 'They've gone downhill.' She held it up so Simon's father could smell it.

'Cost cutting,' he said. 'Inferior ingredients, inferior product.'

'Simon.' His mother twisted around in her seat. 'Smell this. It's terrible.'

Simon leaned forward and took in the scent, nodding. It smelled like perfume as far as he was concerned. His parents' business was to promote beauty products, and they approached it with dogged and cold devotion. Every product was the result of a long, unromantic list of ingredients, fragrances broken down into carbon chains and chemical processes. Each new product tried to recreate something it had no right to be. Simon preferred the smells of real things: baking bread, deep cold dirt. He wondered, sometimes, about the smell of truly plain skin.

A sign appeared as the car rounded a turn. It was a clean sign, smaller and simpler than the others he had seen. All it said, in large blue letters, was Reception. No

3

Hello or Hope You Enjoy Your Stay. Just Reception. This, Simon knew, was their destination. The car began to climb a hill, beyond whose crest was simply blank sky. Simon flicked the button to draw his window down and put his head out. As the wind bent his eyelashes back, he noticed flecks of sand at the roadside. They crested the hill, and there was the ocean. Not blue, but rather a pale grey stripe across the horizon. The town appeared, just as grey, little flat clumps of buildings fanning out towards the water. A piece of land stuck out abruptly from the centre of the town, a foot-shaped bluff, pointing. The place struck Simon as particularly lifeless. A ghost town, perhaps.

The car dipped down into the valley and Simon heard the strange strangled beeping of an appliance in distress.

'Bloody hell.' His father tapped the GPS screen.

'Bill,' said Simon's mother. 'Language.'

'We've only had the thing two weeks and it's conking out. No range? What does that mean?'

'Maybe it means we're out of range.'

'Well, yeah, but the guy said it had 99 per cent coverage.'

'I guess we're in the one per cent then, Bill.'

Simon's mother only called his father by his first name when she was fed up with him. Usually, it was sweetie or honey or, worse, babe.

Simon's father pulled the car to the side of the road, the tyres sinking slightly into the sandy earth. 'Just going to fix this up,' he said to no one in particular. He took the GPS out of its holster. 'If I restart it, maybe.'

'Do you have to?' Simon's mother sounded even more annoyed now. 'The town's just straight ahead.'

4

'I like to know where I'm going. The address is already plugged into the memory.'

'Let's just stop and ask somewhere, can we?'

Simon let his mind wander. It was skill he practised: phasing out his parents' words, blurring the tones of their voices. Focusing instead on something far-off, something unrelated. While the GPS squabble continued, a white shape a little way down the road snagged Simon's eye. A building, a barn, like dozens he had seen that morning. What made it unusual, though, were the rows of gum trees standing like sentries on each side of it. All you could see from the road was stripes of white steel in between the trees.

'There's a farm or something,' he said. 'Just down there.'

His mother snapped her head around. She had a look on her face that Simon knew well, like when you woke up suddenly and weren't quite sure where you were. She collected herself. 'What was that, sweetie?'

'There's a farm just down there,' said Simon, pointing. 'Maybe they can help us.'

Simon's father cleared his throat again. He'd put the dead GPS back in its holster. 'Yes,' he said from his seat. 'Talk to a local. Maybe they'll know about this network problem.' He started up the car. 'Seatbelts on.'

As they drew closer to the barn, Simon noticed a small cottage hidden at the other side. The yard was littered with car parts, a large trailer sitting at the other side of the house, nose tipped upwards. Simon's father parked and switched off the engine. He opened his door and the thick smell of ocean air swirled into the car. It was colder than Simon had expected.

'Come on,' said his mother, unbuckling her seatbelt, reaching back to touch Simon on the leg. His scars tingled.

5

His father had begun to stalk the yard in giant strides, palms pressed into the small of his back, elbows out in wings like a pregnant woman. The red in his beard flared in the low sun. Simon opened his door in time to hear his father say, 'Nice feeling. Quiet.'

Simon's mother left one hand on the car door. 'Is anyone home, though?'

Simon's father strode up to the front door of the house and knocked. Simon felt something flicker in his stomach. A wide spider web flailed in one of the trees by the barn, shimmering reflections metres into the air. There was hardly any wind, but it kept waving.

Simon's father waited a moment, then knocked again. 'No one's here,' he shouted.

'Let's keep going,' said Simon's mother. 'Try somewhere in town.' Simon noticed she had taken off her shoes. She rubbed one foot with the other, stretched out her toes.

'Maybe I'll try the shed.'

'It's okay, Bill, there's probably no one here.'

'Won't hurt to try.' He stepped over a pile of blue netting by the door. 'Might just be working, or something.'

Simon shifted his gaze to the shed. It was much newer-looking than the house, much more modern. It had a roller door at the front of it, like a garage might, but the door was about three times as big. Simon noticed the door wasn't closed all the way to the ground.

'Quite a structure,' said Simon's father. He hit it with the side of his palm. It made a deep clang.

Simon's mother walked towards the shed. 'Bill, that's someone's property.'

'It's solid,' he said, grinning. 'It can take it.' He peered under the door. 'Hello?'

6

Simon was constantly bemused by the way his father treated the world as if it was always glad to see him. He'd told Simon often about his early working days, cold-calling for the company. Knocking on strangers' doors, 'charming' people into buying cosmetics.

Simon's father hooked his hands under the door. 'Simon, give me a hand, can you?'

'Bill, I don't think—'

'We're in the country, Louise. Different rules.' He beckoned Simon over, nodding his head. 'We'll just get this up.'

Simon reluctantly put his hands under the door. His fingers felt dust.

'On three—'

They began hauling up the door. A mechanism squealed horribly somewhere inside. The door was heavy, but eventually began to yield. Simon felt his shoulders stretching in their sockets.

Simon's mother came over. 'Bill, this isn't right!'

Simon's father just grimaced. 'Just a little more.' His cheeks had turned almost crimson, and Simon was close enough to see moisture at the corners of his eyes.

'This is crazy.' Simon's mother had raised her voice. 'Can you just stop for a second and think?'

The door reached Simon's eye line and he could suddenly see what was inside: rows of big shiny tin cans, the kind his mum sometimes got with juice inside, but missing the label. There were maybe hundreds of them, up on shelves like in a supermarket. A spiky black shadow caught his eye. When he tried to follow it, the shape ran out of view. Maybe, he thought, it was the spider, missing from its web. He was about to duck under the door when

7

he felt a hand land painfully on his shoulder. 'Ow!' He twisted his neck to see his mother's fake nails digging into him. 'Why are you—?' He stopped.

A man was standing behind his mother. He had on in dirty yellow overalls, slung up high around his armpits. He was old— Simon thought nearly a grandpa's age— but his cheeks were ridged red with ill-conquered acne. 'Help you?' he said.

Simon's father stood up, smiling. 'Oh, hi. We were just—' He dusted his hands off on his jeans. 'We were just looking for directions.'

'In my shed?'

Simon's father laughed nervously. 'Well, we knocked on your door, and didn't get an answer.'

'We're just passing through,' said Simon's mother. 'We didn't mean to invade your—' she gestured vaguely at the shed, 'but my husband can be a bit ... unthinking.'

'Bill Sawyer,' said Simon's father. He stuck out his hand. 'Nice structure you've got here.' He thumped the shed's wall again.

'Don't really use it that much,' said the man. 'Just takes up room mainly.' He smiled grimly and shook hands with Simon's father. 'Name's Tarden,' he said. 'Jack Tarden.'

'Pleasure. This is my wife, Louise. And my young fella, Simon.' Simon felt his father's hands in his hair. Simon knew he was just putting on an act for Jack Tarden. Going blokey.

'Pleased to meet you, Simon,' said Tarden. 'Looks like you're a bit of an explorer.'

Simon realised he had dirt all down his T-shirt. He brushed it off quickly. He didn't think he liked this man.

'Anyway,' said Simon's mother, checking her watch.

8

'We should be on our way. We've got some time to make up, I'd say.'

Tarden looked confused. 'You wanted directions, though?'

'Doesn't matter,' said Simon's mother. 'We'll find our way. We need to stop somewhere for a meal, anyway.'

'Hold on,' said Simon's father. 'We just need to get to—' he dug his phone from his pocket. 'Got it in an email. Just need to ... dammit!' He held his phone up in the air. 'No mobile coverage either?'

'You've come to the wrong place if you want reception,' said Tarden. He chuckled briefly at what was evidently a well-worn joke.

'You didn't write down the address, Bill?'

Simon's father scratched his neck vigorously. 'I emailed it all to myself,' he said quietly. 'Thought it would be easier to have it all in once place.'

'You said you brought it with you.'

Simon's father waggled his phone. 'I did.'

Tarden laughed again, rather too hard, Simon thought. 'Where is it you need to get to?'

'A motel,' said Simon's mother. 'I don't know which one.'

'Strange name, though,' said Simon's father, still pressing buttons on his phone.

Tarden rocked on his heels. 'Probably the Ottoman,' he said.

'That rings a bell,' said Simon's father. 'Yes.'

'Well luckily,' said Tarden, 'that's just where I was about to go. Why don't you follow me into town?'

Simon's mother turned on her heel and silently walked back to the car.

9

His father shrugged and ruffled Simon's hair again. 'Much appreciated, Jack. Very community minded.'

Simon slipped from his father's grasp and walked off to join his mother. Somehow, this trip was going even worse than he'd expected it to.

They followed Tarden's ute—burnt yellow with rust stains like continents—the five minutes to the centre of town, Simon's mother seeming more anxious with every minute, his father's confidence restoring itself in equal measure. The main street was much as Simon thought it would be. Everything worn, washed out. A nature strip ran down the middle of the street, thatched with dry grass, flanked sporadically on either side with cars parked nose-first at identical angles. There were no lines anywhere on the road, and Simon wondered how everyone knew which angle to park at. All the buildings around them were old: some of them stone, most of them slatted timber, two storeys high, bulging with spindly balconies. As the car passed, Simon tried to make out what was in the window of each shop, but they all seemed fogged up or not cleaned properly. Many were obviously empty.

Tarden drew his ute in to the kerb. Simon's father pulled in behind and got out of the car. The two men stood together, chatting, their shadows sliding up the side of a large brick building. Simon and his mother got out too, keeping their distance.

'Bit quiet out,' Simon heard Tarden saying. 'Always a bit quiet in the cold months. Should see us in summer. Humming, it is.' He led them up the street, nearly around the corner, to an unremarkable shopfront where a small chalkboard was propped up by the wall. Today's Specials was written at the top in looped, even letters. The specials themselves were too smudged for Simon to read.

'Is this our hotel?' said Simon's mother. She had brought her magazine with her. She was rolling it tightly between her hands.

'Yes,' said Tarden. 'Well, part of it. The hotel's behind. Thought you might want to get a cup of tea or something to eat.'

Simon's mother pushed the rolled-up magazine to her chin. 'Well—'

'Cuppa sounds great,' said Simon's father.

'Our luggage?'

'We'll take that out later, sweetie. I'd quite like a cuppa right now.'

'Okay,' she said. 'Whatever.'

Tarden grinned, swung the door open with a strange flourish of his hand. 'Best food in town,' he said. 'Nearly the only food at the moment.' He motioned for them to enter.

At the mention of food, Simon's stomach twinged. He let his mother usher him inside with no protest. The low hum of conversations met him first. The cafe was nearly full. The view was unexciting, though. Nothing more or less than a coastal milk bar: the long counter with stools down one side, the dragon's breath bain-marie, the faded Frosty Boy sign revolving on its tilted axis. Behind the counter, beside the faded menu, were posters for long-forgotten icypoles. A bleached island suggesting summer. A Coke-themed mirror speckled with white. Tables ran along the right-hand wall, some divided into booths, others standing alone, surrounded by flimsy metal chairs.

12

The smell of a deep fryer filled the air. The only difference from any other milk bar Simon had been in was the glimpse of a darker room behind the counter: panelled wooden walls, the orange arc of old lamps.

'Someone'll be over in a sec to take your order,' said Tarden. 'Have a seat.'

Simon's father nodded his head, slowly, taking in the scene. He smiled. 'Thanks, Jack,' he said. 'For everything.'

Simon thought perhaps everything included not reporting them to the police for trying to break into his shed.

'No worries.' Tarden shook hands with Simon's father and went off to the back of the cafe, where a group of men in the same type of overalls sat eating steaming plates of food, hunched over the table with predatory tension.

Simon's parents silently chose a booth, sliding in side by side. Simon sat down opposite, slumping his chin down into his crossed arms. His parents ignored him, and each other, each picking up a menu. Simon took his arms away and let his head rest sideways on the cool of the plastic table. He stared at the tiny hills and valleys of congealed food, missed by the wipes of a thousand sponges. His parents began to mutter behind their menus. Simon tuned their voices out. Somewhere a radio was playing a song with drums that sounded like explosions.

Simon lifted his sideways eyes to the people sitting at the counter, observing the lost movements of their lower halves. Two sets of legs were shorter than the others: one with brown feet and pink thongs that moved up and down like drawbridges, the other even shorter: swinging silver pants and green gumboots. Simon sat up. The brown feet belonged to a girl who looked about the same age as him. She wore a complicated dress with three layers, each one a different shade of grey, wrapping in and around itself like a seashell. A charcoal woollen jumper was tied around her waist. Her hair was a dark brown, cut in crude, lopsided lengths. She stirred at something in front of her with a fork, her back unusually straight.

Next to her was a younger boy with a green ice-cream container on his head and a silver suit and cape, like something you'd wear to school on dress-up day. The outside tread on the heel of his gumboots had nearly worn away. He began to spin a metal milkshake container on the bench, his body swivelling in sympathy on the stool. The girl stuck out her left hand and grabbed his arm. She had a large black sweatband on each wrist, the type a tennis player would use. The boy's body and the milkshake container both stopped abruptly. Brother and sister. Simon could tell.

Suddenly, he sensed a terse silence. He turned his head; his parents were looking at him, expectant.

'What. Do. You. Want?' said his father, measuredly, like Simon was stupid. 'You've got to eat. Choose something.'

Usually, his parents didn't press him any further than they had to, but there was an insistence in his father's voice that suggested he wished to impress someone, probably—Simon guessed— everyone in the cafe.

Simon's mother laid the menu out in front of him; he pointed to something where he knew the kids' meals would be.

'Okay,' said his mother. 'Nuggets and chips. Fine.'

Simon looked back to see the brother and sister at the counter but they were gone. As his parents droned

14

on about trivial work matters, Simon dragged his gaze around the room, noting each detail as it came. It was a trick he had taught himself, pretending he was a spy or policeman, trying to take in everything about a scene in case he had to remember it later.

Strung just below the cafe's roof was the same blue netting he had seen in Tarden's yard. Woven through it were little orange balls, some bleached starfish and, strangely enough, a life jacket. A joke, probably. Or in case the town flooded.

He looked back at Tarden sitting with the other men. He guessed they were all fishermen, back from the boats. Tarden's overalls were the only ones that were bright yellow. The rest of the men were dirty, like they'd been wearing the same clothes all their lives. The men laughed and talked, each one cupping a giant mug with both hands; teabag tags were delicate shapes between their thick fingers.

The food arrived quickly, and Simon's father rubbed his stomach at the waitress with vaudevillian glee. Simon knew this was his father still being a salesman, but instead of selling cosmetics, he was selling himself. 'Great country fare,' he said, accepting his steak sandwich. 'Good for what ails you!'

The waitress smiled. She had a piercing under her lip, and her eyes were different colours. Her nametag read Megan.

Simon's mother said nothing as her salad sandwich was placed in front of her.

'Thank you,' said Simon, smiling at the waitress, who handed him a plate of grey nuggets.

'You're welcome.'

As the waitress walked away, Simon's mother tipped her head to the ceiling, exhaling loudly.

'Sweetie?' said Simon's father. 'Everything okay?'

'Well,' she said, picking up her knife. 'Not really, no.'

'You don't like your meal?'

'No, Bill, my meal is fine.'

Simon's father levered a thick slice of tomato into his mouth. 'What, then?'

Simon's mother put down her knife. Her lips trembled. 'What do you think?' Her voice was too loud, cutting into the white noise of surrounding conversation.

'Sweetie—'

Simon stared helplessly at his plate. This was the moment. He has been waiting for this from the minute they left.

'She's my mother, Bill. It's—' She wrenched a napkin from the metal dispenser on the table. 'You need to understand, but it's quite obvious you can't.'

Simon was sure he could hear people shifting in their seats, heads turning to get a better angle. His mother took noisy, halting breaths. He cleared his throat. The words came out before he realised he was speaking them: 'Can you wait?'

His father turned to him, his mouth a thin grim line. He said, 'This doesn't concern you, Simon.'

Simon's scars began to burn. He went to grab his leg and knocked over the water glass. Ice scattered across the table.

'For God's sake!' shouted his mother. 'Just leave it. Leave it!' She started crying. The waitress reappeared, but Simon's father waved her away. 'We're fine,' he said, smiling. 'Just a little accident!'

16

Simon knew everyone was looking at them now. He slid out of the booth, avoiding his father's gesticulating arm, and went up to the bar. He pulled himself onto the stool he had seen the girl sitting on; it was higher than he realised, and his sandals dangled in the air some way even from the metal footrest. He leant his arms on the counter and, for some reason, he shivered. The waitress brought him a fresh glass of iced water and put it on the counter next to him. Simon thanked her. He watched condensation leach into the thin napkin she had placed underneath the glass.

'What can I get you?' said a scratchy voice beside him.

Simon turned. It was Tarden, thumbs propped behind the straps of his overalls.

'Samuel, wasn't it?'

'Simon.'

'Right, yeah. Simon.' Tarden had a toothpick wedged in between his bottom front teeth. 'Get you a lemonade?' The toothpick moved as he talked, switching up and down like a baton.

'No, thank you,' said Simon, pointing to his fresh glass of water.

'You sure?'

'Yes.'

'Yes, you'd like one or Yes you're sure?' Tarden smiled, stretching his face out: leather taut across a frame. His eyes were grey, wet at the edges.

'I'd better get back to my parents,' Simon said quietly. He was quite sure he didn't like this man.

'Just having fun with you,' Tarden laughed. He reached out and rubbed Simon's hair. His fingers were thick. Somehow, Simon knew that Tarden couldn't feel much

17

with them; they seemed dead against his scalp. 'You not in school?'

'It's holidays.' Simon hadn't even seen his new school yet, but already knew it would be the same as the rest. He turned, trying to wriggle out of the chair, and saw his parents looking at him.

'Sorry, Jack,' called Simon's father. 'He can't sit still a moment.'

Simon shot his father a slit-eyed stare, which was duly ignored.

'Not a problem,' said Tarden, putting his hand on Simon's shoulder. 'The Devil and idle hands and all that. Good to meet a fellow explorer.' He barged Simon back to his parents' table. He smelled of seawater kept too long in a shallow container.

Simon's mother reached out for him. Her eyes were red-ringed. 'Don't just run off like that,' she said. 'We need to know where you are.'

Simon nearly spoke, but his father cut him off with a quick glare. 'Won't say a word while we're in the car, but as soon as we stop—'

Simon slid back into the seat. It wasn't worth the trouble to defend himself.

'Ah well,' said Tarden. 'Good to see some life passing through. Normally just the same faces over and over, once the weather turns. What brings you here, anyway?'

Simon held his breath. He braced himself for his mother's reaction. Tarden rocked back on his heels, comfortably, like he was talking to old friends.

'Actually,' said Simon's mother, 'we're visiting some-one.'

Tarden rocked forward again. 'Really.'

18

'My mother, she lives here. We're visiting her.'

Simon's parents joined hands under the table.

'Who's your mother, then? Might know her.'

'Iris. Iris Shamar.'

Tarden's face dropped, for a moment losing its tautness. Simon's parents—looking at each other—didn't notice. Tarden wiped his hands down the front of his overalls as if they were covered in something he didn't like. 'Iris,' he said. 'Yes.'

'You know her?' said Simon's mother, the edges of her mouth creasing into nearly a smile.

'Well, I know of her,' Tarden said. 'She's up at Ned Gale's place, by the water.'

'Ned Gale?'

'Good bloke. Owns a bed and breakfast. Nice place. She stays there.'

'Sounds right,' said Simon's father. 'Rings a bell.' He brought out his phone again, held it up. Still nothing.'

'Won't have much luck with a mobile,' said Tarden. 'Whole town's a black spot as far as that goes.'

'The whole town?'

'Yep. Council kept saying they'd do something about it, but then they got eaten up by amalgamations, so—'

Simon's father nodded.

'Anyway,' said Tarden. 'I'll let you finish your meal. Just give us a yell if you need anything else.' He turned to leave.

Simon's mother spoke. 'Where is ... where's the bed and breakfast?'

'What's that?'

'The B&B. Where Iris—where my mother is staying. How do we get there?'

'Oh,' said Tarden. 'Right. You just follow this road and there'll be a turnoff on your right. There's signs. Can't miss it.'

'Not far, then?'

'Nah, not even five minutes in a car.'

'Oh, right.' Simon's mother rubbed her hands against her legs.

'Staying long?' said Tarden.

'Ah, we're not quite sure,' said Simon's father. 'It'll depend. Won't it sweetie?' He tried a smile.

'Is there—' Simon's mother let her voice trail off. She looked up at the ceiling. 'Is there anywhere we can go? Beforehand?' She inhaled quickly, as if about to sneeze.

'Um.' Tarden looked at Simon's father, at Simon.

'I mean is there somewhere nice we can go for a while? After we check in. Before—'

Simon's father cottoned on. 'Any local attractions?' he said. 'Sightseeing spots? It'd be a shame to come to this part of the country without seeing what it had to offer.'

'Well, there's the beach, but, at the time of the year, it's not much to look at.' Tarden rubbed his chin. 'There's the Magpie, though. Lovely in the evening. Couldn't really let you leave town without seeing that.'

Simon immediately pictured a giant bird, sitting atop a building in the main street. Brown eyes, wings clenched.

'Right,' said Simon's father. 'The Magpie.'

Tarden bunched up a smile. 'Magpie Lake. Lovely this time of year, specially since winter's slipped in early.

Specially, thought Simon. Specially since.

'Magpie Lake,' said Simon's mother. 'Okay.'

'Go down there myself of a morning,' said Tarden. 'Set some traps. Clear water, yabbies, beautiful. Bit later

20

you get the sunset, too. Pretty spectacular. Be some rain coming in later, maybe, but it should be beautiful about now.'

'Sounds lovely,' said Simon's father, his teeth appearing white from behind his beard. Tarden's hands disappeared behind his overalls.

'How do we get there?' said Simon's mother.

'Well,' said Tarden. 'I usually take a shortcut from my place. It's not far as the crow flies, but it's only a dirt road, pretty rough going.'

'We've got all wheel drive,' said Simon's father. 'They take it over boulders in the ads. Right up the side of a mountain.'

'Well that's the ads,' said Simon's mother. 'Is there another way?'

Tarden nodded. 'Just keep to the main road, like before, but turn left at the servo.' He pulled a hand free, swiped it through the air with his pink palm. 'You'll see a line of trees. Just follow them along. Easy.'

'Thank you,' she said.

'We'd better get settled into our room, then,' said Simon's father.

'They'll sort you out when you pay for lunch,' said Tarden. 'They'll give you a key, then you just head around the corner, where the motel entrance is.'

While his parents said their goodbyes and thank-yous, Simon hung in the periphery. The day—the week, the weeks to come—pushed up against him with an enveloping, empty pressure. He knew he'd never see this place again, but still, this was what it would always be like. This moment would repeat itself interminably, until it wouldn't even matter any more.

The sun crackled low off the windows of the parked cars outside, casting strange reflections on the wall. The light broke through the lace curtains; the shapes moved and grew, like embers from a broken fire.

Simon was in charge of the room keys. His father had presented them as they got back into the car, like some sort of apology. It was always something like this. A dollar coin here, an extended bedtime there. Little gestures that meant nothing to Simon, but a lot, apparently, to his parents. He examined the keys. Two of them, identical, hung off a carved wooden keyring shaped like a turtle. The turtle was surprisingly lifelike. Even the eyes seemed real.

The car rounded the corner, going all the way around the large building that housed the Ottoman. At the other side, it turned into a pub, with a locked double-door, long glass windows, a small verandah. A thin driveway ran up beside it, with a Vacancy sign beckoning them in. The motel was a horseshoe of repeated doorways surrounding an empty, pot-holed bitumen carpark.

Simon's mother sighed. 'This is—'

'This is why they don't have a website,' said Simon's father. 'Looks like we've got the place to ourselves, though.' He parked the car and they got out.

Simon stared at all the identical windows. The sky reflected back at him in a blush of pink and orange.

'Still in charge of that key, Simon?'

Simon said nothing. He held up the key between thumb and forefinger, letting the turtle swing in the air.

'Room eight. You can open the door if you like.'

Simon slumped up onto the concrete landing. It was

lit feebly by a stripe of naked bulbs: one bulb, Simon worked out, for every four doors. He found their room and slid the key into the door. It opened easily, and let out a smell a bit like lavender. It reminded him immediately of the sachets of dried flowers his grandma used to keep in every drawer in her house. Potpourri. Nothing had its real smell, even there.

Simon heard his parents rolling their cases across the concrete. He glanced back at them and his heart stuttered. For a second, something was very wrong. He knew it was just the strange light playing tricks, but for one moment his parents became different people. The shadows on their faces inverted; the familiar shapes of their expressions disappeared. It echoed a deep fear that played on him in silent moments, in dreams: that his parents were strangers, that nothing was real.

'Flick the light on can you, Simon?' His mother waved her hand at him.

Simon shook out the mirage in his head, felt inside the door for the light switch. He found it, and the room lit up in banana yellow. Like any hotel room he could have imagined: a double and a single bed, a desk, a small TV. The forgettable painting on the wall. Simon went in and sat on the single bed, a crumbly feeling. His parents brought their bags in, took inventory of the room.

'Okay,' said his mother. 'Okay.'

'Bit Norman Bates,' said his father, nodding at the painting. Simon didn't know what this meant, probably some artist who liked to paint landscapes with cows.

'How long are we staying here?' he said.

'Don't know,' said Simon's father. 'As long as we need to.'

'Not long,' said his mother. 'Hopefully not too long.'

Simon nodded. He had guessed his grandma was sick, but his parents wouldn't tell him anything else. Something serious, to make them come down here. After not mentioning her for nearly five years. Sometimes he forgot he had a grandma.

His mother lay out on the double bed, her long hair bunching up behind her head, her shoes already slipped from her feet. 'God,' she said quietly. 'This is all—' She said nothing else, just held the back of her wrists up to her eyes.

Simon's father left the bags by the door and sat down on the bed. 'We don't have to see her until tomorrow,' he said. 'We can have a rest, go for a walk. Something.'

Simon's mother held uneven breaths. 'I'm already— this room—' She shook her fingers at the ceiling.

Simon looked up, saw nothing but the sharp spikes of knobbly paint. One of their old houses had the same paintwork. Stalactites or stalagmites, Simon couldn't remember which. He knew his mother didn't like closed-in spaces. She was worse when she was working too much, worse still if she didn't get to the gym. She'd push furniture to the edges of the room. As far as Simon knew, though, she'd never lived anywhere but big cities.

'What about that lake,' said Simon's father. 'The Magpie? We could go and see the sunset.'

Simon's mother nodded. 'The sunset.'

Simon watched the closed curtains. The sun was an orange presence behind them.

'Okay,' said his father. 'Let's go and have a look at this lake. I can take the camera. If it's as nice as Jack said it was, we can get some pics for the calendar.'

25

Simon grimaced. The Christmas Calendar. Every year, his parents would put one together as a gift to send to friends and clients. A series of sentimental family portraits taken with a self-timer, the three of them rushing together in front of random backdrops. Simon always imagined his family as a set of magnets: you had to throw them together quickly before they repelled apart.

His father opened a bag to search for the camera.

Simon's mother rolled over on the bed. She stretched out her arms. 'Simon,' she said, 'Are you coming to the lake?'

Simon shook his head. He knew his mother already knew he didn't want to go.

'Of course you're coming, Simon,' said his father. 'Remember what we talked about?'

He shook his head again. His father had attempted a conversation that morning while his mother was upstairs getting ready. It had still been dark outside, somehow making the new house even more huge. Words like support and difficult and complicated. His father's cheeks had been so red. Each morning, scrubbed almost raw above the line of his beard.

'Leave him,' said Simon's mother. 'We won't be too long.'

'By himself?'

'He'll be fine. Won't you, Simon.'

Simon nodded. 'I'll watch TV,' he said.

His father shrugged. 'Suit yourself, but you could be missing something wonderful.'

Simon's mother got up from the bed. 'He's fine,' she said. 'He's old enough.' She leaned in and kissed Simon's forehead, leaving a cold moist place in the shape of her lips.

'See you soon, champ.' Simon's father held his camera aloft by its strap, like a fisherman with his catch.

'We'll take the key,' said his mother. 'Don't answer if anyone knocks.'

'Okay,' said Simon. 'Enjoy the water.' He heard the lock snib. He walked over to one of the bags and found a book he'd been reading. Then, instead of going back to the bed, he pulled open the curtains. He watched his parents walk to their car, hand in hand, watched them get in, drive away. He stood there for a while, playing a game he'd made up months before. Trying to catch the day losing light, knowing it wouldn't get dark until he stopped watching.

കൗ

Simon's dream slid into wakefulness so seamlessly, like a boat through calm water, that it was impossible to tell one moment from another: the tide of the unconscious, the shore of the real. It was dark; closed eyes and open were so much the same that Simon had to shake his head to remember which was which. When he realised he was awake, he found himself immediately unsettled. At first he put it down to simple disorientation, but there was something more. A forceful thought that had remained an echo in his head.

He was lying on his side, curled up on the very edge of an unfamiliar bed. he scars on his legs itched. He sat up quickly, and the air was suddenly colder. The motel room. He remembered. What time was it? He couldn't focus his eyes, couldn't process the patterns of yellow on the opposite wall. The light bulbs, he told himself. The window. A faint panic began to ripple at his ribs. He got up from the bed. He felt by the doorway for the light switch, but when he flicked it, nothing happened. He tried again, three times more. Nothing. He peered back into the room, at the green glow of the alarm clock by the double bed. 10.02.

He wrenched open the front door, feeling the sensation of the lock popping open. In his mind, he saw his parents sitting outside the door, waiting for him to wake up. All he found was an empty landing. All the other windows in all the other rooms were dark. The carpark was still empty. He stared back into the doorway, registering suddenly his bare feet burning on the cold concrete.

His parents had left him home alone before and come back later than they were supposed to. Working late, dealing with deadlines—but they always let him know where they were. They were casual, negligent in their own way, but they never left him alone like this, not knowing. His mother especially. In his head he heard her voice, the panicked tone she swooped into sometimes, ever since the last time he'd seen his grandma. Maybe they had gone to visit her. But why wouldn't they have said?

It had to be a dream. That was what he told himself. It was like dreams he'd had before: places of no definition, edges of objects ghosting, two or three versions of everything, nothing right. The air scratched at his throat, raking it, leaving a thick, metallic taste. Simon heard his own breathing, became too aware of his lungs filling and emptying. His cheeks burned, his heart pulsed out in corrugated shivers. Something had happened. Simon saw news footage of a car crash, saw a funeral in a large church, saw himself, alone.

He walked quickly into the carpark, to the place he had seen his parents last. His eyes were growing accustomed to the moonless night. He searched the ground, stupidly, for footprints, for some clue. But everything was empty. No sights, no sounds, no feelings he knew. He shouted out, his voice nothing inside the cauldron sky. His mouth ached, with the cold, with words he never used.

'MUM!

'DAD!'

His voice left him painfully, a sob, a bandage ripped

too early. He screamed the names again, but nothing came back. No familiar voices echoing out from the darkness. It was fear now, it was panic. Kids weren't supposed to be lost like this, left like this. He crouched down. The world was ragged, diagonal, spinning and splintering. He pressed his knuckles into the bitumen until he felt a familiar sting of pain. Anything, he thought. Snything real.

He stopped for a moment, still stung with a slim small hope: the voices of his parents returning to him through the dark. There was nothing. No noise. A curious silence he'd not imagined a seaside town might have. Simon tried not to imagine he was truly alone, but no other thought would replace it. It settled in his head, heavy and still. The cold began to take him over. He pictured himself the next morning, frozen like a caveman, trapped in the middle of the carpark, his frosted face staring, twisted, from within a block of ice.

He knew he had to move. He had to get help. He stood up, shivering, taking in nothing but the pale dots of light outside each motel room. The Ottoman, he thought. The smoky warmth of the cafe. Someone would be there. Surely someone had to keep watch over the motel. Maybe his parents were there, eating a late dinner. That was it. They'd come back and parked outside the cafe. His mother had come to check on him, but found him sleeping. They were just eating dinner, not even that far away.

Simon made his way out of the carpark, the soles of his sandals crunching on patches of loosened bitumen. Out on the street, it was easier to see. A high streetlight cast down easy light and as he passed under it, he felt a knot of worry loosen and release a tinge of embarrassment. He had panicked for nothing. A bad thought made worse by the dark, by a place he didn't know. That was all. Only a few steps up the road, he saw the double-doors, the long windows, and remembered what Tarden had said. The cafe was closed at night. His parents would be in the pub.

Light spilled out from the open doors and as Simon got closer, he heard voices. He stepped up onto the small verandah. That strange, warm smell was in his nose. Something had got wet and then dried. A pub smell. He stepped inside. The space was at least twice as large as the cafe, but had the same arrangement: a bar down one side, booths set back into the walls. He scanned each seat in turn for the familiar forms of his parents but these shapes were all strangers. Mostly men. Simon thought he recognised some of the faces from the cafe earlier in the day, fishers changed out of their overalls and into jeans and shirts. A collection of features: one with a clumpy haircut, another a potato-shaped nose. The waitress from the cafe was there, behind the bar, talking to a younger guy who had his foot propped up on a low rail that ran the length of the bar.

That was it. His parents weren't here. He checked every table again. Every face. A few looked back, their expressions blank. Simon's pulse thumped. His scars stabbed with heat.

'Jeez,' said a voice. 'It's the explorer.'

Simon's gut gave a sharp twist. Tarden had appeared behind him, in the doorway.

'Now I know it's not Samuel,' said Tarden. He had replaced his overalls with a denim jacket and jeans. His face was flushed a deeper red by the cold, his eyes

31

watering at their edges. His smile shrunk away as he stepped inside. 'You right, mate?'

Simon felt the beginning of tears. He squeezed his eyes shut to stop them.

'Simon?' he heard Tarden say. Simon opened his eyes. He didn't want to say anything—he couldn't—but then the words escaped unwillingly, like the first squirts of air after a held breath. 'My parents,' he said. 'My mum and dad.'

Tarden said, 'Are they here? Where are they?' He squatted down on his haunches, hands resting on his knees.

Up close, Simon saw Tarden's skin was covered in shallow craters. Simon's body shook before he even felt the tears, little wet strokes at the sides of his mouth.

'Mate,' said Tarden. 'Are your parents not here?'

Simon shook his head.

'Do you know where they might be?'

'They're not here!' shouted Simon. He had finally let out his breath, and now he couldn't control it. Tarden didn't understand. It wasn't that Simon couldn't find his parents—they weren't hiding somewhere where he couldn't see them—they were missing.

'Do you know where they went?'

'They left,' said Simon. 'I didn't want to go. I stayed in the room. They've gone.' Simon kept crying, his words soft and wet.

'They left you in the motel room?'

'They went to that lake. I didn't want to go.'

Tarden put his hand around Simon's arm. 'It's okay,' he said. 'We'll find them. We'll do our best. Don't worry.'

Simon sniffed back tears, nodded, tried to ignore the

32

wetness in his throat and nose. The overwhelming need not to cry in front of people he didn't know.

'Come and sit down,' said Tarden. He guided Simon over to a nearby table. 'I'm just going to talk to someone, okay? I'll get us some help. I'll be back in a sec.'

Simon sat down. He had gone numb. It still felt like he was waking up. Tarden went up to the bar and talked to a large, darkskinned man behind it. They kept looking over at him. Simon could feel other eyes on him, too. All those people he didn't know. The large man nodded, disappeared through a door behind the bar.

Tarden came back over. 'We're getting the police,' he said, 'okay? Nat's going to call the police.'

Simon nodded.

'You want anything to drink?' said Tarden. 'A Coke? A cordial?'

'No.' He didn't want anything. He didn't want the police. He just wanted his parents. He wanted them to come and take him away from Reception.

'Okay.' Tarden drummed his fingers on the tabletop. 'What time did your mum and dad leave?'

'I don't know,' said Simon. 'Afternoon. A little bit after we left the cafe.'

'I'm sure they're okay,' said Tarden. He started biting his fingernails. 'Bugger of a night to be stuck out in, though.'

Simon said nothing.

'What did your dad say he did again?'

'What do you mean?'

'What's his job?'

'They sell things. Both of them.'

'Your mum and dad do? What sort of things?'

'Product.'

'Product?'

'Perfume, lotions and creams,' Simon recited from memory. 'They get other people to sell it for them, really. They just run the company. They've got separate offices.'

Tarden pulled his lips back so his gums showed out. 'Hmm. Couldn't work indoors, myself. Worked outside all my life.' He traced a pattern on his palm. He smiled. 'It's the only life. Fishing. There's yabbies out at Magpie Lake, you know. Seen some the size of a baby.'

This seemed, to Simon, a strange thing to say. He wasn't sure he knew what a yabby was; instead he imagined a lake full of babies, paddling slowly underwater with bright blue eyes, bubbles at the corner of their mouths. Infants asleep at night, on the dam's floor. Curled up in hollow mud shells. 'Don't you get bored?' Simon asked. 'If all you do is fish?'

'That's a serious question,' said Tarden. 'Suppose some people would. Depends on your personality, doesn't it. Me, I like time to think things over.

Simon felt an uncomfortable pressure in his stomach. He hadn't been to the toilet all day, but he stayed quiet.

'So,' said Tarden after a while. 'Your ... grandma. You're visiting her?'

'Yes.'

'She ... I never heard about her having grandkids. Or kids. Or anything, much.'

'We didn't talk to her for a while,' said Simon. 'My mother. We all didn't.'

'Why not?'

Simon twisted his hands in his lap. His mother did this too, he knew. 'We just didn't.' Simon stared at the

34

ceiling, watched a group of moths swing manic loops in the lights.

'So why now?'

'What?'

'Why did your parents decide to visit Iris all of a sudden?'

Simon rubbed at his legs. 'She's not well.'

'Oh.' Tarden pulled his seat forward. 'I'm sorry to hear that.'

'I can't really remember what she looks like,' said Simon, surprising himself with how loud his voice was. 'I can't. She's really not well. I really want to see her.' Simon felt a new sting of tears.

'What's the matter with her?' Tarden put the side of his pinkie finger in his mouth, his wrist bent at an awkward angle. Simon could hear the sound of Tarden's teeth against his fingernail.

'I think,' said Simon, 'she's going to die.'

'Ow—shit!' Tarden's hand shot back from his face. He shook it vigorously. 'Bloody thing,' he said, holding up his finger. The tip was red. A trickle of blood worked its way down the side of Tarden's wrist. 'Always happens,' he said. 'It's this bloody weather.'

'What?'

'Just bit my finger, that's all. Always happens, doesn't it.'

Simon nodded, although he couldn't imagine someone biting their own finger. He thought he saw something else in Tarden's eyes. A faint shadow of fear. He suddenly saw his parents, lying at the bottom of the lake, nestled amongst the babies and the formless yabbies and the mud. Bodies slumped still. Fingers chewed down to the bone.

❦

Simon traced the rings in the pub table where glasses had been put down hundreds, thousands of times. An overwhelming sense of exhaustion had fallen over him, even though he knew he wasn't tired. He stared at the ring patterns until his eyes went out of focus, until the circles swung and swam together.

'That'll be her,' said Tarden.

Simon was jolted from his thoughts. 'Who?'

Tarden nodded his head at the nearest window.

Simon saw a wash of headlights, picking out the dirt in the glass. The headlights switched off.

'Madaline,' said Tarden. 'Police.'

A woman came into the pub, wrapped in a large brown overcoat. Simon thought immediately of a detective, the sort in films. She was younger though, younger than his mother. Her face was pale, and seemed lost between the collar of her coat and the helmet-frame of her black hair. As she got closer, Simon saw that one of her eyes pointed slightly inwards.

Tarden got up. 'Simon,' he said, 'this is Mad—ah, Constable—'

'Senior Constable McKinley,' said the woman. 'Madaline, yes. Simon, you can call me Madaline.' She reached into her pocket and took out a leather wallet. She flipped it open, showing Simon her ID card, a tiny

36

picture of her on it, and smiled at Simon, her mouth lopsided but warm.

'She's the local police officer,' said Tarden.

'But not in official clothes.' Madaline tugged at the sleeve of her overcoat. 'Afraid you caught me just going to bed.' She smiled again, quickly, before her face fell into seriousness. 'Now, Simon. Are you all right?'

Simon nodded, not really hearing.

'I bet things aren't quite right, though, are they.' She held out her hand. 'We'll go back to my house for a little bit, and we'll get this sorted out. Okay?'

'Okay.' Simon took Madaline's hand. She put her arm around him. Simon smelled wood-smoke.

'Thanks, Jack,' she said. 'I'll let you get on with your night.'

'No worries,' said Tarden. 'Hope it all sorts out.' He sat back down at the table. 'I'll see ya real soon, Simon. We can maybe go fishing some time. Get some of those yabbies.'

'Maybe,' said Simon. 'Some time.'

Madaline ushered Simon out of the pub. The cold air hit them, and Madaline drew Simon in beside her. 'You're staying in one of the motel rooms, aren't you. Have you got some warm clothes in there?'

'Yeah,' said Simon. 'I've got a jumper and stuff.'

'All right, well let's walk around there, get some clothes, and we'll leave your folks a note as well in case they come back.'

'Okay.'

They went back to the hotel room and Simon put on a jumper. Madaline scribbled a note on a pad she had in another pocket. She ripped it off and placed it on the bed.

37

'They might have just lost track of time,' she said. 'I've given them my number on here, and the number for the pub. They'll call if they come back. They went off in the car, is that right?'

'Yes.'

'We'll go back to my place and wait there. It's not far. It'll be safer there, seeing as your parents have the keys.' Madaline glanced around the room with a sour look on her face. 'It'll be warmer too.'

Simon let Madaline close the door behind them, let her walk him to her car, let her buckle him into the passenger seat. He tried his best to stay numb, to not let his thoughts overtake him.

'It's not a police car,' he said.

'You mean, no flashing lights and reflective signs?'

'Yeah.'

'I've got one of those, too,' she said. 'Well, my sergeant does. This is still a police car. I know it just looks like a Corolla with pretty bad paint, but don't let that fool you.'

As they drove—slowly, carefully—Simon scanned the road ahead, lit up in grey, running away beneath the car. He felt empty and cold. Grass and bushes crept past on either side of the road, offering only their ghostly edges.

Madaline's fingers were ice-white on the steering wheel. Simon didn't think she seemed as calm as before. She brushed some hair behind her ear. 'Simon,' she said. 'Where are you from?'

'Our new house is on the Gold Coast.'

'Oh yeah, which part?'

'The main part, I think.' Simon didn't really know where he lived. It was the third house they'd lived in at the Coast, and the ninth in his life. When they moved in, only a few weeks before, Simon had got out his father's street directory to try and find their address. His eyes were always drawn to a large blue inlet. Lake Wonderland.

'Must be nice up there,' said Madaline. 'Warm.'

The rattle of the suspension was all that broke the silence. The first unfocused smudges of light rain appeared on the windscreen.

'I'm from up north myself,' said Madaline eventually. 'Used to live out on a farm. Can you imagine?' She laughed, an odd, fast laugh, as if at the strangeness of what she'd said. Simon bunched his fists into the sleeves of his jumper. He didn't see what was so funny about living on a farm.

The car crawled on. The regularity of smaller side streets soon ended and they reached a dark stretch of road flanked on either side by thick coastal scrub. Madaline swung the steering wheel suddenly and Simon thought they would crash into the trees. Instead the car divided a bowing salute of ferns and ascended a steep driveway. The arms of rainforest plants slapped at the windscreen.

'Here we are,' said Madaline. Two wooden lamps lit a porch. A house sat on tall stilts, wide stairs leading from the driveway up to a generous verandah. A man sat beside the door on a bench seat wearing a pea-green coat splattered with a dark pattern of raindrops. He had shoulder-length blonde hair, curled at the ends where it was obviously wet. He stood up as the car arrived.

'This is my house,' said Madaline. 'It's sort of the police station, too, I suppose. But mainly my house. We'll get you something to eat.'

Simon realised he was starving. He wondered what

time it was. The clock on Madaline's dashboard had lost its hands.

'Come on, then.' Madaline tapped Simon on the knee and got out of the car.

Simon opened his door just as the man in the green coat made his way down the stairs to meet them. He let his left hand slide all the way down the railing.

Madaline put her fingers on Simon's shoulders. 'Hi Ned,' she said. 'Thanks for coming out.'

'I parked on the road,' said the man. 'Didn't know how much room you were going to need.' For some reason, he looked at Simon as he spoke.

'Simon, this is Ned,' said Madaline. 'He's a friend of mine. He's going to help us out.'

'Hi Simon,' said Ned. 'Why don't you come inside. I've made us something to eat.'

'Isn't this your house?' said Simon to Madaline.

'Yes, it is,' she said, again with her strange smile. 'Ned's just been stoking up the fire and doing some supper for us.'

'Let's get inside, anyway,' said Ned, peering up at the sky. Thick spats of rain had begun to fall. He led them up the stairs, into the house, to what Simon assumed was the living room.

Four mismatched lamps lit the space: the light they cast joined in strange planes, patchworking the walls into random shades of shadow. There was paper everywhere: manila folders and ring binders stacked in towers on the floor, on a rickety cane hutch, crammed into two giant bookshelves. Even normal-looking books had incongruous pages poking out, swollen with words that were clearly not their own.

'This is where I get my work done,' said Madaline

apologetically. 'Messy, but cosy.' She gestured to the couch, and Simon sat down. She sat opposite in a recliner. Its chocolate-coloured leather was broken into small scales where her arms rested, and where she leaned her head.

Ned cleared his throat. 'I'll rustle up some food,' he said, disappearing into another room.

Madaline leaned forward in her seat, her dark hair reaching down to shadow her cheeks, her fingers pressed together in a steeple. She had a small trail of pink dots up the inside of her arm. Insect bites. She stared right into Simon's eyes, trying to see inside him. He shifted on the lumpy cushion.

She said, 'I want you to understand, Simon, that we'll all be doing our best to find your parents. I want you to know that.' She leant over and pressed her palm to his knee. She kept it there, and kept looking at him.

'I want to go home,' said Simon.

Madaline bit her lip and let out a quick breath from between her teeth. 'I know,' she said. 'I know.'

Simon realised no one had told him it was going to be okay. If it was a movie, they would have. They would make promises. We'll find your parents if it's the last thing we do. Everything's going to be fine.

Ned came back into the room, holding a large tray. Simon smelled toast and his stomach growled. 'Brought us some sustenance,' said Ned, sitting down beside Simon on the couch. The tray had a blue plate in the middle of it, and on the plate was a pile of toasted sandwiches, golden with butter, molten cheese leaking from the edges. An enormous glass sat beside the plate, filled nearly to the top with Milo. 'Toasted cheese and mustard,' said

41

Ned. 'Perfect midnight snack.' He took a red napkin from under the plate and handed it to Simon.

'Is it midnight?' asked Simon. He felt a tiredness lurching inside him.

'Maybe close.' Ned glanced at his wrist, even though he wasn't wearing a watch.

'Eat up,' said Madaline. 'You must be hungry.'

Simon picked up a sandwich, and it was perfectly warm. He bit into it, a small bite. The butter melted gently against the roof of his mouth—he felt it, he could almost see it. The cheese was creamy and the mustard was sharp. It was the best thing he had ever tasted. He smelled the flavours as he ate them and felt a shudder across his shoulders: his senses beginning to return. The rain had come up; now it was hammering a loud pattern on the roof.

Madaline cleared her throat. 'There's not much we can do tonight. I'm sure your parents are safe wherever they are. I'll drive out to the dam tonight, and if I don't see anything we'll start a proper search at first light.'

'You might find them tonight though?'

'I may do. The car might have broken down out at the lake, or something. I'm sure it's nothing to worry about.'

Simon pictured his parents, huddled together inside the car. Light, in streaks, appearing at the windows: the safety of sunlight, the reassurance of police blue and reds.

'Simon,' said Madaline, 'you're going to need somewhere to stay tonight.' She leant forward in her chair. 'I don't want you staying by yourself in that motel room.'

Simon took a sip of his Milo. He crunched the undissolved malt with his back teeth. He imagined a brontosaurus, grinding branches and leaves.

42

'I've asked Ned if he can look after you,' said Madaline. 'He's got a bigger house than mine. It's sort of a hotel, but his family lives there too.'

'The Gales' place,' said Simon. He remembered the name, the image of a strong wind blowing.

'That's right.' Ned cocked his head. 'You know my last name.'

'Tarden told us,' said Simon. 'At the cafe.'

Madaline put down a corner of a sandwich. 'You spoke to Jack before your parents went missing?'

'Yes. At the cafe.' Simon suddenly remembered the connection. 'My grandma is staying there,' he said.

'Your grandma?' said Madaline. 'Where?'

'At the Gales' house. That's why we were coming here.'

'Who's your grandma?' said Ned.

Simon thought this a very strange question. He heard her voice again, in his head, echoing through an empty house. 'My grandma,' he said. 'Iris.'

Ned's mouth stood open. 'She's never mentioned—'

'We were coming to visit her,' said Simon. 'My mum and her haven't spoken in a long time. But she called us … and she's sick. All mum wanted was—' Simon felt a fire flick yellow in his stomach: not pale like lamplight, but sharp like a flashing sword. He saw a dizzy wide sky, streaked with clouds, and knew his parents were not under it. The world spun. He smelled dust and hand cream. A spider-spout of vomit scuttled at his throat, a warm jumble that fell from his mouth and wet his chest in mustard coloured clumps.

Madaline jumped from her seat and put a napkin to his lips. 'Poor thing,' she said kindly. 'You poor bugger.' She put a hand to Simon's brow.

43

'I'll get a towel,' said Ned quietly. He got up, and as his arm brushed past, Simon could not ever remember his parents doing this. Tending to him. Simon's breath was sour and hot when he finally breathed in. His tears, when they came, were cooling.

The rain had set in steadily, dropping down layer after layer, cloaking everything, in the dark, but the basic shape of the house, its two wide-set storeys. Ned drove up as close to his front door as the driveway would allow. 'We'll have to make a run for it,' he said.

Simon took a deep breath. 'Okay.' Another step away from the familiar: beyond Ned's car, beyond the next open door. His jumper was stale with vomit. His panic had abated, his tears had dried, but something blanket-like had settled on his mind. The tug of dead-tiredness dragged at his eyes.

They sprinted from the car. Simon felt the rain in the small of his back, then streaming down his legs and arms. In a few blind moments he was standing on a porch, shocked to be in a dry place, the rain still falling inches from his face.

'Quite a downpour,' said Ned. His long hair, warped by the moisture, sketched out at strange angles like loosened hay. He shook one arm of his giant green coat and reached down to a flowerpot on the ground, into the soil, to dig out a key. 'People usually put the front door key underneath the potplant,' he said. 'Thought I'd outsmart them.' He tapped the side of his head, leaving a tiny clump of soil.

He ushered Simon inside and closed the heavy door

behind them. The clatter of rain disappeared as if shut inside a suitcase.

'Welcome,' said Ned.

They stood in a large alcove. The floor was patterned with tiny tiles, spread in a blue and white seashell spiral. The effect was whirling water, glittering back an imaginary sun. Beyond the tiles was a hall with a polished wood floor and a straight staircase. Red-wine dark, impossibly old. Water dripped from Simon's elbows.

'We'll get you settled,' said Ned. 'I'll show you around properly tomorrow.'

Simon followed Ned out to the hall and the house opened over him. He peered up through the staircase, at the roof, dim and shadowy. He imagined thick spider webs lacing the ceiling, the patient lure of some ancient, awful creature. He spun his head at a silhouette arcing across the floor, at a girl standing underneath an archway. Her hair was dark and uneven, and her dress—Simon recognised the layer-dress of the girl from the cafe. She looked at him with suspicious, sleep-muzzled eyes. She said, 'What's going on?'

Ned took a moment to answer, as if equally confused by the girl's presence. 'Audrey,' he said, 'this is Simon. He'll be staying with us for a little while. Simon, this is Audrey, my daughter.'

The girl rubbed her eyes. 'I know you,' she said to Simon. 'You were at the Ottoman.'

Simon nodded. 'You were sitting at the counter. With your brother.'

'How do you know he's my brother?' Audrey took a few steps forward. She had strips of fabric tied to her wrists where the sweatbands had been.

46

'I don't know,' said Simon. 'It just looked like he was.'

'He is,' said Ned. 'That would have been Julian. My son.'

'We call him Gin,' said Audrey, 'like the drink. It's quicker to say. He won't mind if you call him that.

'We can all meet each other in the morning,' said Ned, 'but I think Simon should get to bed now. We all should.'

'The boys have been watching TV with the lights off.' Audrey did a little dance on her left foot. A toe showed through her sock.

'Well that's all right for tonight,' said Ned, 'but can you get them to go to bed now?'

Audrey stuck out both her hands. 'Are you left or right handed?'

Simon stared at her.

She insisted. 'Which hand do you prefer?'

'I'm left handed,' he said.

'Interesting.'

'I'd better show Simon to a room,' said Ned. 'You can meet properly in the morning.'

'Okay,' said Audrey. 'Goodnight, Simon.' She fluttered her hand at him like a hummingbird's wing.

'Goodnight,' said Simon.

Audrey disappeared under the archway. Ned began to climb the stairs. 'Your grandma's on the second floor,' he said. 'I'll get you some extra blankets so you can sleep in her room.'

Simon didn't move. 'I don't ... won't she be asleep? I mean she's—' He didn't want to say sick.

'Probably.' Ned paused. 'You want to see her, don't you?'

Simon scuffed a foot against the carpet. 'I don't

know.' He ached for something familiar; he could hardly remember his grandma's face. He wanted to see her with his parents. He wanted them all to be together.

Ned came back down the stairs. 'There's another room on the same floor,' he said, 'if you'd rather wait until tomorrow. If you'd rather have your own room.'

Simon nodded, the prospect of a bed almost a sweet taste on his tongue. 'Yes,' he said. 'I'd like my own room.'

At the top of the stairs, the rain smacked a windowpane like an angry hand. A glass cabinet displayed painted plates, teapots and a large open book with black-and-white drawings. Down the hall were definite signs of life. A trail of odd shoes littered one side, gumboots and thongs and sneakers. A large piece of red material lay scrunched up in the middle of the hall, with some metal jacks and a ball sitting on it.

'As you can see,' Ned bent down and rolled it all into a bundle, 'Gin's been this way recently.'

Simon thought suddenly of his parents. He wondered if they had left a trail behind them. Like Hansel and Gretel: breadcrumbs, being washed away by the rain.

Further down the hall, Ned opened another door. He flicked the light and a dim light spilled out across him onto the landing. 'This can be your room,' he said. 'It's all made up.'

Simon peered in. A giant freestanding wardrobe filled up most of one wall. In the centre of the room, occupying one half of a huge bay window, was a queen-sized bed covered with a thick patchwork quilt. A seat was cut into the other half of the window, a crescent moon shape covered with a light, fuzzy fabric. On the other side of the room was a small dressing table and chair. The whole space had an ancient, unused feel. Simon saw himself: a reflection in the window. He was surprised at how small he seemed.

'Anyway,' said Ned, 'it should be comfortable enough. He ran his hands along one of the walls, slowly, as if waiting for it to change temperature. He turned to Simon. 'How about I get you some clean clothes? We can wash those other ones for you. I'll be back in a tick.'

Ned left and Simon wandered around the room. Everything felt too large, too adult. He sat down on the bed. Instead of springing beneath him, the mattress collapsed silently like a giant pillow.

When Ned returned he placed a muddled mass of clothing on the end of the bed. 'Best I could do at short notice,' he said. 'We'll get you something better in the morning.'

Simon thanked him, and shuffled his weight on the bed, unsure of how familiar he was allowed to be. His mother's absence, his father's, hurt like a headache.

Ned stood awkwardly. 'If you need me, I'm just downstairs. I'll leave the light on outside for you.' He walked to the door and turned, pushing his hair back from his face. 'Look, Simon—I—' His face tensed, then slumped back. 'Is there anything else you want?'

Simon wanted to brush his teeth. He wanted his own pyjamas. He wanted his father to walk past the door with a cough and a reassuring shadow. He shook his head.

'Okay, well I'll wake you in the morning. Try to get some sleep.'

Ned closed the door quietly, leaving Simon alone, sealed in like an insect.

Simon reached over to the pile of clothes and pulled

out a large purple jumper. He took off his old jumper, his T-shirt, his shorts and sandals, pulled the new jumper over his head. It smelled of must and aftershave and reached to well below his knees. His pyjamas for the night. He switched on the lamp that sat on the edge of the window seat, turned off the overhead light and pushed the pile of clothes onto the floor. He slipped under the sheet that was tucked tightly under the doona. Sank his head into the big pillow, ancient goose-down enveloping his ears.

He closed his eyes, imagining he was in a cocoon. Imagining daylight was trying to break in, to mark the end of his nightmare. He wanted to wake to real life: in the back seat of his parents' car, driving home. But the imagined world would not stick. Unfamiliar senses overpowered him. The smell of the quilt, mothball-sharp. The thick salt of swallowed tears. The relentless pounding noise of the rain, impossibly heavier than ever.

He was still in a strange room in a strange house in a strange town. Lost. He opened his eyes just as the lamp flickered out, leaving behind only a ghastly darkness.

Madaline blinked her eyes she heard bat's wings. An empty mug sat before her on the kitchen bench. Her hand had been poised above it for nearly a minute, holding a teaspoon heaped with instant coffee. The decision to overturn it was somehow absurdly hard. The coffee, hauled from the depths of her cupboard, was old and infected by moisture: the odd-shaped granules repulsed her, how they clumped together into moon rocks. Still, she needed it. For the first time in years, the base of her throat sung with a need for nicotine, and she knew coffee was all that would quiet it.

It was proper coffee she craved, though, a thick stovetop brew. She almost smelled it on her fingers, the tang of a cigarette and the bitter hit of caffeine. A cruel sense memory: Ned and Stephanie, their smiling faces. A backyard afternoon, brimful of birdscreech.

Sweet smoke blown into clear salt air, countless cups of fresh hot coffee. All her adult addictions gathered at a table. She added the scene to the collection of ragged thoughts circling inside her head.

The cordless phone lay at the edge of the kitchen counter where she'd placed it half an hour before. Tommy's number rolled through her head, and a vision of his sleep-scrambled face, a flare of his frequent sore-headed rage. Officer in Charge—that was a laugh. Tommy was hardly able to maintain himself, let alone an entire town. Madaline ground a knuckle against her eye. Was she any better? She'd already failed to do the simple things right. She'd taken almost no information from Simon. Couldn't bring herself to, the way he was sick all down himself, flinching when she tried to help. All she had was two names. No description of what they looked like. No idea what car they drove. The most likely explanation stared her in the face: that they had simply abandoned their son. Tommy would tear her to pieces for the mistakes she'd already made.

Reasons, she heard in her head. Everything has a reason. That shaky mirage called Police Training shimmered into view. Those shards of psychology copied eagerly to her notebook, single sentences she would pore over on the evening train, deciphering her own writing, trying to obscure it from the cramped eyes of strangers, as if they would take the wisdom from her. She wondered now—as she did then—whether anything was truly without reason. A senseless killing, as the papers often said, a senseless act.

She finally turned over the spoon, dropping the coffee into the mug, adding two pellets of sweetener. She flicked on the kettle for the fourth time, blankly watching the orange light that she knew would flick off in a matter of moments. She thought about the power she was sucking from the grid, thought about the rain, heavier than ever, covering everything like a blanket. The kettle boiled, the light switched off. Madaline poured water into her mug. She watched the coffee hurl itself against the side of the cup, abandoned into half-dissolved faecal blobs against the ceramic lip. She pressed the back of her left hand against her mouth, feeling something rise in her throat.

Through the flywire window, she heard the awning

on her back verandah flap despairingly against itself like some tired bunting at a country fete. A flash of lightning illuminated, for a moment, the rest of her yard: the blank concrete slab, the lush thicket of ferns and fruit trees closing in around it. She swallowed whatever sour thing had tried to rise. She had to do something. She pictured the night ahead of her as she continued not to act. Hours of selfpunishment, worse than anything Tommy could dish out. Her eyes becoming iron-chained drawbridges, refusing to yield to a battering of sleep. All night, every mistake she had ever made, replaying in her head. The regrets, the missed chances, catalogued crisply and lined up like tabs in a filing cabinet. A finger running over them, flicking each in turn.

She seized the phone from in front of her, brought it up to her face before she could change her mind. She ignored the flashing message light, pushed out the sound of her mother's voice, her question, stored, waiting for as long as it would take. She punched in Tommy's number.

The tone burred, cracking with the usual static. After five rings it picked up.

'What?'

Madaline knew he had call display. 'Tommy,' she said. 'It's Madaline.'

'What.'

'There's been—' she struggled with the proper way to say it. 'Something's happened. A boy ... his parents have gone missing.'

'What boy? Madaline, it's fucken God knows what time. I'm trying to get some well-earned.'

'They arrived in town today. Iris's family. Her daughter.'

53

Tommy cleared his throat in a wet rattle. 'Iris's daughter?' He lowered his voice.

Madaline pictured Tommy's wife beside him, sleeping. 'Apparently, yeah. They went out to the lake, left the boy—Simon—in a room at the Ottoman. Never came back.'

'Whaddya want me to do?'

'I don't know. I sent Simon to Ned's place for now. Should I call it in?'

Tommy sighed. 'If you want. They'll probably turn up. Probably lost on a side road. Where're they from?'

Madaline stirred her oil-slick coffee with the handle of the spoon. 'Somewhere up the Gold Coast.'

'No doubt about it then. Lost. Fucken hell. You been out to Magpie?'

'Not yet.'

'Yeah, well. This weather—it's your funeral. The roads'll be shot.'

Madaline took her mug and went back to the living room. One of Ned's sandwiches still sat on the couch, the toasted triangles resting side by side, a suspension bridge of cheese linking them together. 'Yeah,' she said. 'I don't know.' She took a quick slug of coffee, wincing. The boiled water burned the top of her mouth, which somehow pleased her.

'They're probably bogged,' said Tommy, 'or the road's under. They'll be fine for a night.'

'Should I log it in?'

'If you want. Won't be looked at till tomorrow anyway, if ever. They see a low-priority pop up from our district, they put it straight in a special file called Not a Fucking Chance.' He yawned. 'We can chase it up in the morning. If I ever get back to bloody sleep.'

54

Madaline slumped into her leather chair, crossing her legs at the ankle, sighing to the ceiling. She caught her free hand plucking at a stack of paper by her chair. How many times had she promised herself she'd clean the room up? 'All right,' she said. 'I'll be down at the Ottoman first thing so I'll probably see you there. Sorry to bother—'

He hung up.

Madaline hauled a handful of paper onto her lap and let the pages flick over. Words jumped out at her—randomly, illogically. They had all begun to look like this. Cases, reports, statements. She leant over and picked up one half of Ned's sandwich. She took a bite from one corner, washed it down with another gulp of awful coffee. Why had she brought Ned into this? She knew exactly why.

There was another itch, another addiction: the bulging ringbinder held together with cracking rubber bands, sitting just under the couch. A schoolgirl's hiding place. Like a diary with a plastic lock. Madaline got off the chair and slid the folder out. Just the cover—the awful photographer's-background sponged grey, that was all it took. Her fingers shivered as she rolled off the rubber bands and opened the cover. The first page, pale blue, inside a torn plastic sleeve. She could have sketched it in her sleep. Case File : Disappearance : Stephanie Rhelma Gale. The thick black letters were an open grave. Nothing in the world could have made her feel worse.

Hand over hand. That's the way it'd always been. Small, repeated tasks producing the greatest results. Jack Tarden leant his weight back, feet bracing. He'd discovered a place where his boots could fit, where he could wedge himself impossibly into the slimy surface even as the waves slid up over them. The surf roared in around the bend in the cliffs but was quickly diffused by the angle of the rocks, the natural protection of the cove. The tide was rising, though. Tarden's ankles flooded with ice as the water found its way through the tiny rip in his trousers. He grimaced, but never let himself complain.

He would never allow himself to sell out like the others. He plied his craft the way others had done for decades, the true pioneers. He knew most of the fishermen would be only now stumbling from their houses, sealing themselves in climate-controlled utes for their short trip to the wharf, where all their boats clogged together, identical. He pictured their bulging figures, bodies wrapped in thick layers of artificial fleece, minds streamlined for profit and warmth. Chugging out in their boats to the same, overfished sections of the ocean. He was sorry for them, mostly, denying themselves the truest pleasure of what they did for a living.

Tarden's view from the cove was pure. No sense of the land, just the water. The sight of an empty ocean always inspired and scared him. The sun cracked at the horizon, and Tarden hauled the first pot up among the first long fingers of light. There was nothing—nothing—like the sight of the brass latches drawing towards him, gleaming from just below the water line, then the fizz as the pot broke the surface and the air was filled with the sound of streaming water, the bracing briny smell, the promise of the tell-tale shadows lurking behind the wire.

This was pure joy, a clean high: the morning's first catch. The first pot was a fiver, a good weight. Tarden hauled the pot onto its end, unlatched the lid. He threw away some weeds and a handful of nippers clinging, unfathomably, and as always, to the outside. He splashed some water back onto the rest—five crabs, healthy morning-first fellows with strong new shells of umber iron. He removed his left boot, placed it behind him, then picked the up the top crab with a strong starfish grip, reaching already to his pocket for the gnarl of fishing twine he kept there. The creature fought like a horse's heart. Tarden felt all of its strength travel up from his fingers, up his arm, through his chest. This one had struggled against life, he thought, and won. They always came to him, the strong ones, the water-spinners, the sand-movers, the underwater poets. No one else knew them but him. He held the crab down with his left foot, wrapping it in the twine, tying back its claws and legs.

Three more pots came up, and then the sun, a grey egg poaching in the white morning sky. These early winter sunrises were nothing but one black piece of paper placed before another. Not that he minded: Tarden's eyes strayed only to the sea, to the lake and the creeks. Less light was all that winter meant: he didn't mind the cold. Of course, the other fishers started later each day in

57

winter, complaining about the weather, spending more time drinking.

He collapsed the pots, threw them back into his boat that he'd anchored just before the rocks. The crabs, nineteen in all, went into a plastic tub. He motored slowly out of the cove and around the bend, making sure no other boats could see him. The cove was his place, and his place only. The rocks and the curve of its entrance meant it was nearly invisible to someone going past it, but still, you couldn't be too careful. No one could know it was there.

It was a good twenty-minute journey back to the wharf. He pulled a tarpaulin over the pots and his haul, shielding it from the air and from any prying eyes. He sat back and let the current guide the boat while he reached beneath his seat and took out his aluminium water flask. He took a slug of water and squinted out against the growing glare. He rested his free hand back on the tiller and put his feet up against the side of the tub. He felt the vibrations of the crabs testing their new surroundings, their gentle tapping on the plastic. These were the weaker ones, the ones he hadn't bothered to tie up. The crabs never grew frantic—never—and this was what Tarden liked most about them. Gracious, graceful creatures. He never liked to think too far into their future. Luckily, he had always been able to switch off that part of his brain. For better or worse.

He felt a dull ache in his finger, the one he had bitten the night before. He studied the ragged quick, noticing that one side of it, near the square edge of his fingernail, had stayed white, almost translucent. His skin was covered with many such strange markings. He had lost count of what they all meant. He thought of Robbie's arms, his shoulders, somehow untouched by the many imperfections of time. He had not been at home when Tarden left that morning. Nothing new there, he supposed.

The wharf drew into view and Tarden cut the engine, letting the tinnie drift with the current. He liked to watch the trawlers setting out and returning, wondered if he would ever own such a boat. Probably not in this lifetime, not while his craft was ruled by the bottom line, rewarding speed over quality.

Tarden watched the shimmer-mirror of the water's surface and thought of the young lad and his parents. They had seemed like nice people. But still.

The night had come into Simon's room. Not from the outside, from the black cavity of nature beyond the window, but from within: dark vacant shapes that grew like living things from tiny cracks and overlaps. Dark creatures had crawled, with their rich shadow flesh, along and up the walls. Drawing closer to Simon with each breath he took. They'd entered his eyes—ink stains leaching outwards and in—and when he closed them, they were inside him. His familiar dream demons shrouded themselves in dim cloaks, growing impossibly large, filling every space with fresh edgeless fear.

Somehow, these shards of sleep propelled Simon into a new day. He cowered in one corner of the enormous bed, sheets and quilt pushed back away from one another. His first moment was a sharp intake of breath. The light coming in the window was wrong: a weak light like a failing afternoon, nothing like what a morning was. Then he remembered the room, the house. His body was itchy without movement. He got off the bed and moved to the seat at the window. He looked out at a beach, sunken down behind sand dunes covered with a spiky grass.

Tall trees poked up too, stringy eucalypts and whippet-thin firs. Directly below, Simon saw a green splash of garden surrounded by a fence. Spidery salt crystals had hatched in each corner of the window. He felt the wind rattle the frame intermittently. He hugged himself in his strange woollen jumper, bending his knees up to his chin. The window seat was large and surprisingly comfortable, and he settled back in its softness. He sat for some time watching the morning mist shift between the trees, revealing colours and shapes and lines he would not normally have seen.

There was a sudden clunk, almost as if a rock or something just as heavy had been thrown against his door. He sprang off the seat and walked cautiously across the room. He put his ear to the door but heard nothing. Maybe someone else staying in the house had gone into the wrong room. Maybe someone had found his parents.

Maybe it was his parents.

Simon turned the doorknob slowly. It creaked in protest and Simon thought perhaps it was locked. He tried again, harder, and still it resisted. There was no sign of a lock or latch. He put both hands on the doorknob and tugged and the door flew open with sudden ease, sending him staggering back into the room. Before he could regain his balance he felt something hard fly into his stomach, knocking him to the floor, his left leg crumpling under him painfully. He glimpsed a flash of the ceiling as his body was lifted and crashed against the floorboards and a dull wedge jammed itself into his back. His body sand with one folding pain.

'Don't move,' said a croaky voice near Simon's ear.

It was a person, pinning him down, knee in his back. A set of bony brown fingers dug into his right shoulder. A rubber sole squeaked.

'What are you doing in here?' said the voice. It sounded old, but Simon could tell it belonged to someone young.

'I was … staying the night,' was all Simon could think to say with his cheek pressed against the floor.

61

'You can't stay on this floor,' said the voice. 'You can't stay in this room.'

'But Ned let me stay. He gave me some clothes.' Simon felt the pressure increase on his back. 'I'm only staying for … a bit,' he added.

'What?' said the voice. 'This is Ned's jumper.' Fingers felt at Simon's sleeves. 'And those are my trousers.' The voice's owner leapt off Simon's back. Simon unsprung his body and sat up, aching. A thin boy who looked only a few years older than him was crouched over the pile of clothes. He was pulling out different items and sorting them into piles. A pair of khaki trousers was draped over his shoulder, identical to the pair he was wearing.

'Unbelievable,' said the boy. 'Unbelievable.' His voice was strange; it rattled and rasped as he talked, like coins shaken in a tin. The tone of his speech was split in two, one a high echo of the other. He turned his face towards Simon. 'Where did you get these from?' he said, holding up the trousers.

'I told you—Ned gave them to me.' Simon rubbed his sore shoulder.

The boy's face turned into a sneer. His whole body was brown but Simon thought he wasn't a black person, just tanned. And dirty. Grime had made a home in his lines and creases, giving him wrinkles like an old person. He was scarily skinny too, his body bent at strange angles. His bones pointed out from his skin as if they had been fired from some painful internal machine. 'How do you know Ned?' the boy asked.

Simon's head began to spin. 'He let me stay here. Madaline and him let me stay. I lost my parents, okay?'

The boy's sneer fell away. His face resumed an inert,

62

sallow expression. 'You lost your parents? How did you do that?' He dropped the pile of clothes and sat cross-legged on the floor.

'I didn't mean to,' said Simon, then realised this was a stupid answer. 'They went for a drive to the lake. And they haven't come back.'

'You're lucky,' said the boy. 'What's your name?'

'What do you mean I'm lucky?'

'My name's Pony.'

'Pony? Like a horse?'

A rolled-up sock hit Simon on the forehead.

Pony's voice dropped. 'Don't make fun of my name or next time it'll be a rock.'

Simon scrunched the sock in his fist. 'My name's Simon Sawyer,' he said, sitting cross-legged as well.

'Well my name's just Pony.' He stood up. 'My parents died, so you're lucky you just lost yours.'

'I'm sorry for your loss.' Simon had heard his mother say this sometimes.

Pony made a dismissive sound with his mouth. He sat on the edge of the bed, kicking the air with thick boots covered in gaffer tape. 'Simon the Pie Man,' he wheezed. 'Simple Simon.'

Simon didn't like Pony at all. He was like all bullies: never content to let anything lie.

'Where's Ned?' said Simon.

'Making breakfast. What's up with your leg?'

Simon's face burned. He pulled the jumper down to cover his shins. His scars began to itch. 'Nothing,' he said. 'What's up with your voice?'

This was how Simon always got into trouble—standing up for himself at exactly the wrong moment.

63

He tensed for retaliation, but instead of striking out Pony just laughed, a dry sound like a prize draw on an old game show, like a thousand envelopes rolling in a barrel.

Pony kicked his heels against the bed. All he said was, 'Welcome aboard, Simon Sawyer.'

Madaline swung the steering wheel harder than she needed to, pulling up just shy of the pavement. Lost in her thoughts, she had found the main street nearly past her when she realised where she was. Her tyres made a short squeal, but the only witnesses were other cars, seemingly rusted onto the road exactly where they were always parked. The town that never changed. She shut off the ignition and took a deep breath. The rain had lent a plastic sheen to the pavements, and bubbles of dirty water welled in the seam of the car's window.

Her hands seemed browner against the sky-blue of her shirtcuffs. Her winter uniform, retrieved from her cupboard that morning, still sealed in its dry-cleaner's bag. The unfamiliar weight of a heavy belt at her hips. She had tried, earlier, to think of the last time she'd worn her full uniform. Even when the District Commander visited, every few weeks, she was not compelled to wear it. Tommy's personal rules of 'country policing' included a relaxed dress code, and he held enough clout in the district to have this pass unquestioned. She fingered the coarse weave of her navy trousers, a heavier fabric for winter. Her hat sat next to her on the seat, smelling of dry-cleaner's chemicals, hiding beneath its plastic rain cover. Shower caps, they'd called them once. She had even changed into police-issue shoes, hiking boots with metres of laces, instead of her usual black sneakers.

She stepped from the car, the breeze teasing her bare neck where she'd gathered up her hair into a short, unsuccessful ponytail. The glare off the street pierced her sleep-clogged eyes. She felt a sort of unbalanced sickness as she stepped over the large puddle she had unerringly parked in and up onto the footpath, avoiding a loose slab of concrete that had slipped out of place, its lip mounting the kerb. Bitumen spit—the remnants of the last half-hearted council works—lined a lamp post. She stepped into the shade of an awning, refocusing on a wagon-train of ants circling cautiously the rim of a public bin.

She walked the few metres to the Ottoman, clearing her throat as she pushed open the door. Inside, the air was full with frypan haze. She sensed the same things as always: the smell of brine and the sour edges of old beer leaching from the bar next door, the fat squeak of bacon cooking. There was always something about the cafe, a layer of something that hadn't quite been cleaned. The always-present group of fishers had dragged three tables together to sit against the back wall. There seemed more of them than usual, crowded together like a single mass.

Madaline took a seat at the main counter. She could see the top of her head in the reflection of a Peter Jackson ad. Someone had scrubbed out the brand name, but she knew it was there. Megan was behind the counter, squeezing chocolate syrup into a tall glass. 'Morning,' said Madaline, in what she hoped was a friendly way. Megan always seemed pissed off about something.

'Hi,' she said, not bothering to look up. Her hair hung in front of her eyes: black-tipped blonde strands.

'How's things?'

Megan shrugged. She bent down to get milk from the fridge and Madaline glimpsed the tattoo at the base of her spine: blackbirds.

'Is Nat in?'

'Cooking.' She motioned a hand to the door that led to the kitchen. 'Can you get him for me?'

Megan stood there, stirring the milk and syrup together until it turned a dull brown, regarded Madaline with her different coloured eyes.

'Can you get him?' Madaline repeated. 'It's important.'

Megan skulked off and Nat appeared moments later. His face was covered in a sheen of sweat, as it often seemed to be. He wiped his brow with the arm of his shirt. 'Dressed up for us, Mads.'

Madaline smiled grimly. She hated that contraction of her name. 'Something like that.'

'Some rain, ay.'

She nodded.

'You here bout those people? The kid's parents?'

'Yeah. Need the key for the room they stayed in last night.'

'Gave em to Tommy X-Ray. Swans in here first thing, full uniform, same as you.' Nat chuckled.

Madaline blew out her cheeks. It was like he went out of his way to infuriate her. 'Tommy's been in already?'

'Yeah, said he was heading down to Magpie. Should be back through any time.'

'Right.' Madaline took off her hat and placed it on the counter. 'Guess I'll wait.'

'You want something to eat?'

'Thanks.'

Nat headed out the back again and Madaline settled

onto the stool. Tommy X-Ray. That ridiculous nickname. A legacy from the hostage case that made him a hero in his first posting. Happened years ago, in Coffs Harbour, but everyone in Reception knew the story like it was their own. She picked up a newspaper someone had left on the counter, but it was one of the Sydney tabloids, already a week old. It was hard keeping up with things here: newspapers only got dropped at the servo every few days in the off-season, and heaven help you if you wanted a TV signal for the nightly news.

Madaline sensed a quick silence cut through the cafe. She swung around to meet the inevitable staring eyes of the fishers who dropped their gaze quickly to their drinks. Except Jack Tarden, who shot two nervous glances at her. She grinned briskly in his direction, knowing it would throw him. She already knew he had told them all about the isappearance. Probably worked out the mistakes she'd already made.

Nat came back, carrying a bowl of muesli and yoghurt, and a mug trailing steam. His wide brown fingers nearly dwarfed the bowl. 'Sorry,' he said. 'I would've put some fruit in, but I've been bought out this morning.' He nodded his head at the back wall. 'No fry-ups. Whole town's on a health-kick now, apparently.' He put down the bowl and the mug.

'Doesn't matter,' said Madaline. She wrapped her hands around the mug, letting the sting of plain boiling water transfer to her skin. 'You're good enough to me as it is.'

'Don't you forget it.' Nat took out a lemon from somewhere behind the counter and cut it in half with a small knife. 'Bon appetite.'

Madaline picked up the lemon half and squeezed it

into the mug, watching as it blossomed milky clouds in the water. She sipped it and could already feel her head beginning to clear.

'Morning, Senior Constable McKinley,' said a quiet voice.

Madaline felt someone sit on the stool next to her. She turned around. 'Morning, Robert James Kuiper.'

Kuiper mock-winced. 'Okay. Madaline. How's ... everything?'

Madaline took a mouthful of muesli, swallowed it too soon. 'I'm fine, Robbie,' she said. 'How're they biting?'

'Biting?'

Madaline threw out an imaginary line.

'Ah, the fishing, yes.' Kuiper smoothed down the front of his pressed shirt. He wore a peaked tweed cap, which was certainly odd, but Madaline knew him well enough not to comment on it. 'Well,' he said, the clipped South African vowels precise, 'there are plenty in the sea, if that's what you mean.' He smiled at her. His teeth were like little bones buried in his gums.

Madaline could already feel the patronising heat rising. She decided to wrong-foot him. 'I was actually hoping to get your help this morning. With the search.'

'Oh yes?' Kuiper drummed his fingers on the table. Knuckled tanned a deep brown.

'I assume you've heard about this disappearance?'

'Who hasn't?'

'I wanted you and Jack to help with the search this morning. I know Jack's an SES volunteer.'

'As am I.'

'Really?' Madaline couldn't help but smile.

'Why so shocked?'

69

'Just can't see you in an orange jumpsuit. Well, actually I can.'

Kuiper's face darkened. 'That's very droll.'

'You think you and Jack could get some people together? We need as much help as we can get.'

'I thought Tommy would be taking care of all this.' Kuiper accent made his consonants bite.

Madaline's fingers tightened on her spoon. 'Well, Tommy isn't here, so I'm asking you.'

'We're keeping it local, then?'

'For the time being, I suppose.'

'Well I'm sure we'd be more than—' Kuiper trailed off as Tarden's hand landed on his shoulder.

'Morning Madaline,' Tarden said. 'Any news?'

'Not really,' she said. 'Just talking to Robbie here about organising a search party.'

'For sure. Long as the roads are okay. Fair bit of water when I went down the wharf earlier on.'

Kuiper arched his back, and Tarden removed his hand.

'We'll have to see,' said Madaline. 'I'm just waiting for Tommy, then we can get moving.'

'No, well we'd be happy to help,' said Tarden. 'That poor kid.'

Madaline's chest tightened. 'I'm going up to see him soon.'

Tarden propped his hands behind his overalls. 'Sure they haven't got far.'

'Well, that's what we all hope. You guys right to get some searchers together?'

Kuiper yawned. 'Don't worry about us,' he said. 'We're well versed in this particular scenario.'

'Right,' said Madaline, her voice thinning out. 'Yes.'

'Well,' said Kuiper, getting off the stool. 'Guess we'll see you out there.'

The two men walked back to their table. Madaline stared at her unfinished breakfast. A keyhole burn of indigestion flamed at her throat. She sipped at her lemon water and flicked through the newspaper, waiting for the unlikely moment her appetite returned.

There was a familiar phlegmy cough behind her: Tommy Parker, in a new uniform, fixing her with a sour squint. Whatever Tommy wore looked like it had seen better days. His navy trousers shone with strain; he'd pulled them halfway up his gut, exposing his non-issue white circulation socks and moulding his crotch into an unpleasant wedge. Lit from behind, the sparse stalks of his hair seemed to be alight. He hauled himself onto a stool.

'Morning,' said Madaline, folding up the paper.

Tommy slumped onto his elbows. 'Went down there earlier,' he said.

Conversations with Tommy always seemed to start halfway through, and end around the same point. Madaline often wondered how his wife put up with him. Perhaps she was just used to it.

'Went down where?'

'The lake. Took the four-wheel-drive down to have a look. Check the roads were okay.'

'Oh yes?'

'No car for one thing.'

'No car?'

'Roads were driveable at least.'

'There was no car at the lake?'

'Tea please love.' Tommy raised his hand at Megan, who raised a hand back.

71

'Tommy?'

'Hmm?'

'At the lake. The Sawyers' car wasn't there?'

'Like I say.'

Madaline blew out a long breath. 'You don't think they wentout there?'

'I think they went there, but I don't think they stayed there.'

'Why's that?'

Tommy reached into his shirt pocket and pulled out an evidence bag. 'Found it at the carpark.' He threw it onto the counter.

Madaline picked up the bag. It held a set of keys attached to a wooden keyring. She upturned the bag to see it better. 'A turtle.'

Megan came over with Tommy's coffee. He had his own mug they kept behind the counter, a big white mug one with the words # 1 DAD printed on in red. His daughter—who had kids herself now, who had long ago fled Reception for a suburban city life—had given it to him before she left.

'Ta,' he said. He took a long sip, slurping it in.

'Hey,' said Megan. 'That's one of ours.' She reached over and took the evidence bag.

Madaline was about to protest before she understood. 'Is this a room key?'

'Yeah. They all have a different animal. This is ... room eight.'

Tommy put down his mug. 'Room eight,' he said, nodding.

'That was their room, wasn't it,' said Madaline. 'The Sawyers.'

72

'Yeah,' said Megan, handing back the bag. 'Fucking hell.'

Tommy shot her a glare.

'Sorry,' she said, 'but fucking hell.'

'We're going to have to check the room,' said Madaline. She took out her wallet.

Tommy put up a hand. 'Can you let an old man finish his coffee first? An old man who's already done an hour's honest work.'

'Jesus, Tommy.' Madaline eyed Megan, who took the hint and began to walk to the other end of the counter. 'Jesus,' she repeated. 'This could be important.'

Tommy wiped his mouth, the white bristles at the corner of his lips. 'Settle down, Senior Constable. I chased up the rego and called it in.'

'But that doesn't—'

'Ten dollars says they're picked up by the afternoon. These parents—dopeheads, probably—they're already halfway home.'

'You think they're junkies who drove a few hundred kilometres to abandon their kid?'

Tommy shrugged. 'The criminal mind is not a very clever thing.'

'I just don't think we should discount other options.'

'Well, my current option is finishing my cup of coffee. Maybe having another.' Tommy took a long slurp from his mug.

Madaline sighed.

'Listen.' Tommy wiped his mouth with the back of his hand. 'Madaline. I tell you this for your own good: you overthink things. You always want to look for more.'

'So?'

73

Tommy's grey-coated tongue darted from his mouth to catch a coffee drop. 'What you have to understand,' he said, 'is that there's no great mystery to what we do. It's boring. It's fucking monotonous. We shovel the shit left behind by desperate, stupid people.'

'I don't think—'

'It's bloody depressing, but it's true. And it means the most obvious answer is usually the right one.'

Madaline ground her fingernails into the palm of her left hand. She knew what was fucking monotonous, and it was sitting right next to her. 'So we don't investigate it?'

Tommy downed his coffee in another gulp, pushed the cup back on the bar. 'I'm just saying don't tie yourself up in knots.'

'Look, when Stephanie Gale—' Madaline knew her mistake even as she said it.

'This again?' Tommy threw up his hands. 'Bored wife goes off for a swim and never comes back. You say big fucking mystery? I say big fucking ocean.'

Madaline felt her stomach tighten. 'Fine.' She got off her stool. 'I'll check the room.'

She slid the keyring off the counter and walked purposefully towards the door. The worst thing was, she knew he was right. She already knew what she'd find in the hotel room. Another dead end.

The house creaked like a ship. Simon half expected to hear icebergs shrieking along a hull, an engine rumbling far below. He slid his hand down the balustrade. Pony clomped down the stairs in front of him, swaying. He had let Simon wear his spare trousers—green soldier's pants with pockets stitched into every corner—and now the pair of them matched, although Simon still had on Ned's purple jumper.

As it turned out, Pony had thrown a rock at Simon's door. He kept a collection of them in his pockets—flat skimming stones—for what reason Simon had no idea. About Pony's person were also concealed various chains, sticks and pieces of string. He had proudly shown Simon but had declined, when pressed, to elaborate on their purpose.

Pony led Simon to the kitchen, down the stairs and along a passageway, through a set of swinging doors he opened with straight-locked arm. Ned stood at a monstrous steaming stove, his hair tied back with a thick black band, a frypan in each hand. The gas hotplates ran in two rows, four at the front and four at the back. He turned around and gave Pony a confused look. 'You're up early,' he said, 'for a weekend.'

'Yeah,' said Pony. 'Just felt like it.' He swung himself up onto a chair beside a huge wooden table. It was made of dark brown wood and lacquered. Simon stayed in the doorway, unsure of what he should be doing. He coughed. Ned looked at him, Simon thought, the way you might look at a shadow, then he blinked and shook his head. 'Simon. Oh, I completely ... I'm so sorry.' He turned and wiped his hands on a nearby tea towel. 'How did you sleep?'

'Well. Thank you.'

'Come in. Sit down. You've met ... Pony?'

'Yes, I have.' Simon took a chair across the corner from where Pony sat. It was wooden, too, and heavy.

Ned took one pan off the stove. 'Simon, there's ... been no word on your parents yet. I'm sure Madaline and everyone will be doing all they can. There'll be search parties I suppose. That sort of thing.'

Simon nodded. All along the kitchen window herbs grew in thick green plumes.

'I'm making breakfast,' said Ned, 'if you'd like some.' Before Simon could answer, he swung his body back to the stove, just as one of the pans began to hiss frying butter. 'Can someone pass me a few tomatoes?' he said over his shoulder. Pony didn't respond, so Simon looked around for where they might be. 'Over there,' said Ned, 'in the crate.' He pointed to the corner. Simon saw three large wooden crates. He hopped off his chair and peered inside one. It was filled with crackly-skinned brown onions. The next one held potatoes. The third, finally, tomatoes. He handed three to Ned, the fattest and reddest he could find.

'Good man.' Ned sliced the tomatoes in half with an immense shiny knife, letting the halves fall into the steaming pan. Simon watched their red skins shrink with the heat. 'Can't have a fry-up without good fresh tomatoes,' said Ned, grinning. Bacon followed. Mushrooms. Beans. Mashed potato balls. In the other pan, Ned cracked six eggs. He did them two at a time, with one hand, breaking one shell against the other. The yolks fell in perfect circles.

Simon's parents only ever ate muesli, sitting silently across an empty table.

Pony had spilt orange juice on the table, and sat staring at a squadron of ants conducting reconnaissance around it, traversing the grooves in the wood. 'Gonna rain again today,' he said.

'How do you know that?' asked Ned, moving all the food onto a large metal tray. Pony made a tyre-air noise with his mouth. 'Winged ants. See? They're not normally on the move unless something's going to happen. Usually rain.'

'Better leave the washing for tomorrow then I guess.' Ned brought the tray over to the table and placed tongs and a spatula next to it. 'I'll whack some toast on and then go and raise the dead.' He looked at Simon quickly. 'Audrey and Gin, I mean. You guys help yourselves while it's hot. Pony knows where the plates are.'

Ned left through the swinging doors. Pony slid reluctantly off his stool. He opened a cupboard beside a large set of pantry doors and removed some plates. He said, 'Of course, ants can mean any sort of change. Rain's just one sort.' He took a handful of cutlery from hooks on the wall. 'Might have something to do with your mum and dad.'

'What do you mean?'

'Animals pick up on these things.'

'Do they know where my parents are?'

Pony sat down heavily and lanced a forkful of bacon. 'You'd have to ask them, wouldn't you.'

'That's stupid,' said Simon.

Pony just shrugged and began to spade food from the tray to his mouth. Simon, manoeuvring at the edge of the frenzy, felt like a bird picking food from between a crocodile's teeth.

With a squawk, the swinging doors opened. Simon turned around to see the little boy—Julian, Gin—rush in wearing a blue and red costume, arms outstretched, hair slicked into a Superman curl. He stopped when he saw Simon, his flight hovering in mid-air. Ned came in behind him.

'Gin, this is Simon. He'll be staying with us for a little while.'

'Why?'

Ned smiled weakly. 'Remember? We talked about Simon. He's visiting.'

Gin regarded Simon with X-ray eyes. 'Do you know who Clark Kent is?' he said.

'Yes,' said Simon. 'He's Superman when he's not Superman.'

Gin nodded. He looked around before resuming his flight, landing at a seat on the other side of the table. His red socks were so long that the ends folded back under his feet.

Ned went back to the stove and the girl, Audrey, came in. She wore a blue mesh basketball singlet over a yellow skivvy. The layered skirt remained.

'Good morning Simon. I hope you slept well.' She took the seat beside him. 'Would you like some juice?' She looked at him with her head tilted, like someone watching goldfish. 'Seeing as Pony didn't get you any.'

'Simon and me wear the same trousers,' said Pony matter-of-factly. 'Simon Sawyer and me.'

Audrey rolled her eyes. She went to the fridge and came back with a container of orange juice and two glasses. 'I'm sorry about your parents,' she said. 'Do you think they'll come back?'

Ned cleared his throat. 'Perhaps we should just eat, Audrey. Would you like some banana?'

'Yum. Simon will have some too, won't you Simon?'

'Maybe after I finish this,' he said, pointing to his plate.

Audrey quickly wiped orange juice from her lips. 'No, Simon, you have to have it with this! Banana and bacon.'

'Banana and bacon?'

'It's weird,' said Gin.

'She's weird,' said Pony.

Audrey drum-rolled the table. 'They're stupid. You'll love it.'

'Maybe Simon can try a small bit,' said Ned. He peeled two bananas, cut them lengthways and placed them in the pan. Simon had to admit it smelled pretty good.

Gin squelched mushrooms under his fork. 'How long are you visiting for?' he asked.

Simon rotated his glass of juice. 'I'm not sure. I don't know.'

'People visit the hotel,' said Gin. 'But they all have to leave sometime.'

'I suppose they do,' said Simon.

'It's my birthday tomorrow, are you coming?'

Ned said, 'That'll do, Gin,' and brought the pan over to the table.

Simon thought the banana looked mushy and delicious.

It had crispy brown strips down its edge. Audrey showed Simon how to wrap the bacon around it. The first forkful made him murmur. It was the best thing he had ever tasted.

They finished breakfast and Ned washed up while Gin rinsed and Audrey and Simon dried. Pony wiped the kitchen table distractedly, absorbed in his own middle-distance.

Ned's hands were immersed in angry steaming water. 'So,' he said to Simon, 'what did you think of breakfast?'

'It was great,' Simon replied.

'Dad used to be a chef,' said Gin. His Superman sleeves were rolled up above his elbows. 'Everyone likes his food.'

'Well,' said Ned, 'I used to be a caterer. Slightly different to a chef in a restaurant. I cook for the guests here now sometimes, but only breakfasts. Mainly it's just us.'

Simon rubbed a fork through his tea towel. He said, 'Am I your only guest?'

Ned's hands stopped moving under the water. 'Well,' he said, 'not really. There are a few ... permanent guests, I suppose. It's always less busy in winter, anyway.

'Megan stays with us,' said Pony, 'In summer. When she has work.'

'Who's Megan?' said Simon.

'She works at the Ottoman,' said Ned. 'She waitresses. And helps out here when it gets busier.'

'She stays in the next room over from me,' added Pony.

Audrey snorted out a laugh. 'Pony's in love with her,' she said. 'And he never leaves.'

Pony rolled his eyes. 'Whatever.'

Ned shook his hands dry in the air, cutting off Pony's inevitable response. 'Pony's more family now, really, than a guest.' He pulled the plug from the basin.

'And Iris.' Pony's voice mixed perfectly with the sink-water curdling in the plughole. 'Don't forget Iris.'

Ned cleared his throat. 'Yes,' he said. 'Iris has been with us a while, too. She's like family as well, I suppose. Well ... have you finished the drying yet Audrey?'

Audrey had the large breakfast tray in her hands. It dripped water at her feet. Nearly,' she said. Simon stood ready with his tea towel. He sensed a need for duty and calm.

'Just leave the tray if you like,' said Ned. 'I've got a few things to do, but Madaline—Senior Constable McKinley—is coming by soon, Simon. She can let us know how everything's going. I'll get some clothes for you, and maybe Audrey can show you around a bit more.'

Simon nodded. Before mention of his grandma, he had forgotten she was here, under the same roof. He still wasn't sure he wanted to see her, not without his parents. What he wanted, more than anything else, was to see Madaline coming up the driveway in a proper police car, his parents in the back seat, smiling, running towards the house to see him.

'Can I go and fly?' asked Gin. 'In the garden?'

Ned checked his watch, which, Simon noticed, still wasn't there. 'That's fine,' said Ned, 'but clean yourself up before you come inside.'

Gin shot off back through the swinging doors. Ned followed him, smiling.

Pony sniggered. He stretched his tree-stick arms behind him.

81

'What's so funny?' Audrey dropped the breakfast tray upside down in the sink.

Pony pointed at the table in front of him. In the pool of his spilt orange juice, the flying ants were floating. He flicked them with his finger and their suspended bodies spun, wings broken, slowing to a stop in their amber ocean.

Audrey never stopped spinning. She jumped around Simon like a humming top.

'This is so exciting,' she said. 'No one ever comes here in winter.'

Simon followed her down the hall from the kitchen. Her hair was strange; it seemed to wisp and dance with its own life.

They walked back past the front door. Simon noticed a small raised desk in a recess by the doorway he hadn't seen the night before. An old looking silver bell, a town crier's bell, sat on the desk next to a discreet sign that said Reception. The blue tiles at the entrance seemed even bluer in the daylight.

Audrey pointed down a corridor to their left. 'That's where we sleep,' she said. 'I mean, Dad and Gin and I each have a room.' She led him into a large dark room with two giant bookcases flanking the entrance. Big brown leather couches were scattered everywhere. It felt to Simon like he was walking through a giant chocolate box. A small television nestled nearly out of sight in a corner.

'This is the living room,' said Audrey. 'It's for the guests, really, but we use it all the time. Also, we're not allowed to watch TV after seven at night.' There was a hint of pride in Audrey's voice. 'Are you allowed to watch TV, Simon?'

83

'I suppose so,' he said.

'And your parents don't mind?'

'I don't think so.' The truth was, his parents never really forbade anything. Mainly because they weren't around to forbid it.

'TV's bad for you,' said Audrey. 'I prefer music.' She walked over to a tall window that looked out onto the front garden. Next to the window was a small wooden phone table and an old-fashioned black telephone. Audrey spent a few moments staring at it. She lifted her shoulders back. Without warning, she quickly hoisted the receiver from its cradle and slammed it back down.

Simon jumped. A sharp ping tumbled-turned in his ears.

Audrey sniffed. 'What sort of music do you like, Simon?'

Simon righted his breathing, which had skewed sideways with the shock of the phone.

'I'm not sure,' he said. 'I don't really listen to music much.'

'That's strange. I thought everyone listened to music. I like Rossini.' Audrey hummed a staccato tune, and mimed a bow and arrow at Simon's head. 'I've got lots of records,' she said. 'They're so much better than CDs.' Her feet shuffled light, easy patterns as she talked: more a boxer than a ballerina.

Simon studied the bookshelves, which were lined neatly with sombre spines. 'Have all these books been read?'

Audrey shrugged. 'I'm not sure how I'd know that,' she said, knotting her brow. Sometimes the guests read them. Dad doesn't really read. Besides, they look better all in a row, don't you think?'

'I suppose.' Simon's parents didn't own any books, except boring ones about changing your life or getting rich. No stories. Back at home, he had twelve different library cards. He had never seen so many books outside a library. 'Do you think I'd be able to read one?' he asked.

'Maybe.' Audrey had turned around to face the window. She appeared not to stare at the view, but up at the pane itself. She said, 'Do you know what's going to happen to you, Simon?'

Simon ran his fingers down a row of books. 'What do you mean?'

'Do you know how your life is going to turn out?'

Simon turned around. 'How would I know that?'

'Well, some people think it's all mapped out for you already, and you just follow along, like a join-the-dots.'

'I don't think my life's a join-the-dots.'

Audrey made a vague noise of agreement and placed all eight fingers against the window's glass. The morning light shone through, evenly and calmly, tricking Simon's eye so it looked like Audrey's fingers were the only thing holding the outside world together.

A hazy despair rose in Simon's mind. The weight of isolation grew heavy about his head. He didn't know anyone now. He didn't know anything. There were no points of reference left, just him. His lungs filled with a thick, irrational fear.

'I want to see my grandma,' he said. 'I want to see Iris.'

Audrey sighed. She turned her head to Simon, her eyes vexed with some hidden question. She looked a lot like Gin, Simon thought: somehow, in whatever way it was that resemblance shimmers through a family. He wondered if anyone ever saw the features of his parents

85

appearing in his face. He certainly didn't see his face in theirs.

'I guess you can,' she said. 'If you want. She gets up late, but we can knock on her door.'

'Yes,' said Simon. 'Please.' He knew he had offended Audrey somehow. 'You can show me the rest of the house later, though.'

Audrey's face brightened. 'Yes I can, can't I. Come on then,' she said.' She skidded out of the room on pretend skis, and Simon followed. She walked right up the centre of the staircase, arms outstretched, so her arms brushed each banister. The light was brighter at the top of the stairs. Through a porthole window, the sun chewed thoughtfully on fat clouds. Simon peered closer and saw Gin running past in the garden below.

'This floor is where the guests stay,' said Audrey. 'Pony and Iris stay here too.'

In daylight, Simon saw the walls were covered in white and green wallpaper, striped thick and thin like a humbug. Simon asked, 'How many people can stay here?'

'There are six rooms. Seven, if we need to. When we kick Pony out.'

'Isn't it weird, having strangers in your house?'

'Not really,' said Audrey. 'I'm used to it, and it's how Dad makes his money. Besides, everyone has strangers in their house.'

'No they don't. I don't.'

'They don't have to be people you can see,' said Audrey, as if explaining the deadly obvious. 'No matter where you are, there are other people.'

'You mean ... ghosts? I don't believe in ghosts.'

'That doesn't matter. Some people don't want to see

them. And, sometimes, they don't want to see you.'

Simon made a dismissive noise. 'Our house is brand new. No one else lives there.' Simon remembered the cold flat smell of fresh paint, the dead sound of all the empty rooms.

He walked over to a cabinet. The light reflected off the glassso he couldn't see what was inside. Audrey was strange—this was the conclusion he had reached. How could there be ghosts everywhere? He surely would have seen one by now if there were.

Audrey came up behind him. 'So what is it you believe in, then?'

'What do you mean?'

'Well if you don't believe in ghosts, what do you think is out here—' she swept her arm theatrically above her head '—apart from you and me?'

Simon thought of ghosts riding the air currents that swooped from Audrey's arm. They all had improbable howling faces. Simon knew he believed a little bit in God, but this was something he had confessed to no one. He certainly wasn't going to tell Audrey. houghts of God were only for late-night ceiling stares and moments when silent spaces scared him. And definitely not for people he'd just met. 'I don't know if anything's out there,' he said, 'except for maybe molecules or atoms or something.'

Audrey's lips fizzed. 'There's too many of them to count,' she said. 'So why bother?' She walked away from Simon, plunging her hands into hidden pockets in her skirt. 'I thought you were smart, Simon. Apparently not.'

Simon's scars began to buzz. 'Where does your mum sleep?' he said, immediately regretting it. He had already guessed Audrey's parents had divorced. His stupid words, coming out, as usual, at the worst possible time.

Audrey's reaction was not one Simon expected. Audrey's features—instead of widening with shock, or puckering with anger—simply receded, like water into a sponge. 'No,' she saideventually. 'It's just us.' She ruffled her left hand deep into her hair.

'I'm sorry,' said Simon, 'I didn't mean—'

'Iris's room is on the end at the left,' interrupted Audrey. 'You can find your way I'm sure.'

'Audrey—'

'See you, Simon.' She clomped back down the hallway without giving him a chance to respond.

Simon was left alone in the empty corridor, with its invisible ghosts and misspoken words.

Ned's house always reared up on you before you realised it was there. Its colonial arches appearing first above the rise of the hill, then the rest of it, a castle, an outpost. It had been built as a postmaster's house, or so Ned had told her, back when Reception was a whaling town. Sometimes, the house seemed to hang out off the edge of the land, clinging impossibly to the air.

Madaline had been here first four years ago: her first seaside summer. She'd come straight from Sydney, from a place she'd felt filled with manic boredom. Two years following orders, following protocol, making career progress by simply having no other purpose in her life. She'd been running, of course, from an old life, and had taken the posting in Reception as something of a compromise: halfway between the polluted crush of now and the humid cloak of then. Ned and Stephanie Gale were the first to welcome her, perhaps enjoying the companionship of someone close to their own age, perhaps sensing her vulnerabilities. Just the view, the house appearing, had filled her with a gladness she hadn't known for so long. That feeling was faint now, nearly washed away.

She felt another pang of memory, her first night in her new house. Bare walls and a single bed: space waiting to be filled. Flicking on every light in the house, clapping her hands to test the echo. It had reminded her, more than anything, of the single, spotless lock-up Tommy had shown her in the police station attached to his house. If we do our job right, he'd said, we'll never have to use this. Tommy, even then, was a country cop diffused to cliché: tyre-truck stomach, orange fingertips, a drinker's rippled gaze. Above his desk was framed newspaper clipping of his famous hostage case. He was so different: stout, still, but strong with it, his eyes bearing dark intensity. Tommy X-Ray. The person she knew now—her boss—was an old man treading water till retirement. The saddest thing was he had lost his perspicuity, the one trait that had really set him apart. The way this morning he had already decided the Sawyers had done a runner. The easiest option for him. Madaline parked her car, adjusted the rearvision mirror. She caught herself checking her hair and slapped the mirror back into place. At least Tommy's integrity had taken twenty years to leach away. Hers was gone inside a fortnight.

A blur came at her from the other side of the house. Ned's son, Gin, dressed as Superman. A mud-spattered red cape flew out behind him. He seemed, in fact, sodden with water. His outfit was stained dark, sticking to his skin. What was once—Madaline guessed—a carefully formed cowlick, was now a thatchy mess. She saw Ned's face in Gin: a bright eagerness, an important detail.

She got out of her car. 'Gin,' she called. 'Hi!'

Gin stopped in his tracks and then started running towards her. 'Hi,' he shouted. 'I'm Superman!'

Madaline walked up the hill towards him. 'I can see that.'

'And you're a policeman!'

Madaline ran her fingers across her starched collar.

'Well, yes. Police officer. It's a bit cold for a swim, isn't it?' She motioned at the darkened S on his chest.

'Have you found Simon's mum and dad?' Gin came up to her, but stopped a few metres away. He squinted at her through one eye.

'Not yet,' she said. 'But it won't be long.'

Gin nodded his head, a resigned movement. Madaline felt a familiar tightness in her chest. She had given Gin the same false promises about his own mother. She wondered if he still remembered.

'Is ... your dad here?' she said.

'Think so. Want me to go get him?'

'Sure.'

'I'll fly back to the house, okay?'

'Okay.'

'But will you watch me fly back?'

'Sure.'

'But you promise?'

'Yes,' said Madaline. 'I promise.'

Gin turned around and ran back to the house, arms outstretched. He was acting, Madaline thought, insulating himself. Always adding a layer.

She wondered how Audrey was. Madaline had seen reports from counsellors, from teachers, but they didn't tell her what she really wanted to know: whether the hollow space that grief had scooped out of the little girl was beginning to fill again. No amount of training could have prepared Madaline for what she saw Audrey go through. It was as if a light had been switched off inside her mind: she'd been shrivelled, submerged by her loss. It was clear she had worshipped Stephanie, never far from her side. After disappearancewas replaced by probable death, Audrey had filled a bathtub, climbed in and refused to leave. Madaline, sent to interview her, knocked on the bathroom door—talked through it—for nearly ten minutes, before forcing open the lock. Audrey was still, lying down, her face the only part of her above the water line. Her waist-length hair drifted in the water as if it was the water, swirling strands covering the surface completely. It was only when Madaline said her name that Audrey's eyes opened, that she raised herself up and it was clear that her hair was no longer attached to her head. Her patchy skull turned and the girl met Madaline's eyes. The hair in the water began bleaching red and Madaline only realised what had happened when Audrey's arm emerged, holding a pair of heavy fabric scissors, her wrist hatched black, her arm streaming blood.

It was this image that stained Madaline's dreams, more than any other.

Simon put his ear to the cold wood of the door, like he had seen in the movies. He couldn't hear anything. His grandmother's room was, as it turned out, only two doors down from his. He strained as hard as he could to listen. He wanted, somehow, to hear Iris's steady breaths, wanted to recognise her instantly, even from such a tiny detail. He was worried no one had roused her the night before. Worried that her sickness was a deep, debilitating disease. What if she had wasted away? What if she was nothing but a skeleton sunk into sheets?

Simon held his breath and knocked at the door, gently, with a bunched index finger. The sound was nearly deafening in the quiet of the hall. He felt suddenly, impossibly out of place. He flexed his legs, ready to leave, but no voices protested, no feet came running across the floorboards. No sound at all, in fact, except the growing rumble of distant waves.

He tried the door handle, but pushing against it he felt a great resistance. More than a lock, perhaps: almost as if something heavy had been pressed against the door. Suddenly, then, a voice from inside the room, so familiar that Simon's breath caught in his throat.

'Who's that?' said the voice.

Simon's mind spun back to the glare of a window, his starfish hand pressed against it. His scars itched: he imagined criss-cross lines linking each of them. Join-the-dots. This was his last chance to run away. To keep running until he found a home. 'It's me,' he said. 'It's ... Simon.'

Silence from behind the door. Then a scraping sound. 'Simon?' Iris's voice was weak.

'Yes,' he said again. He had the strange sense of being an imposter, like he wasn't Simon, or at least wasn't the Simon he was supposed to be. 'It's your ... grandson.' The word was so strange.

'Just a minute,' called Iris. The scraping sound came again, closer this time. 'Turn the handle to the left. Turn it the wrong way.'

Simon opened the door. The room was bathed in light, the soft grey of the day baking through a bay window at least twice the size of the one in Simon's room. The rest of the space was almost bare. A double bed, a small desk at one wall. The desk was made of a strange dark wood, polished to a raspberry gleam. The bed was the same, the red frame nearly hidden beneath a soufflé of pastel bedclothes, numerous puffy doonas and fringed bedspreads, pillows like layers collapsing. But he couldn't see Iris anywhere. 'Hello?' He stepped into the room. He thought of Audrey's ghosts: disembodied voices, furniture shuddering, unaided, across the floor.

'Simon.' His grandmother's voice was close, frail, quiet, as if by his ear.

He felt a chill. 'Where ... where are you?'

The door swung back, only slightly, and Simon saw her. Somehow hidden in the only shadow that escaped the window's light, in a long white embroidered gown, was his grandmother. The nightgown was like a lace curtain, layering her body completely except for her

94

head. Her hair was different—the familiar grey replaced with blonde, light like balsa wood—but her face was the same: the fine features and wide cheeks she'd given to Simon's mother, the elegant, confident sweep of her eyebrows that lent themselves to surprise and sadness. She appeared, somehow, to be younger. She drew out her arms to Simon, her hands unfurling from beneath her gown. Her fingernails were tipped with dark purple polish.

'Simon,' she said. 'It's been so long.'

Simon let himself into her embrace. Her arms were so strong they crushed his nose into her stomach and all he could hear was the leaf-rustle of starched fabric and the round smell of sandalwood. His senses of her, still present, even after all the years. He let out a sigh, which he realised too late was so full of sadness that the tears choked his throat.

'Everything will be fine,' Iris said, patting Simon's head. 'Everything will work out.'

'They've gone,' cried Simon, bunching up his fist just under his eyes. 'They've gone.'

'I know. I know.' She stroked his hair. Simon felt as helpless as he'd ever been in his life.

Iris led him to the bed and made him sit on the edge facing the window. Without thinking, Simon let himself flop back against the soft snowfall of pillows. He stared at the ceiling. How did he feel so comfortable with someone he hadn't seen for so long? His grandmother sat down next to him. She didn't say anything, just let him sit with his thoughts. He liked this.

'Grandma?' Simon tested the word out as he said it.

'Yes, Simon?'

'Do you think ... do you think Mum and Dad will come back?'

'Darling, I know they will.' Iris lay back on the bed, pushing some pillows down to the opposite end to rest her feet on. Simon noticed she had the same purple polish on her toenails. 'They probably just wanted an adventure.'

'An adventure?'

'You know, a break from the ordinary.'

'But ... why didn't they tell me? If they were going on an adventure?'

Iris stretched her limbs out, shivering her skin. 'Sometimes you just have to get up and go. That's what makes it so exhilarating.'

'Exhilarating?'

'Yes. The worst thing you can do is think about it. You just go.'

'But didn't they think of me?'

Iris sighed. Her body sunk further into the sheets. 'It's all ... cycles,' she said. 'It goes around and around.' She pushed back her hair. 'I was the same.'

Simon turned his head to look at her. She'd closed her eyes, and with it, her spark disappeared. She was his grandma again, the person he remembered. Fragile, fearful, a force of weakness.

'It's my fault,' she said. 'You came here because of me.'

'You said you were sick. You said—' Simon couldn't finish the sentence. He couldn't bear to think that Iris was his one remaining link to something he knew, a link that would soon disappear.

Iris kept her eyes closed. 'I know what I said.'

Simon sat up in the bed. 'But we hadn't seen you in so long.'

96

'Well, that was my fault too.'

Simon watched a tear fall from his grandmother's eye. She reached out and found Simon's leg. Her fingers traced his scars.

She said, 'I disappeared too, Simon. I disappeared to my own adventure.'

Simon felt, for the first time, a deep unease. 'Where did you go?'

'I sold the house—that awful house. I travelled. I had to cut away everything that I was. You probably can't understand, but I had to.'

Simon nodded.

'I couldn't stay, Simon. Where I was, what I was ... I was hopeless. Truly hopeless.'

'No you weren't,' Simon said quietly.

'Your mother,' Iris wiped away another tear. 'I was a failure to her, and to you. I was a dead-end.'

Simon remembered what it felt like when he landed. When all the air escaped from him and all he could feel was the sun and thecold dirt, as if he no longer existed on the earth. Before the pain flooded up through him, the deep sense of being broken. And the sound of a boiling kettle, so loud from the house, screaming to be removed from its place.

A knock at the door made them both jump.

'Iris!' Ned's voice came through the thick door. 'Is Simon in there with you?' There was a panicked edge to Ned's voice; Simon wondered if Audrey had told him he was.

'He's in here,' said Iris. 'Everything's fine.' Her eyes had flecks of red. She wiped them with the back of her wrist.

'Madaline will be here soon,' said Ned. 'She just wants a quick chat.'

Simon wondered why Ned didn't open the door. 'Okay,' he said. He got off the bed and looked back at Iris.

'You go,' she said, waving her hands at him. 'She's probably going to tell you she's found your mum and dad.' She smiled. 'We'll talk later. I'll be here.'

'Okay,' said Simon. 'Thanks for—' He trailed off. Iris had already drawn a doona up around her and turned away.

❧

The sand was winter tight, so dry it nearly crackled. Tarden turned his boot to an angle and scraped across it, watching the grains crumble like stale breadcrumbs. He sometimes thought he was building his own desert island here, behind the house, the crabs bringing with them their part of the sea. He wedged the plastic tub between his stomach and the old freezer. A familiar pain shot across his gut as he tugged at the freezer lid, but this was as much a part of his routine as anything else. He knocked away the padlock with his free hand. The freezer lid refused to open, its rubber seal stuck fast. As he tried to wrench it the tub slipped and he cringed at the sharp crack as it hit the side of the freezer. He felt water spurting against his arm and knew the side had split.

He put the tub on the ground; the sand beneath leached quickly dark. He took off the lid and the crabs were tumbleturning, colliding. One had its claws free, holding fast to the legs of another. Tarden swore at himself for trying to take a shortcut: they deserved better than this. They deserved to have their final moments cloaked in calm, even if not comfort. He used both hands to prise open the freezer, shielding his face from the inevitable briny stench. He bent down over the tub, reaching in with a wide grip and hoisting the unbound crab from the water. It came out with two legs seized in each claw, a limb thief. He wiped his brow with the back of his hand.

Three more legs floated in the tub, along with a twisted gnarl of twine. A stupid mistake. He'd let his focus slip. Let those other thoughts cloud his mind.

He slammed down the freezer lid in anger and the sound echoed, a deep metallic chime, recalling the mellow ring of steel drums. The only music he'd heard for years, the Jamaican who they'd let work in the kitchen who'd hammered tiny dints into metal bowls. He'd been allowed to keep the bowls, to everyone's surprise, and would play them some nights when curfew lapsed. The sounds would sweeten the stale air trapped between the walls, replacing that voice of despair that sometimes overtook you. He wondered how many lives the sound had saved.

Tarden inhaled the ocean air deeply; he still remembered to count his blessings. A pair of butcher birds chortled together down at the fence line. The breeze had picked up again. The mistletoe—like waterfalls high in the weeping gums—whistled and rushed. He stood for a moment, letting every one of his senses take itsfill: a practice he had promised himself, once a day for the rest of his life.

There was a sudden sickly humming. The freezer's motor struggling. Tarden drew his hands down over his face. It was all too much sometimes, these little details, all adding up. Every week he promised himself he'd talk to Robbie about buying a new freezer and new equipment. It wasn't much to ask. But every last dollar had to go into the shed, with the promise of so many more dollars to come. He threw up his hands, appealing to no one but himself. He started to walk back to the house, defeated already by the day. He stared back at his abandoned crab tub. He'd caught by far the best haul of the morning. It was a daily ritual, the fishers meeting at the Ottoman to compare hauls. Even the blokes from the trawlers sometimes turned up in their shiny utes and monogrammed polo shirts. He'd told them all that morning about his catch, his crabs as big as dinner plates, heavy with good meat. It was a pissing contest, really, but Tarden was still proud of the envy in the other fishers' faces. He didn't have to go on about what price he'd get. For him, it was the satisfaction of hard work rewarded.

In a daze, Tarden swung open the back door with his foot, then cursed himself. Even though the door hung three-quarters open no matter how hard you kicked it, Tarden hated to take his home for granted. In the kitchen, the fridge buzzed like a blizzard. It was on its last legs as well. He swung it open, the bottles in the door rattling, the buzzing growing louder. One day it would just conk out, and then what would they do? All that technology sitting across the yard while the house and cars slowly fell apart. They hadn't taken a holiday in over two years. But there was always something new to buy: better storage, better transportation. Always problems to anticipate, always complications to rectify. It was never easy. And now another headache: the car Robbie had brought home last night. A huge, stupid fuck-off complication.

Tarden took a bottle of lemon cordial and sloshed some into a glass. Once he would have drunk it with white spirits. Today, he simply mixed it with cold water from the fridge. He downed it in two gulps. He caught a subtle shift in the whine of silence. A television?

He took his empty glass down the hall. Robbie's bed was behind the open door, up against the wall, so all Tarden could see were his brown legs, crossed at the ankles. The ridge of Robbie's foot had a deep purple bruise across it

101

where he'd kicked the towbar of the car that morning. The small black-and-white TV he kept on his desk was showing a game show. On the screen a contestant sat behind a panel with a question superimposed below her. The static made it too hard to read.

'What's the question?' Tarden said, stepping into the room. Robbie, he saw, wasn't looking at the television: his eyes were fixed on the book lying flat in his lap. It was one of the classics he got sometimes in the mail, tightly bound in fake leather, titles stamped in gold down the spines. He wore his jeans but had taken off his shirt.

'What question?' Robbie spoke without looking up.

'On your quiz show there.'

Kuiper raised his head to the television, folding his arms across his chest. 'That's a news report,' he said. 'Nations warring, people starving. Et cetera.' He snorted a humourless laugh. He shifted his legs up under his body to let Tarden sit down. Tarden felt his warmth still present on the sheets. The room smelled of whatever sweet state came before decay.

'Shouldn't we think about getting back to the Magpie?' Tarden said.

Kuiper stretched, yawning a dead man's yawn. His muscles shivered. 'Reckon we'll head out in twenty,' he said.

'What about the car?'

Kuiper gritted his teeth. 'It'll be safe for a day.'

'You sure? What about tyre tracks?'

'Relax. It pissed down last night. The road's mud. If it blows over, we get a car, or we sell it. If not, we dump it, make a nice bonfire.'

'I guess.'

102

'All we've got to do is keep it local,' said Kuiper. 'Keep it all in town, everything'll be fine.'

Tarden put his glass down on the floor. 'I just think—'

'Bit on edge, Jacky?' His demon grin. 'Want to take the edge off?'

'Nah. You know I don't … fuck, especially not today. We gotta be careful. You said so this morning.' The TV's reception went completely, the picture dissolving to a froth of ants.

'I don't mean that,' said Kuiper. 'I know you're Healthy Harold now.' He shifted his weight to move his legs out from under him. Lay back, placing his calves on Tarden's lap. 'I'm saying we can find a way to relax.'

Gin met them halfway down the stairs. He came running, making sputtering noises with his mouth like a failing fighter plane. He was covered in dirt and soaked through. 'Madaline's here, Dad,' he shouted, running at Ned full pelt. 'She's a policeman again.'

'Don't!' said Ned, holding out his arms to stop Gin cannoning into him. 'Have you been under the sprinkler?'

Gin looked up to the ceiling. 'No.'

'Shower,' said Ned. 'Now.'

'But I'm a crime-fighter.'

'A crime-fighter who's been told many times about playing under the sprinkler.' Ned ushered his son down the stairs.

As they reached the bottom, Simon noticed Madaline standing in the doorway. She had on a proper police uniform, which made Simon feel safer. She had a black backpack in one hand.

'Hi Simon,' she said. 'How're you feeling?'

'I'm okay.'

Madaline came into the house and took off her hat. Its brim reminded Simon of a platypus's bill.

'You can use the dining room,' said Ned. 'First door on the right.'

'All right,' said Madaline. 'Shall we?'

Simon followed her down the corridor and past the kitchen and through a panelled wooden door. The first thing he noticed was the thick spread of dark green carpet. It seemed to suck the light from the room, made the air a weighty curtain draping the cavernous fireplace on the main wall, sagging solemnly from the gold frames of the paintings. It was nothing like the rest of the house, Simon thought, it was older. Stuck in a different part of history.

In the middle of the room was a large wooden table just as big as the one in the kitchen but perfectly square. The wood was the same gloomy ruby as Iris's bed, its surface so deep and polished that Simon imagined the same hand rubbing it with a soft cloth for centuries.

Madaline stood at the window staring through the gauzy curtain. 'We'd better start,' she said. She put the backpack down. 'Do you want a seat, Simon?'

Simon took the chair next to hers.

Madaline opened the backpack and placed a battered black exercise book, a pencil case and a tiny tape recorder on the shiny table; it seemed wrong to Simon to give such ordinary objects a place on the ruby surface.

'Myself and Senior Sergeant Parker—that's my boss— went to the Ottoman Motel this morning. We went to the room you and your parents were staying in.'

A flash of fear. Simon remembered the moment his parents' faces shifted under the motel lights and they became other people.

'They don't seem to have gone back there,' said Madaline. 'Everything was the same as when we left it. We have to keep—just for now—we have to keep everything there the way it was, for evidence. But I did bring you some clothes, and a book.' Madaline reached into the backpack and pulled out a large see-through plastic bag. A couple of Simon's T-shirts were in there, some underwear, a pair of trousers. 'I didn't know which ... how many—' Madaline fluttered her fingers. 'There was a book as well.' She placed Simon's book on the table. He had chosen it for their destination. The Reader's Dictionary of the Sea. He had bought it in an op-shop, intrigued by the cover, a picture of a huge wave with a ship stuck at the bottom of it, its nose upturned. Simon had always imagined the wave a giant mouth, ready to swallow whatever was foolish enough to drift inside it.

'Now, Simon,' said Madaline. 'I need to ask you a couple of questions now. This isn't an official interview, which means that nothing you say will leave this room unless you tell me it can. Do you understand?'

Simon nodded.

'Good. There's nothing to worry about here. If you don't want to answer any questions, or you don't know how to answer them, you don't have to. All this is about is you telling me as much about yesterday as you can. Anything at all, even if it seems unimportant. Okay?'

'Okay.' Simon knew he had to pay attention. But as his eyes relaxed, staring into the table's surface, dark lines started to crawl into his sight, stealing in from outward angles. Tiny spidery figures and shapes seemed to follow each other in constant motion, only stopping when Simon moved his eyes just to either side of them. He slowed his eyes, trying to catch them, but the figures would not come into focus. He moved his finger slowly above the polished surface, and they fell away, shrinking into shadow.

Simon felt a pressure on his arm. He looked over. Madaline's fingers were pressing gently on his skin. Her fingernails had flecks of white, little ships in a ridged pink sea.

'Simon,' she said. 'When you're ready.'

He looked over at the tape recorder. Through a translucent window on its cover, he saw two wheels of a tape churning.

'I don't have to use the tape if you don't want me to,' said Madaline. 'It's only so I don't forget anything.'

'No,' said Simon. 'It's fine.'

'All right.' She clasped her hands in front of her. 'What time did you and your family arrive in Reception, Simon?'

'I don't know,' he said. 'The sun was still up, but it was low.'

Madaline scribbled something in her worn exercise book. Simon thought the police were supposed to write in a black notebooks that flipped over at the top. 'How long had you beentravelling for?'

'We left after breakfast. Maybe eight o'clock?'

Madaline nodded. She pulled a folded piece of paper from her book. It was a map, dotted with place names, criss-crossed in read and black lines like a medical diagram. The top of it was the tall triangle Simon knew was Queensland. He also knew Reception was somewhere below the border, the wormy black line in the middle of the page that traced its way towards the coast, turning into a frantic squirm when it saw the egg-blue sea. 'Reception is here,' Madaline said, pointing to a small bubble of coastline.

'It's not on the map.' Simon looked closer.

'Well the name's not. But it's there.' Madaline put her finger on the map above the border. 'This is the Gold Coast. Do you recognise any of the towns between here and Reception?'

107

Simon scanned his eyes down the map as Madaline traced the highway. He tried to match a town's name to his memory of the road signs he'd seen. 'I'm sorry,' he said. 'I don't know.'

'That's okay.'

Simon's head felt suddenly empty, as if the previous day was a dream he'd had and already forgotten. He gave Madaline descriptions of his parents, the car, the town they'd stopped for morning tea, but the details had disappeared.

Madaline leant back in her chair. She stretched her neck and Simon heard tiny clicks. 'Maybe we can talk a bit about when you got here. You visited the pub, didn't you, the Ottoman?

'Yes.'

'Did anything unusual happen while you were there?'

'We had lunch, even though it was too late to have it.'

Madaline smiled. 'But nothing strange or scary happened while you were there? Your parents didn't do anything, or say anything that might have worried you?

'No,' said Simon. 'I don't think so.'

Madaline smoothed her hands across the paper of her book. 'Some ... people I've spoken to who where at the Ottoman yesterday afternoon said your parents had an argument.

Simon's scars burned. Was this the reason they didn't come back? Because they disagreed?

'Do your parents often have arguments?'

'Not really. Maybe.'

'Do you know what they were arguing about?'

Simon sighed. He thought about Iris, huddled under her sheets. The fear in her voice. 'I don't know,' he said.

'I was sitting at the counter I think.' He felt his cheeks getting hot. 'Why are you asking me about this? They haven't disappeared just because they had an argument. That doesn't make sense.'

'It's all right, Simon.' Madaline put her hand back on his arm. 'We can stop this any time you want. You just tell me.'

Simon felt the sting of tears. 'Why does everyone talk so much? Why doesn't anyone want to just find my mum and dad?' He felt the world stretching away from him again, an empty world that went on forever. There was no safe place to return to once the interview had finished. No normality. This was the way it was now.

It should have been his mother's hand on his arm. His parents should be home, should be here, but they weren't. Not any more. Simon's shoulders shook, the bottom falling from the earth, and him falling through it.

He felt Madaline's arm close around his shoulders and watched his tears drop to the table's surface. Against the endless depth of the polished wood, the tension of each tear wavered, unbroken for an instant, then scattered absently like so many stars: seeds strewn by God against a darkened sky.

Tarden let his finger ride the air current that flashed past the driver's window. His hand surfed the wind for a beautiful moment before a rogue gust pushed it back to the edge of the sill. His other hand rested lightly on the steering wheel, two fingers to keep the car on the bitumen. They'd had to take the long way to the lake; the dirt track that ran from the back of the house was slush after the rain. The familiar beauty of the landscape never failed to captivate Tarden. His childhood, those days when memories first formed, had been framed by steel, by the static shadow-shapes of the urban fringe. Coloured in rail-yard greys, hemmed by highways in every direction and reminded of his boundaries by the burnt-out cars that never made it out. The bush, that mythical quarry for terms like scrub and sea and outback was nothing but an abstraction in those days. And yet, here he was, twenty, thirty years later, truly knowing what the country was, his discovery all the sweeter for the extra freedoms it contained. And Robert Kuiper, a man he could have never imagined, here with him.

Robbie, Tarden had to admit, had chosen a rural life for business, not pleasure. He was a man whose veins pumped harder with more bodies around him, with less space to live in. Although Robbie spoke little of his early life, Tarden had pieced together snatches of speech and intimate, near-sleep whispers. He had a blurred image of a large family, a childhood fortressed by money, an unimpeded view of opportunity in a country of skewed privilege. Robbie's upbringing went some way to explaining his innate, almost ravenous, sense of entitlement; he and his family had suffered much, Tarden gathered, since apartheid's demise.

He knew Robbie had once been a confident, bulletproof spirit. The head of his own company, a shining light of commerce. It saddened him deeply, this listless, apathetic, shadow of the man Tarden imagined he once was. Even when they first met, in the grey-washed light prison— where every spirit was inevitably dampened—Robbie was a rare point of brilliance. Sharp where other minds were blunt, alert where others slumped; attractive in a way no one else had ever been.

Tarden glanced over. 'Right there?'

Kuiper shrugged, staring into his lap. He was wearing the same black shirt he'd been wearing for the past three days. 'Hungry.'

'Really? We only had breakfast a couple of hours ago.'

'Yeah. Well.' Kuiper brought his hands up to his face.

Tarden stared straight ahead at the road. Without realising it, his fingers had hardened to the steering wheel. The thing he was most worried about how much Robbie was using. Ever since the kid's parents had arrived—and the complications that came with them—Robbie had been on edge. More on edge.

Kuiper reached into the backseat and came back with a sunmelted chocolate bar. 'Want one?'

'What sort is it?'

'I dunno. Something.' The wrapper had faded to a light brown.

111

Kuiper tore off the top with his teeth and spat it out. 'Mars Bar,' he said, with a mouth full of caramel.

'I'll be fine,' said Tarden.

'Come on,' Kuiper said. 'Helps you work, rest and play.' He waggled the moist end of the bar at the corner of Tarden's mouth.

'I said I'm fine.' Tarden brushed away Kuiper's hand.

'Suit yourself.' Kuiper went for another mouthful. 'Ah, fucking hell.' He put the half-finished bar on the dashboard to peer at his shirt. He found the dropped chocolate and tried to rub it off. White, chalky stains began to appear.

'Fucking thing,' he said. 'How am I supposed to eat one of these fucking things without it dropping all over my fucking shirt? Piece of shit!' He spat on his fingers and rubbed them against the cotton, then picked up the Mars Bar and threw it out the window. 'This wouldn't have happened if I could've fucking eaten at home.'

Tarden had been following Kuiper's snack food tragedy with some amusement. 1Don't worry about it. It's only a bit of chocolate.'

Kuiper sneered at the dashboard. He ran his fingers through his hair. 'I'm not worried,' he said. 'Only a bit of chocolate.'

Tarden looked back at the road.

'It's just that I don't like being dragged out on a perfectly good—' Kuiper's hands flailed, '—whatever the hell day it is. Couldn't even have a shower. I mean, why are we even bothering to go out there? It's not as if anyone's going to—'

'You told Madaline we would. Besides, everyone else is going out to help.'

'I say a lot of things, Jack. It might surprise you to know I don't follow up on all of them.'

Tarden took a hand off the wheel and rubbed the back of his neck. 'I just think it's a nice thing to do for the kid, if no one else.'

Kuiper slid back in his seat. 'Nothing nice about it. We're only doing it to make sure this thing doesn't get any more complicated than it has to.'

'You've got to feel for him, though, don't you? And Ned ... it can't be that easy.'

Kuiper wheezed out a laugh. 'Well I guess I'm what they call objective. I don't spend as much time fraternising at Ned's house as some others.'

'That's not fair.' Before the words left his mouth, Tarden regretted rising to the bait. He hadn't told Robbie about Iris being related to the Sawyers. He shrugged. 'I help out where I can. Ned's a good man.'

'Surely they don't need that much help. What is it you're really after, Jack-me-lad?'

Tarden breathed out heavily. 'I'm not going to continue this conversation.'

'And why is that?'

'Firstly, Robbie, because it's a stupid question, and secondly, because I know your brain's halfway up in the ether.'

Kuiper spat out the window. He bit his lip, then laughed. Kuiper leant his head against the window. 'The funny thing,' he said, 'is that some people can't see what's right in front of them.'

Tarden returned his eyes to the road, silent.

The water from the lake gleamed like metal, glittering through the trees, reflecting back what little sunlight there was into focused, knife-sharp flashes. Simon sat in the back of Ned's blue station wagon. Gin was in the front passenger seat and Audrey sat next to Simon in the back. Pony had disappeared when Ned went looking for him, and Simon was somehow disappointed not to have him here as well.

They followed the faint dust-spray of Madaline's Corolla as it threaded its way carefully along the rain-pocked road. Audrey's hand brushed his as they drove over a pothole. She seemed to have forgiven him for his words about her mother, about not believing in ghosts. Gin had changed into a new outfit. Red T-shirt and shorts, with Flash Gordon written in comic book writing on both. ed's hair made its way through the gap in the driver's headrest, blonde strands ruffling in the wind.

Underneath his borrowed jumper, Simon's borrowed shirt was beginning to itch. He had left his own things in the plastic bag Madaline had brought; he would put on proper clothes when he was back with his parents. He put his cheek up against the door, but it was harsh fabric, not the warm leather of his parents' car. He watched the sky. It was bare of snaking powerlines but shapes still fractured the clouds: snarling, palsied wolves and dragons.

Audrey tapped him on the shoulder and put an

114

envelope in his hand. On the envelope, in triple-layered writing, was his name. Simon remembered how he used to write like this sometimes, holding three textas together at once, writing like a rainbow.

'What's this?' he said.

'Just open it.'

Simon opened the envelope and some glitter fell out onto his lap. Inside was a card, with leaves pressed to its front. Audrey grinned at him.

Dear Simon, You are cordially invited to Julian (Gin) Gale's 5th Birthday Party. Venue: Our House. Time: 11am-3pm. Please RSVP to Audrey Gale, 1st Floor.

'Thank you,' said Simon.

'You're welcome,' Audrey replied. 'It's tomorrow. You and your mum and dad can come.'

Simon smiled.

They rounded the lake, and they came out at the top of a gravel carpark. A dozen or so cars were parked. Simon didn't recognise any of them, except for Tarden's yellow four-wheel-drive. Simon's whole body jolted. Where was his parents' car? He felt a fresh squirt of panic. Maybe Madaline had taken it as evidence as well. Maybe there was more than one carpark.

Ned parked the car. He turned around in his seat. 'Simon,' he said, 'we don't have to stay here. Any time you want to leave, you just tell me.'

Simon nodded. His face felt like a cold flannel.

'He'll be fine,' said Audrey. 'Won't you?' She picked up Simon's hand and squeezed it. 'There's nothing to be scared of.'

Ned and Gin got out. Simon undid his seatbelt and sat for a moment with his fingers on the door handle.

115

'It's really okay,' said Audrey. 'We're all here to help you.' She had a mole at the corner of her eye that Simon hadn't noticed before.

Simon got out of the car. Magpie Lake was a white place: not light, but bleached. Nothing like the postcard picture he had imagined: it was grey water and naked granite, weary winter grass. He stared out across the lake.

Groups of people had gathered below the carpark. They'd formed tight circles on the grass, mostly men. Fishermen, Simon guessed, who knew the lake. They were smoking, laughing, drawing shoe-patterns in the dirt. Schoolchildren waiting for their teacher. Simon noticed Jack Tarden talking to two other men. One was thin, his neck bent down like a vulture, wearing a peaked cap. A trail of cigarette smoke whispered from his fingers. The other man was large, with curly black hair, wearing a blue and black chequered shirt that was dark in waves where his sweat had stained it.

Madaline busied herself in the boot of her car and emerged with large rolls of paper and a megaphone. Gin was walking along the top of one of the wooden barriers that fenced the carpark, his arms outstretched for balance.

Audrey came up next to him. 'They'll probably use a grid,' she said.

'What do you mean?'

'Well, what they do is divide a map up into a grid, and then every grid gets a number. You cross each number off on a list so you know where you've looked.' She made cross-patterns in the air with her fingers.

'How do you know?'

'I've done it before.'

'When?'

'I just have,' she said. 'And that's how you do it.'

Simon imagined black lines running away from him, down over the rocks. 'What about the water?' he said.

'The water?'

'How do gridlines work on the water? You can't walk across it to check.'

'No,' said Audrey, 'of course you can't do gridlines on the water. That's just stupid. What a stupid thing to say.' She turned around and walked away down to where Gin was balance-beaming.

Simon walked over to where the other searchers were gathering—most standing in a large semicircle around Madaline's car. A large piece of paper was spread over the bonnet, weighted down by a megaphone and what looked like a walkie-talkie. Simon counted twenty-three people, the rising wind tugging at their clothes. To the edge of the group, the waitress from the Ottoman was looking off into the distance, slowly revolving the piercing under her lip.

A little further away, Madaline and Ned were talking to Tarden, along with the thin smoking man and the fat checked-shirt man. Ned saw Simon and beckoned him over. 'We're about to start the search,' said Madaline, 'and I just wanted to know how much a part of it you wanted to be—whether you want to go with one of the teams, or just stay here.' She made it sound like a playground game.

'Are you using a grid?' said Simon.

'A grid?'

'On a map. Are you using a grid on a map?'

Madaline's face looked half-amused, half-worried. She

117

said, 'Something like that. We're going to have different teams search different parts of the dam. We're going to lead one each.' She motioned to the others. 'You know Mr Tarden of course.'

Tarden nodded. 'Jack,' he said, 'please.'

'This,' said Madaline, 'is Mr Kuiper. A friend of Jack's.'

The thin man smiled at Simon. He had thick lines under his eyes, and at the corners of his mouth. 'Hello, Simon. A pleasure.' He had a strange, high-strung voice, and an accent Simon didn't recognise. Kuiper, thought Simon. Viper.

'This is Mr Patterson.' Madaline gestured at the fat man. 'He owns the Ottoman.'

'Call me Nat.' He smiled at Simon. His skin was brown and soft, like Madaline's leather chair. Curls hung over his forehead like the tendrils on ferns. 'Pleased to meet you, Simon.' He reached out his hand and Simon shook it. Nat's fingers were brown, but his palms were pink.

'Nat's going to lead one of the teams,' said Madaline. 'His family used to live around the mountains out this way.'

Simon looked at Nat, wide-eyed. 'Really?'

'A while ago,' said Nat. 'Before I was born. I'm sure it's all up here somewhere, though,' He tapped his head.

Kuiper suddenly began to cough violently. He doubled over, hugging his waist with his arms. He quickly straightened up and cleared his throat. 'Sorry,' he said. 'My allergies are hell this time of year.' He wiped an invisible tear from the corner of his eye. 'Where were we, Madaline?'

Simon felt Kuiper's sharp accent cut through him.

Madaline took off her hat and put it under her arm. 'Well,' she said, 'I just wanted to talk to Simon about what he wants to do this morning.' She crouched down,

118

so her eyes were at Simon's height. 'Do you know if you want to come along with any of the teams?'

'Yes,' said Simon. 'I think so.'

Ned rubbed his hands together. 'I was thinking that maybe Simon could come with me,' he said. 'I could take the other kids as well, just down around the shoreline. Nothing too hectic.'

'That might be good,' said Madaline. 'Simon, does that sound okay? Going with Ned and Audrey?'

Simon thought for a moment. 'All right,' he said. 'But how will we know if another team has found my parents?'

Madaline removed a metal whistle attached to some string from her pocket. 'Each leader has one of these.' She strung the whistle around her neck. 'If anyone— when someone—finds your parents, all they have to do is blow on the whistle. You'll be able to hear it for miles out here.'

Simon looked out at the surrounding hills. He imagined the sound of a whistle circling the dam. 'Okay,' he said.

'Good lad,' said Ned, zipping up his green jacket so it closed up just under his chin.

'All right,' said Madaline. 'Let's go.'

They made their way over to Madaline's car, where the rest of the search party were waiting. Simon's stomach pitched and reeled like a wave-tossed boat, but his head was somehow clearing. Any sense of fantasy, of imagination, was leaving him. This was real. This was his answer. The pain of not knowing would be replaced by one overpowering truth: everything, eventually, had to end.

⁀

Madaline smoothed the map out, realising too late that what she thought were wrinkles in the paper were really tracings of the lake's edge. The map Nat had brought was old: hand-drawn, photocopied more than once; some lines had two or three sketchy echoes, others faded in and out of clarity. Still, the general shape of the lake was there. It did look a bit like a bird. Not a magpie, really; maybe a hunched and curious vulture. In the top righthand corner the lake fed into a thin channel that squirmed out towards the sea.

She picked the megaphone up off the corner of the map, and the paper flapped up violently, snapping like a loading sail in the wind. She jammed one hand against it as she tried to activate the megaphone with the other. Where the hell was Tommy? He was supposed to have arrived before her to get everybody ready but no one had seen him.

Madaline heard the whine of feedback and spoke into the megaphone. 'Hello?' Her voice blared out and the searchers fell silent. There weren't nearly enough people for a proper search. Pathetic numbers, really. Kuiper and Tarden had done no more than trawl the back tables of the Ottoman, but it was better than she could have done herself. Some of them had on their orange SES jumpsuits but had them rolled down to the waist, meaning easier access to cigarettes, and a subtle indication that it wasn't a real emergency. Nat was here, which was good, and Megan: a closed Ottoman meant a better turn-out than she had feared. They were bored bodies, Madaline thought, looking for something to do between the tides. She recognised all the faces, even if not the names. They were faces she'd dealt with, come up against, especially in the winter months; by late April, the phone calls would start at night. Mostly just boredom and bravado; most of them settled down after she arrived, happy for the attention. If they wanted to take it further, she'd cuff them and issue a few threats, but she hardly ever had to use the lock-up. At most, they'd get a summons to appear up at Byron or a tongue-lashing from Tommy for wasting everybody's time.

Madaline didn't like to admit it, but she was secretly glad of these outbreaks of real police work. Perhaps she welcomed the attention as well. None of them were bad people, really, they'd just become stuck in a life that offered no change and little reward. Not that she could talk.

A familiar blue and white four-wheel-drive came down into the carpark. Tommy's face was red behind the wheel. He parked and stepped carefully out onto the gravel, pulling on a reflective vest. Everyone had turned to look at him.

He waved his arms down at them as if discouraging applause. 'How are we all?' His blinked his eyes profusely. 'This dry wind,' he said. 'Bloody hell.' He came up into the circle of searchers, pulling a squashed pack of cigarettes from his back pocket. He lit one, sheltering his body from the breeze. 'Madaline,' he said. 'This is your operation. Just pretend I'm not here.'

121

Madaline gritted her teeth. The lazy bastard hadn't changed. Ever since she had arrived, he had treated her not as a welcome addition to Reception's police presence but an excuse to do less himself, to be a police officer only when it suited him. The first days of Stephanie Gale's disappearance had been the worst. The way he constantly threw responsibility to her, the junior officer. Back then, the world was not the freezing edge of a winter lake but the apricot arms of summer sand, stretching endlessly in both directions. The dark mass of the bluff, the beckoning crash of warm-weather waves. And Ned, in his perennial green jacket, despite the baking heat. Madaline in a uniform of even fresher fabric.

Had she known her feelings for him then? Probably not. So why had it all seemed so hard? Why had a routine search started to feel like the slowest torture? It came back to her often, the memory of those first days. The same emergency service jumpsuits, the same expectant faces. They shot into her mind with the strange warm glow of ancient photographs.

Madaline found herself talking, her voice suddenly clear: 'Thank you all for coming this morning. As you have no doubt gathered, time is of the essence this morning. We have two missing persons who were last seen heading for this site at approximately six o'clock yesterday evening. Bill and Louise Sawyer, both of the Gold Coast, took a room at the Ottoman Motel with their son, Simon. They left him in the hotel room, heading to Magpie Lake.'

A different photograph flashed into Madaline's head: a stretch of cane fields, a cleared track narrowing back to the horizon. Her father, leaning on a shovel, foot propped up on the blade. The only way she could ever remember him: arms crossed like a single muscle against his chest, eyes etched into a permanent squint. A grimace, a fortress.

'Their car was not parked here at the lake, but we have reason to believe they are still here. Bill and Louise are both in their mid-to-late thirties, and have no experience in bush survival. We are to assume, unless we learn otherwise, that they are both in the vicinity of the lake. I have appointed four—' she shot a glance at Tommy, '— five team leaders, along with myself, to guide the separate teams to different areas around the lake. Please see me to be allocated to a team.'

Her mother, sprawled on a cane chair. Christmas Day. The sweat from a true tropical summer shining her brow. In the warm Polaroid wash, her face reduces to shapes: fat circles of mascara, wedges of lurid eyeshadow, the fractal damage of self-crimped hair. Madaline, behind the lens, taking her very first picture.

'Your group leaders will each have a map of the area they will search. Please stay with your teams, and report to your leaders anything you think is pertinent to the search. Leaders will alert me to any significant developments, otherwise we will reconvene back here in three hours. Remember water, remember a hat. This is a mostly contained area, and I am confident it will be just a matter of time until we find Bill and Louise. Any questions?'

The wedding waltz. That stupid tradition. Every face in the crowd blasted by a too-bright flash. Madaline with her back to the camera. Her hair is longer, plaited down below her shoulders. Will's face wears a look of

123

rare contentment. The smile that stretched his lips ever since she told him yes. What the camera can't see—what history didn't record—was Madaline's animal groan, barely covered by the music, her tears misconstrued as happiness: her mortal fear that she'd made the worst mistake of her life.

♥

Back near their new house on the Gold Coast there was a pretend beach. Instead of sand there were small smooth stones that clicked and shrieked when you walked across them. The rocks sat beside a long pontoon that ran from the back of their house and jutted out into a canal. On the second afternoon after they'd moved in, Simon had gone with his father to the pontoon to watch the flat orange sunset spread across the rooftops on the opposite shore. His father had his new camera slung around his neck, the oversized lens sticking out from his chest. The pontoon was covered in a rough ridged carpet that smelled salty and wet. The beach-stones were deep black, slippery as whale's eyes, the water milling around their edges. His father had picked up a handful and was at the pontoon's edge, skimming them across the water.

Simon had asked if they could go swimming in the canal. People don't go swimming here, his father had said, throwing his last stone. Simon let his gaze settle on the soft chop of the canal waves. A sadness overcame him: the thought that no one had ever dived into the water, nobody had ever swum with those waves to start a journey to the sea. The knowledge that this new place was no different from any other; it was just a new set of boundaries to settle within.

The water of Magpie Lake was quite clear up close, the colour of cold tea. A line of fine pale sand ran just past the

125

shoreline, disappearing eventually into shadow. Simon bent down and dipped his hand beneath the water. He sank his fingers into the sand, releasing a swollen cloud of white that roiled in the gentle tide. The water was icy, but felt good against his hand. He thought perhaps the lake was friendlier in smaller pieces.

Simon's mood had improved. Madaline had spoken with such authority, such certainty, that it was impossible to think his parents would not be found. She was in charge now and he finally had hope. Like she'd said, they had no experience in the bush. How far could they have gone? Simon pictured his parents wandering out from the bush, flanked by searchers, clothes muddied and egos dented. It might almost be funny. He wished he'd helped Madaline more when she interviewed him. He wished he'd said important words into the tape recorder, remembered important things she could have written in her book.

Gin had removed his shoes and was already wading, knee deep, a little further out. He was pushing his hands through the water, palms down, as if trying to wipe the surface clean. Audrey remained some way up from the shore. For some reason, she hadn't wanted to come down to the water and Simon wasn't about to argue with her. Ned strolled along the foreshore a little way ahead, hands behind his back. After an initial burst of combing through the grass, none of them had wanted to keep going. It didn't matter to Simon: he knew his job now was to stay here and wait. His ears strained, waited, for the sound of a whistle.

He wondered how long they would stay in Reception after his parents were found. He hoped they could stay for a little while, hoped his mother could spend some time with Iris. Perhaps they could all stay at Ned's house, stay in one of the rooms. It would be like a real holiday.

Still squatting, Simon took his hands out of the water and wiped them on his trousers. He felt a hard lump at the side of one leg, then remembered he was wearing Pony's army pants, with all the pockets. He found the pocket with the lump in it and pulled out a flat black stone the width of a tennis ball. He had a strong urge to throw the stone, skimming across the surface of the lake, the way his father had done at the canal. But then he thought of Pony, who seemed to keep stones like other people would keep seashells. He put it back in his pocket.

Just back from the sand, the ground was mostly grass, but in some places it had ripped open like torn material. Underneath the grass were slabs of speckled rock pecked and cobbled with spiky ridges. Around the exposed patches, some of the rock had crumbled away, broken off in horizontal tiers like layers on a stack of pancakes. Simon went over and picked a piece up. As he moved it in his hand, parts of it gleamed in the dim light; it was full of semi-transparent flecks, little minerals sunspot-dotted. Simon opened one of the empty pockets in his trousers and dropped the piece of rock into it. He walked back to the shore, feeling the weight bump rhythmically against his leg. After a moment, he went back and put another rock in the opposite pocket. That was better. Balanced.

'What are you doing?' Audrey's voice floated down from the grass bank where she was sitting with her legs crossed.

Simon spun around. 'Nothing,' he said. 'Just waiting.'

'Aren't we even going to look at the map?' she said. 'I thought this was supposed to be organised.'

Simon walked up the slope to where Audrey sat. 'I don't think we're old enough to do a proper search. At least, Gin isn't. So we'll just stay here and wait.'

'How is waiting supposed to help?'

Simon shifted his weight. He said, 'It's just a matter of time.'

Audrey blew air upwards with her mouth, making her fringe flop up and down. She blinked, three times, quickly. 'So if we just wait here, everything's supposed to work out, is it?'

'Yes,' said Simon. 'We just have to wait.'

Audrey sniffed noisily. 'You don't see it, do you. You're not even worried.'

Simon looked at the red under Audrey's eyes. 'Have you been crying?' he said.

Audrey stared intently past Simon. 'No. Why would I be crying?' She rubbed one eye with the back of her thumb.

'Are you okay?' Simon stood in front of her. He tried to block the sun so it wouldn't fall on her and make things worse.

'I don't even know why you're worrying about me,' said Audrey. 'You don't even care that your mum and dad are out there and they might not turn up or they might turn up dead or it might be you never know, and you're so calm and boring about it!' Tears began to fall on Audrey's singlet.

'It's okay,' Simon said. 'Madaline will find them. And you don't have to worry.' He tried a smile, but it didn't quite come.

Audrey's shoulders shook. 'No she won't. She won't find anything. No one will find anything.'

Simon felt a ribbon of uncertainty shiver through his stomach. 'How can you say that? How can you know that?' He didn't mean to sound so angry.

Audrey's mouth formed a bitter curve. 'Because nobody just disappears. There's always a reason. Maybe they were sick of you and wanted to leave you here. Why is their car not here?'

'What?' Simon bit his lip, so hard that he felt pain behind his ears.

'They probably wanted to get away from you, so they left you asleep in the hotel and drove away.'

'No!' Simon's voice trembled.

'They're probably sitting at home right now, laughing at you.'

Simon felt the burn of tears in his own eyes. When he looked at Audrey's stupid face, he knew that he hated her. He thought of the worst word he knew.

'You're a stupid shit!' he shouted, spitting the words at Audrey's eyes. His blood thumped in his head as he ran away from her, ankles breaking in his stupid borrowed shoes. He flung them off with his feet and didn't care where they landed, he had to get away.

Away from Audrey, away from the lake, away from the town. He had to get back home where his parents were and make them let him stay.

Tarden squinted at the copy of the map in his hands. It had been shrunk down on a photocopier, making its sketchy lines even harder to see. Not that he really needed it. He had travelled over the lake often enough, albeit approaching it from the other side. Just beyond his fishing cove, he had discovered a slim estuary that led directly through to Magpie Lake, winding through a long tributary. It was a maze: the water spread out like curling fingers, arriving at more dead ends than continuations. He had explored it for a week before he worked out how to navigate it. There were good crabbing spots along the way, muddy mangrove shores where the creatures were often left exposed for easy trapping. The last thing he wanted was the other searchers finding it. Even more so now.

He had volunteered to take a group out to the opposite shore, taking a large dark boulder as their landmark. The tributary was close to it, but he figured he could keep prying eyes away. This was just another reason to waste some time, lead his group on a fruitless search. But he had hours to kill. The groups were not meant to reconvene until a quarter past one, and Tarden was already sweating. He should have changed into shorts, should have brought a water bottle with him. His natural habitat was the early hours of the day or the waning hours of the afternoon. Mid-morning was a time for rest, for quiet things.

The sun had returned, wiping most of the thick cloud away, drawing the steam up from the landscape. Still, the wind was strong; tree seeds coptered down around him in alien invasions. Tarden wiped twin glugs of sweat from above his eyebrows. He'd caught the kid's face: Simon Sawyer. Those sad hopeful eyes.

The thing that most troubled him, though, was Robbie, who was leading a group at the other side of the lake. Any other day, he wouldn't have cared as much, but Robbie's composure was always shot when he was coming down. Couldn't he have just taken a break for one night? He was stressed, sure, but all he had to do was stay off it for a couple of days, make the trade, get on with their lives. And his walks now, too. Each night, leaving later and later, taking longer and longer to come back. Except last night. It was Tarden who'd come home late, to find a strange car idling in the yard.

And Robbie wasn't supposed to be like this. The Robert Kuiper he'd first met was the most level-headed person he'd encountered. Back then, Robbie read books, he'd meditated: kept the Zen, he liked to say. Somehow nothing fazed him, not even the inevitable horrors that befell a white-collar criminal thrown in the deep end. Drugs had been a foreign concept to Robbie then. He would have dabbled in a casual way, but juggling numbers had been his real vice. Tarden had spent countless hours teaching him the ins and outs of the trade, the correct lingo, the ways and means of that particular dark world; it was not an achievement he felt good about. But if not for those long conversations, who knows if they ever would have stayed together? Then again, they wouldn't be in quite so much shit now, either. Tarden knew it was a moot point.

He was too enamoured, too loyal, too stupid ever to have cared.

As his mind wandered, Tarden's feet followed unconscious paths through the bush. He had stuffed the map in his back pocket, let the landscape guide him. His group followed him, in a line, whacking the grass with long sticks. The progress was excruciating. The bodies corralled from the Ottoman, had mostly signed up for the SES years ago in fit of short-sighted empathy. After the bushfires in '94, fits of goodwill shot through small towns like Reception, but they'd never really expected to be called out. That morning they all grumbled about not being back in time for afternoon drinks, but Robbie had the bright idea of roping Nat Patterson in, meaning the pub wouldn't be open till everyone got back. The seeds of Robbie's guile still sprouted; it wasn't in Nat's nature to refuse a mercy mission. Everyone had a weakness, and it was Robbie's gift to know it. He had a strong influence over the locals. If Reception hadn't long ago been absorbed into the faint sprawl of an amalgamated council, he would have been a natural fit for mayor. Well, perhaps not.

That girl was here too, that waitress Megan. The one Robbie always talked about. She had been to their house once; Tarden was sure Robbie just did it to taunt him. He suspected the bastard had given her a sample, too. Particularly stupid, considering she spent half her time up the coast and worse still, she'd attached herself to one of the drivers.

This, though, was the greatest of Tarden's worries. What preyed most on his mind was the thought of Iris— his Iris—wasting away in silence. She had never told him.

When he thought of her sickness, whatever it was, his stomach cinched like a drawstring bag. Louise Sawyer was Iris's daughter; Simon was her grandson.

Tarden shook his head, trying to clear his thoughts, trying to return his attention to the patch of ground in front of him. The last thing he needed was to lose concentration. He needed to lead the team away from the hidden estuary and deep into the bush, where he'd make sure they found nothing at all.

೮ನ

Simon stumbled forward in his socks, not caring what he stepped on. He was the one who was lost, not his parents. They were back at home, laughing, drinking wine, enjoying life without a son they never wanted anyway. Audrey was horrible and stuck-up, but she was right.

The sand and rocks and water had disappeared, and Simon found himself threading through spiky grass and tough tall shrubs with gnarled branches, curled up like bodies protecting themselves from unseen harm. He smelled camphor and pine, felt fine dust on his tongue. He heard wind—the whipping fins of thin leaves—but no insect noise, no cicadas buzzing like he expected there would be: their absence seemed as sudden as sunshine.

He stopped by a tree with a natural saddle, leant his body back against it. The stones in his pockets felt solid against his legs. At the corners of Simon's thumbs, the skin had dried and turned hard, leaving a pattern of white triangles. He picked at them with the nails of his index fingers while he decided what to do next. Before long, a burrowing pain distracted him and he looked down to see a trickle of brown-red blood snaking to each wrist. He bent to his knees and willed the blood further on, but it had already dried. Simon didn't notice Ned until he heard the crack of his footsteps emerging from the taller grass behind him. Ned's jacket was covered in leaves and

he seemed out of breath. 'Simon,' he said. 'Thank God.'
He brushed down his jacket. 'Where are your shoes?'

Simon said, 'They're not my shoes.'

'Audrey said you ran away.' Ned came closer. His face
fell. 'The blood, Simon—your hands—what happened?'

Simon glanced down. He must have started picking his
thumbs again; the trickle of blood had become thicker. It
looked like he was a robot, and the blood was his wires.

'They just got dry,' he said. 'They're okay.'

Ned took Simon's hands. 'Your thumbs,' he said.
'They're all cut up.'

Simon pulled his hands back. He raised one hand to
his face. All down the side of his thumbnail, the skin had
been pulled away, leaving it exposed and raw. It stung in
the wind.

'We should get you back to the carpark,' said Ned,
blowing hair from his eyes. 'We'll need to fix up that
bleeding.'

Simon remembered Jack Tarden's finger, how he had
bitten it bloody. 'I can't go back to the carpark,' he said.

'Why not?'

'Because ... because I can't.'

Ned put his hands in the pocket of his coat. 'It's okay,
Simon,' he said. 'If you don't want to stay, I can drive
you back.'

'You don't understand.'

'Actually,' said Ned. 'I think I do.'

Simon felt the reckless heat of tears pressing again. He
was so sick of crying. 'You don't know!' he found himself
shouting. 'My mum and dad have gone and they've left
me here and they don't care and they wish I'd never been
born and they don't even love me and—' Simon closed

135

his eyes to stem the wave that was surging up inside him. The word love ripped at the back of his throat, like some part of him being torn away. Without thinking, he reached out for Ned's jacket and—without knowing why—wrapped his arms around it. He felt Ned's hands patting him on the back.

'It's okay,' Ned said softly. 'You know that's not true. Where ... why do you think that?'

Simon didn't want to say, but he did. 'Audrey said so.'

'Audrey?'

'She told me Mum and Dad left me here and went back home.'

'Oh, Simon, no. Audrey makes things up sometimes. She shouldn't tell lies like that—it's a really silly thing to do. She didn't mean it.'

'But our car isn't here. It isn't at the lake.'

'Maybe your parents parked it somewhere else. Maybe they decided to walk.'

The tears suddenly sprang from Simon's eyes. 'But I called Audrey a shit.'

'Hey,' said Ned, hugging Simon tighter as he pressed his wet face into his jacket. 'Don't worry about that. I think everyone's just getting a little too excited.'

Simon dug his fingers in to Ned's back. 'I don't want to be here,' he cried. 'I don't want to.'

'All right,' said Ned. 'Maybe we should just take a rest for a minute.' He gently pulled Simon away from him and they sat down on the ground. 'Simon,' he said. 'I think I know why Audrey got upset with you, and why things are maybe a bit strange at the moment.'

Something in Ned's voice made Simon's shoulders relax. He had not realised he was clenching his body so tightly. He had not realised he craved something real. All he had felt, ever since he arrived in Reception, was that the truth was hiding from him. Everything was like an echo.

Ned took a deep breath, and worked the toe of his shoe deep into the soft ground. Here, just below the surface, was soft sand, sprinkled with mineral colour. Above it, among the blanket of weeds, were tufts of wispy red grass, shaped like sea anemones.

'A few years ago,' said Ned, 'nearly two years ago, someone else went missing here. Not at the lake, but at the beach, near the headland, near my house.'

Simon saw the bluff clearly in his mind, remembered it from his first view of Reception: an angry foot lashing out at the ocean.

'It was my wife, Simon. That's who went missing. Audrey and Julian's mother.' Simon's mind processed Ned's words. He pictured them stretching out, like a train track. 'She was swimming,' said Ned, 'She would go swimming every day. The same place, the same beach. And ... it was like she was there one minute and then—' He opened his hands in front of his face. 'That day, she never came back. And then there was just a space where she used to be.' He smiled grimly.

Simon continued to stare into the ground. He said, 'Did they search for her ... your wife?'

'Yes. Everyone did. Madaline did. Everybody helped.'

Simon realised now why Audrey knew so much about searching, why she was so upset. He asked, even though he already knew the answer: 'Did they find her?'

Ned sighed. 'You've got to understand, Simon, that it was so different. It was summer—such a hot summer—

and the sea, the tides ... it was impossible, right from the start.'

'She wasn't ... no one found her?'

Ned nodded his head. 'We don't know what happened. She—Stephanie—she left us.'

'I'm sorry for your loss,' said Simon. He felt so sad for Audrey and Gin.

Ned smiled. 'Thank you,' he said. 'That's very kind.' He rubbed his hands together to shake off some sand. 'That's why Audrey might have been a bit strange about things. She was ... very upset when her mum went. She was quite a different person before it happened.'

'Because she doesn't know what happened.'

'I think so, yes.'

Simon sat and let the silence grow. It came up to meet him with the solemn steps of a friend he didn't have to greet. He pictured gentle waves at an ocean's edge, leapfrogging each other like a family of brothers, settling their scores on the sands of the shore.

Audrey had not moved from where Simon had left her. She'd drawn her knees up to her chin, peering at the world from underneath her uneven fringe. Simon guessed that memories of her mother—the not being able to know—made up that part of her that swung and bobbed against what people normally did. Her strange behaviour was a protest, perhaps. She saw Simon and Ned coming; her eyes mined the ground for some hidden meaning. Simon noticed Gin, some way out in the water.

'Mind if we join you?' Ned sat down in front of her on the grass. Audrey stayed silent. 'Simon told me about what happened.'

'So what?' Audrey puffed out her cheeks.

'I told him why you might be upset.'

'How would you know why I'd be upset?'

'I'm sorry I called you a name,' said Simon. 'It wasn't nice. And I'm sorry about your mother.'

Audrey's eyes shot up. 'What about her?'

Ned put his hand on Audrey's arm. 'I told Simon about how your mum disappeared. I thought he'd like to know that we've all been through the same thing.'

Audrey formed a fist around her right index finger. She said, 'That wasn't why I was upset,' but it didn't sound like even she believed it.

'It helped,' said Simon, 'to know about the gridlines.'

Audrey's mouth wavered. 'Really?'

'Yes. It's good to have you helping.'

Audrey sat up straighter, shook her hair back. 'Thank you, Simon.'

Ned cleared his throat. 'Perhaps you could apologise, Audrey, for the untrue things you said about his parents?'

Audrey stood up and put a hand on Simon's shoulder. 'I apologise, Simon.' She screwed her mouth up, like she was thinking. 'I shouldn't have said those things.' She stuck out her left hand. 'Friends?'

Simon took her hand, which was soft and cold. 'Friends.' They shook, and Simon was glad he had washed the blood off his fingers already. The bleeding had stopped.

'All right,' said Ned, 'I'm going to get the thermos from the car. Does anyone want a drink or something to eat?'

Simon waited for Audrey's answer.

'No thank you,' she said. 'Simon and I have something to discuss.'

'Yes, I'm fine,' Simon agreed.

'Okay then.' Ned got up and dusted off the back of his jeans. 'Back soon.'

Audrey started walking to the water's edge. She climbed a small rock and jumped off it. Her layered dress made her look a bit like a bat, flying in the daytime. Simon met her where she landed.

'It was different, you know,' she said.

'What was?'

'When my mum went missing.'

'Your dad told me.'

'There was a sniffer-dog down at the beach. Gin wanted it to catch a Frisbee. It didn't make any difference. We had to pack up half the house—the bits that she used.'

'The bits she used?'

140

'Some of the furniture, things she was halfway through.'

Something snagged in Simon's mind. 'Did your mum ... make things?'

'Yes,' said Audrey. 'She made things from wood.'

'Did she make the table, in the dining room?'

'When did you go in the dining room?'

'With Madaline. She interviewed me.'

'Madaline?' Audrey's face darkened, then just as quickly relaxed. 'Stephanie. That was her name. She was a sculptor. She used to make us animals, when we were littler. She was always carving.' Audrey picked up a pointed stone from the ground and began whittling into her palm. 'Just because she disappeared,' said Audrey, 'doesn't mean your mum and dad have.' She smiled, and Simon thought her smile was the small start of something good.

They walked together down to the water's edge where tall stalks of grass stuck out, mud-caked into spider's legs. 'I don't miss her, anyway,' said Audrey. 'I just got used to it.' She weighed the whittling stone in her right hand. Making Simon jump, she rushed her arm over her head and hurled the stone up into the sky, out across the water. 'I don't miss her,' she said again, as the stone shrilled through the air in a high arc. It finally landed, making a pleasant white dash in the water.

'Bet you can't do that,' she said.

Simon smiled. 'Bet I can.'

'Okay,' she said. 'Furthest throw wins.'

Simon looked around and found another stone. He'd played cricket at one school. He was sure he could throw better than a girl. It would be easy.

'Get ready to lose,' he said, like someone out of a

movie. He wound up and let the stone go. As he released it, he realised his grip was too weak, and it went out too flat and wobbly, crashing into the water like a diving plane.

Audrey threw another one—a small and round: a water stone—and it went even further. She laughed. 'There's no way you can throw further than me.'

A quick anger buzzed in Simon's stomach. Just because he was lost, just because Audrey could make up the rules, that didn't mean she had to win. He had to beat her. They each threw three more times, and each time Audrey won. 'You're not trying,' she kept saying, even though she knew he was. On the fourth go, Simon remembered the rocks in his pockets. He had forgotten about them. He thought of Pony. He reached down and got one out. Its weight felt right in his hand.

'What's that?' said Audrey.

'My secret weapon.' He turned the rock over in his hand, enjoying its glint, its glittering jewels. 'I've been saving it up.' He turned it over in his hand until it nestled snugly in his grip.

'It's too big,' said Audrey.

'No it's not. There's no rules about that.' He turned around, stepped back and readied his arm. He knew his throw would be enormous. He could picture it sailing over the lake completely, tracing a superhuman path that would set a record. He pictured the rock hitting one of the trees on the opposite shore, lodging in halfway up its trunk. He would show Reception what he was made of.

He ran four steps, leant back and hurled his arm forward with all his strength and all his anger and all his sadness. Just as he did, a voice rang in his head, as

142

clear as air itself. An uneasy feeling: his mother's voice: You need to understand, but it's quite obvious you can't. Simon felt a weight leave his fingers. His vision skewed, his body stuttered forward as he regained his balance, but when he listened again the voice was gone. His eyes settled easily on a spot on the horizon, but the uneasy feeling was still there. Something wasn't right. Something wasn't where it was supposed to be.

The rock.

Simon was off-balance again, spinning his head in every direction for signs where the rock was coming down. It hadn't fallen in the water because there was no sound, no splash. He searched the sky, eyes flicking. Perhaps he had thrown it to the other shore. Perhaps he had won— but then he saw it—a dark spinning shape, a full stop falling through the air. It was too fast to follow and all he heard was a dry noise as he spun around and saw Ned falling like a shot solider, his white thermos cup, his sandwich, crashing against the ground. Ned collapsing, crumpling, his body with no apparent memory of how it was supposed to land. And then stillness: a patch of red, growing slowly, like a handprint against Ned's hair.

Audrey screamed. Not a quick shrill shout but a slow moan. Simon's body was frozen in a flashbulb pose of expressed energy: shoulders bunched, body hip-swivelled, face contorted with effort. He couldn't see the rock, only what it had done.

Ned lay on the ground in an impossible spiral shape. His arms and legs curved somehow in the same direction, as if his body was circling in on itself. But what Simon noticed most was the bright stain that was breeding red tendrils in the thatch of Ned's hair. With a self-taught-trick, Simon tried to convince himself that the blood was paint that had fallen from above, descending on Ned from a puncture in some stratospheric balloon. But he knew the only thing that had fallen from the sky was the rock he had thrown.

Audrey fell silent; she turned her head to Simon. Her face showed little: except her eyes, which simply said I fear this. They turned together, and their bodies moved slowly forward. As they approached, Ned's body seemed to loom unevenly towards them. Neither of them could measure a response. There was nothing to compare it to.

Ned's body heaved and Simon's breath stopped in his mouth. Ned's arm dragged itself towards his head, his fingers searching out the dried blood and the gash beneath. He climbed slowly to his haunches, hair swinging before his face, grained with dust and twisted into thick dirty ribbons. Audrey held out her hand—too far away for Ned to take it—and let out what was a cry and a question. Ned didn't seem to hear it, or perhaps he couldn't. He rose to his feet, both hands rising to his head; blood began to run down the inside of his forearms, dripping in measured doses from his elbows, making dot patterns on the bone-white rocks below. The dots followed him as he staggered forward, connecting hissteps together. He looked up and met Simon's gaze, as if remembering something important. When he removed his left hand from his temple, a fresh complaint of blood spilled free. Ned's mouth opened to speak, and what Simon heard was, 'I remember,' though he wasn't sure if Ned was even making words. Then, with a loud exhalation and a final widening of his eyes, he collapsed again.

Audrey sprang to her father's side with the reflexive quickness of panic. She grabbed Ned's jacket, bunching it up in two little fists. She shook him, tried to pick him up. Her arms strained, but Ned remained where he was. She turned to Simon. 'Why did you do this?' she said, her voice not wet and wavering, but so dry that her words cracked in her throat.

'I didn't!' said Simon hopelessly. 'I didn't do anything.' He thought of his mother's voice, how it had appeared from nowhere.

'You threw the rock!' Audrey cried, shaking Ned's jacket. 'It's my dad!' Then she wept, whooping sobs, sucking in air that never satisfied her breaths.

Simon grabbed at his thoughts. Here came Gin, splashing towards them in the water. He didn't want Gin to see. But what about the rest of the people, scattered all around the dam, scores of them, more than enough to help, but too far away. What was it Madaline had said? Communication ...

'The whistles!' he shouted.

'What?' Audrey's entire face burned red.

'Every group leader has a whistle.'

Audrey seemed to understand. 'It's around his neck.' Simon crouched down to help, but Audrey slapped him away. She put her fingers up to Ned's throat and tried to work her hand underneath his collar. Simon made himself look into Ned's eyes. They weren't focused on him. They weren't focused on anything. His eyelids were broken blinds, sagging sadly.

Audrey was trying to force down the zipper on Ned's jacket. She had to push her hand against his chin, her fingers staining red. Eventually the zip came loose and she pulled out a small plastic whistle. Trembling, she unclipped it from its length of cord. The side of the whistle that had been resting on Ned's chest was covered in blood.

'What do we do?' said Audrey. 'It won't work like this.'

Simon took a deep breath and grabbed the whistle from her hand. He pulled the bottom of his T-shirt out from under his jumper and rubbed the whistle as hard as he could. When he brought it back to his face, it looked nearly clean.

'Should I try it?' he said to Audrey.

Audrey nodded her head.

Simon put the whistle to his lips, and he could taste the smell of old money. He took a breath and blew as hard as he could. The whistle spluttered, but that was all. Simon closed his eyes. It wasn't going to be like this.

146

It wasn't. He hit the whistle against the side of his leg, again and again. Something had to go right, eventually. He put the whistle to his mouth again and blew. And a piercing, trilling, beautiful sound shot out into the winter air, its pure echo ringing out. Simon blew it, over and over, harder each time, until he felt his last breaths leave him, the last efforts of air clawing at his lungs to remain.

Madaline hadn't always hated hospitals. Her childhood self had been intrigued by the secret world of healing sickness. She had been fascinated by X-rays, how you could see inside someone, transforming them to ghostly tracings, seeking out a broken bone or the dark evil of illness. She blamed the handsome doctors of her mother's guilty afternoon soap operas, somehow even more glamorous than the privileged heiresses and boat-hopping playboys. They were the ones who put things right. Hospitals, in those impossible lens-softened worlds, were the noble purveyors of justice and rightness.

That was before afternoons with a television's were replaced by after-school trips to waiting rooms; lounge-room lace curtains replaced by thick hospice. That repeating pattern of brown bare trees she still saw sometimes when she closed her eyes. Her father, looking lost in his own body.

Madaline locked her legs out straight in the plastic chair and had unconsciously hooked her thumbs over the top of her belt, a classic police pose. They'd taken Ned through to emergency straight away because of her uniform, although once the triage nurse looked at his head, the injury was enough. The look in the nurse's eyes had been sceptical.

'He was hit by a stone.' It did sound unlikely, but there was nothing Madaline could do except set her mouth in a grim line and hand Ned over. The bandage she'd wrapped around his head was already sodden with blood, and he slipped in and out of consciousness. She'd sped all the way from Reception, hurling them seventy kilometres up the highway, all the while talking manic rubbish to Ned. Now he was in safe hands, and all she could do was wait. Thinking, he could have died, could have disappeared from the world so easily.

Audrey and Gin sat beside her. Audrey had not said a word the whole way. She'd sat with Ned in the back seat, cradling his head in a towel, looking desperately sad. Madaline had had to prise her hand away from Ned's as they wheeled him away.

'Do you know the Green Lantern?' Gin swung his legs on the waiting room chair.

Madaline looked at him. 'Do I?'

'Yes,' said Gin. 'Do you know why he's the Green Lantern?'

'To fight crime? To do good?'

'No,' Gin's mouth twisted up in thought, 'do you know, um, how he's the Green Lantern?'

'Oh,' she said, 'how he became Green Lantern. No, I don't.'

'He made a ring from a meteor,' said Gin, 'that fell from the sky.'

'I see.' Madaline remembered Gin when she first met him: a little ball of energy. Wouldn't stop running. He seemed devoid of colour, now. Immersed too deeply in his own fantasies. His eyes lost somehow in his face.

Madaline heard a metallic chime, and it took her some moments to identify her own ringtone. All her messages coming through. Every time you left town, all your calls

149

would catch up with you. She unclipped the leather pocket and took out her phone. Ancient police issue, a brick of a thing. All the messages were from her mother, of course. Same time each day, six-thirty in the evening. Madaline pictured her mother sitting in her perfectly rustic kitchen, leaning back on the old church pew, third or fourth glass of wine in hand. Always the same wine, a blistering local red, a roundhouse of tannins. Those kohl-rimmed eyes fixed on apoint on the wall as Madaline's phone rang and rang.

It was another form of avoidance, Madaline knew. Something else to ignore, hoping it would disappear. Then: what if something happened to her mother—an accident, like Ned? Who would rush her to the hospital? Who would notice if she choked alone in the kitchen or keeled over in the garden? Who would care if she slipped into the bath with a pair of fabric scissors?

Madaline realised she was bleeding. She'd been scratching her arms, a pattern of midge bites that machine-gunned up her arm. She turned to the kids. 'I'll be back in a sec, okay?'

Gin nodded his head. Audrey said nothing.

Madaline got up and looked across the waiting room. Yes, there was a public phone, the large metallic box propped up on a table, the token plastic shield protecting it from God knows what. She dug a hand into her pocket. If there was nothing there she wouldn't call. She fumbled out a two-dollar coin. Shit. She put it in the slot and dialled her mother's number. She kept her finger poised above the phone's cradle as the line burred over and over.

She hardly needed a reason to press it.

'Hello?'

150

'Hi, Mum.'

'Madaline. Mads. Darling. How are you?' Her mother's voiceseemed rushed. Madaline pictured her in patchwork overalls, in her gardening shoes, hands covered with black northern soil, the phone wedged between cheek and shoulder. 'What's wrong? You're not calling from home?'

'I'm fine,' said Madaline. 'I'm ... calling from a hospital.'

'A hospital? What's the matter?'

Madaline enjoyed the panic in her mother's tone. 'I'm fine,' she said. 'Just a work thing.'

'Oh good. Just a sec though, I'm covered in dirt.'

The line went to hold. Gentle piano music. Madaline tapped her fingers on her holstered gun while her mother made her wait.

'There we are. Now, Mads, how does it take you this long to call your mother back?'

'You know,' said Madaline, 'work.'

'Oh, surely not. That little town can't have that much crime. It's not exactly Midsomer Murders, is it?' She laughed, a melodious chuckle that Madaline had no doubt she'd practised. There was silence for a few moments, then, inevitably, 'Why don't you come home, sweetie? I've got this whole house, and it's like you've forgotten—'

'God, Mum, you wonder why I don't call you.'

'Oh, I know. Fighting your battles.'

'I've been here four years. Fighting my battles? What does that mean?'

'I worry about you down there. Especially after that poor lady, the horribleness—haven't you had enough?'

151

Madaline ground a palm into her eye. The horribleness. Her mother's shorthand for anything that needed forgetting. Her husband's death. Her former career. Stephanie Gale's disappearance: a time in Madaline's life she regretted, every day, involving her mother in.

'Everyone asks after you. They want to know how you are, Mads, and I can't tell them anything.'

'Everyone?' said Madaline. 'All those friends I've never met? Is it pottery classes still, or dream-weaving this week?'

Her mother sighed down the phone. 'I'm trying to move on with my life, Madaline. It would just be nice to see you do the same.'

'Oh for fuck's sake, Mum. You want me to move on by coming back home? Become a good farmer's wife, child on each hip, dinner on the table?'

'There's no need to swear. And I still see Will down the street sometimes. You did a—'

Madaline slammed the phone down, her chest heaving with angry breath. She looked around and realised people were staringat her, Audrey and Gin regarding her with a mix of suspicion and wonder. She tried to remember why had she cared whether her mother was alive or dead. It didn't really matter either way.

Through the car window Simon could see Iris waiting. She was swathed in a bright orange sheet, her eyes ringed in black makeup and her hair pulled back. It made her eyes appear larger, her cheeks shovel-sharp. Simon could not remember his grandmother looking like this.

'Iris will look after you here,' Tarden mumbled. He had the corner of his little finger clamped in his teeth. 'I've got to get back to the Magpie, okay?'

Simon nodded. He undid his seatbelt and opened the door. Iris came towards him, her body held in the shape of a hug. 'Come here,' she said. 'Come inside.'

Simon felt himself move towards her embrace; he wanted to let himself collapse into his grandmother's arms. But he stood still, remembering she was a stranger now. Another part of this town he wished had never existed. Iris let him go and ushered him inside.

'I'm cooking,' she said. 'Come into the kitchen and I'll make you some tea.' The kitchen. Simon tasted banana and bacon on his tongue, his body remembering.

He followed Iris down the hall. From below the saloon doors, he could see Pony's legs tangled under one of the chairs. Iris pushed open the doors and ushered Simon in.

Pony looked up briefly; he was running a spoon distractedly around the rim of a cereal bowl—whatever was inside it was long gone. 'Simon Sawyer,' he said, as if reciting Simon's name off a list. Simon felt the weight of stones in his pockets and a shiver went through him.

'Sit down.' Iris busied herself at the counter. The folds of her orange sheet made wispy sounds as she moved. She put a kettle on the stove and lit the gas with a whoosh.

Simon sat down opposite Pony. 'Are you having more breakfast?'

Pony shrugged. 'I like cereal.'

'Do you have sugar, Simon?' said Iris.

'Two please.'

'Sugar's bad for you,' said Pony.

'Everything's fine in moderation,' said Iris.

Pony made a face. 'What are you doing today, Simon Sawyer?'

'I don't know,' said Simon. 'Staying here I guess.' He dreaded the moment when Audrey, Gin and Ned came back. Or maybe Ned wouldn't come back.

'I'm going into town,' said Pony. 'I fixed up my bike so it only takes me a few minutes.'

Simon looked out the window above the kitchen bench. Above the plumes of herbs, the sky had darkened. 'It's going to rain again.'

'I don't care about rain,' said Pony, staring into his empty bowl, as if it might magically refill itself. 'I've ridden my bike in floods before. In monsoons.'

The kettle squealed and Iris turned off the heat. 'I doubt that very much,' she said. 'I've seen army tanks washed away in monsoon floods. I don't think a young man on his bike would stand much of a chance.'

For a moment, Pony seemed genuinely chastened—not a state Simon had thought possible—but then he shoved himself angrily from the table.

'You haven't even seen my bike now I've fixed it,' he said. You don't know what it's like.'

Iris poured hot water from the kettle into two mugs. 'That's true, Miles, but I can't imagine it's any heavier than a tank.'

Simon was confused. What were true miles? Was that how you were supposed to measure a bike ride?

'I don't want to know what you imagine!' Pony shouted. 'You're just dirty and everybody knows it!'

He grabbed the spoon from his bowl and bunched it into his fist like a dagger. He opened his mouth, about to say something more, but instead plunged the spoon into his pocket and stalked out of the kitchen.

'Miles,' Iris called after him. 'Don't be like that.'

She meant the name Miles, Simon realised. Was that Pony?

'He's a strange boy,' said Iris. 'But then you would be, I suppose.' She looked at Simon, conspiratorial, as if they'd talked this way together every morning for years. 'Hasn't had an easy time.'

Simon stared at his hands.

'Simon?'

'Hmm?'

'Are you okay?'

'Hmm.'

'Listen,' said Iris. 'What happened was an accident. You shouldn't feel bad about it.'

'But what if he—' Simon again saw Ned's body, crumpled. 'What if he—'

Iris put her arm around Simon. 'He'll be fine,' she said. 'He'll just be in shock. Trust me. People have survived much worse.'

Simon burrowed his head into the soft fabric of her clothes. 'I feel so bad.'

'They'll all be okay. Ned, and Audrey, and Gin. Everything will be okay. Once your mum and dad turn up, everything will be fine.'

'My mum and dad—'

'They'll turn up,' said Iris. 'They have to.'

Tarden screwed up his eyes, banishing a repeated memory. He shook his head and he was back where he was supposed to be. Chipped sideboard, zigzag carpet, grandfather clock. His sister's painting looking down at him from the opposite wall: still the same mournful mountain, a sky clenched with Newcastle blue. He heard his voice, shimmering into clarity, saying, 'It wasn't an easy time.'

'I can imagine.' Madaline McKinley sat under the painting, in the uniform she had started wearing again. Tarden wasn't quite sure how he had got here. It was his house, he knew that. But what was she doing here, a copper, for crying out loud. Something else tugged at his mind.

'There's no—' Madaline was talking again. 'I mean, it's never going to be easy, is it.'

Tarden tried to regain his composure. He wasn't drunk, or high. He just got this way sometimes: unsure, disorientated. He wondered at Madaline, if she knew more than she was letting on. He had never known her to lock anyone up, but the amount of paperwork cluttering up her house—she'd have something on nearly everyone in the town.

She looked at him, smiling. That left eye that wasn't quite straight, it bothered him. The cops he'd known were all symmetrical. Not good looking, but always in tedious proportion. Madaline was attractive enough, but

157

she had this accumulation of imperfections. She didn't look entirely regular. So far, she hadn't touched the busted-up exercise book in her lap.

'It's only that you know the lake, Jack. Better than most. And we just need to keep at it.' She stressed her words with the tap of a pen.

He wondered if she already knew about the inlet. 'I thought we'd take a break,' said Tarden. 'After—'

'Ned's fine,' she said. 'Concussion, a deep cut—a few stitches and some Panadol.'

Tarden bent his jaw. 'Worse than it looked.'

'Exactly. And it shouldn't mean we give up on the Sawyers. Imagine how that poor kid's feeling now.'

Tarden tried not to think about Simon. Just wasn't worth it. 'Way I see it, if they haven't turned up by now I reckon they must have done a runner.'

Madaline shifted in her seat. 'And nothing turned up after I left with Ned?'

'Nothing,' Tarden said. 'We kept up for another hour or so. No sign. Who gets lost out there, anyway? There's a giant landmark right in front of you.'

'That's just it, Jack. They didn't know the area at all. Might seem strange to you, but these people don't have any sense of the place.'

Tarden thought of train tracks, burning tyres.

Madaline said, 'Was it you who suggested they visit the lake, Jack?'

'Who told you that?'

'But you did tell them about the Magpie, when they arrived in town?'

'I talked with them, yeah, but you can ask anyone at the Ottoman—I was only there a few minutes.'

158

'Simon seemed to think you gave his parents directions to Magpie Lake.'

'Well I did, but I—' Tarden knew he had lost his touch. Used to be he could run rings around these people. 'I was the one raised the alarm,' he said. 'You saying it's our fault they got lost?'

'Our fault?' Madaline pulled the cap off her pen.

Tarden's mouth was dry. 'My fault. 'Cause I told them where Magpie was.'

'I'm not accusing you of anything,' said Madaline. 'It's just that you were the last person to talk to the Sawyers. Means I need to talk to you.'

'Then why're you asking me about all this other stuff. The old stuff ... doesn't even—you can't think I'm still like that?'

Madaline drew her notepad up in front of her to screen her moving pen.

Tarden knew he was fucking things up. He'd answered the door to Madaline only twenty minutes before, and his head had been perfectly clear. When did Robbie get back? Where was Robbie?

'This is all just normal procedure,' she said. 'I just want to get the facts right in my mind.'

Tarden watched her eyes move around the room. Fuck, fuck, fuck. He cursed himself for letting Madaline in so easily, so amiably. She'd become such a part of the landscape, he'd almost forgotten what her job was. Stupid. There was a way of dealing with cops—giving them what they wanted without telling them anything at all—but that skill that had left him it seemed.

She looked at him. 'You go out to Magpie Lake quite often, don't you.'

159

'I'm there sometimes,' he said, wary. 'Got some yabby traps there.'

Madaline nodded, without any noise of agreement. 'And Kuiper—Robert—does he ever go out there with you?'

'Sometimes. Depends on how busy he is.'

'Sometimes? Meaning ... a couple of days a week? Every second day?'

'I don't know—couple of days each week I guess. When he feels like it.'

'Did you both go out there yesterday? Did you go out there last night?'

Tarden reached his hand down to the floor and felt around for his cup of tea. He leaned his head over the armrest: the mug wasn't there.

'Jack?'

'What?' He was sure he'd made tea.

'Did you go out to Magpie Lake last night?'

Tarden felt the rising sting of bile in his throat. 'He just—I don't—'

A throat cleared. 'Jack was at the pub. Anyone'll tell you. I was at home.' Kuiper stood in the doorway, half hidden by the darkness of the unlit hall. He lit a cigarette with a snap of his hands. He smiled at Madaline then looked over at Tarden. 'Jack,' he said, 'I wish you'd woken me up. I didn't realise we had a guest. Could have saved us all some time and bother.' He turned, blew smoke into the shadows.

Tarden wondered how much Robbie had heard. How long he'd been waiting to make an entrance.

'Hi Robert,' said Madaline, not looking at all surprised to see him. 'I was just finishing up with Jack here. Just having a chat to tie up some details.' She tapped the pen: details.

'So I see,' Kuiper said. 'I'm just glad we're all here to help out the young lad.' He smiled.

Madaline closed her notebook. 'As I say, just finishing up.' She stood up abruptly, compelling Tarden to do the same. 'Thanks for your hospitality, Jack.' She handed him an empty mug. Tarden eyed it suspiciously, as if she'd conjured it from thin air. 'Anyway,' she set it down on the arm of the chair, 'I'm sure I'll see you soon. Have a nice day, both of you.' She pushed past Kuiper, who made no effort to move. The front door opened and closed.

Kuiper curled smoke from his nostrils. 'So nice to have guests, isn't it?'

Tarden sat back down. 'She just ... came in. I didn't think it was anything serious, but she kept at me. Like an interview.'

Kuiper put a palm to one side of his face. 'Jack,' he said softly, 'it's one thing to let a copper into your house—but to start blabbing about your bloody murder trial?'

'I didn't mean to,' said Tarden. Had he? Robbie must have been listening the whole time. 'I just ... I forgot who I was talking to.'

Kuiper stubbed out his cigarette in the ashtray on the sideboard. 'Didn't the fucking uniform give it away?' He clamped his hands down on the chair Madaline had been using. 'Didn't that give you a fucking clue?'

Tarden felt a headache pressing at his skull. He wished he was out in the boat, not stuck in this airless house. A thorn of annoyance suddenly jagged. 'You could have come in earlier,' he said, 'instead of just waiting out in the hall. I mean if we're in this together, we're—'

Kuiper narrowed his eyes. His hair had fallen down over one eye: the other, Tarden noticed, was ringed red. He said, 'I get the impression, Jack, that you don't understand quite what's at stake.' He sighed, pushing his breath out too quickly. 'I chose this place because it's quiet. Because nothing ever happens.' He took a step closer. 'This isn't just another dumb-fuck small town joke, something that'll blow over in the morning—'

Tarden realised too late. Robbie wasn't just bent; he was at that stage where your mind teetered on a cliff of reality, desperately trying to claw its way back from the horrifying edge. Tarden remembered what it felt like, what it made you do. The rush from dead calm crashing rage. 'Robbie, I know.' He kept his voice low. 'We just have to—'

'You think it'll be o-fucking-kay if we just give it time, Jack? Well, that's not how it is. There's just so much money ... it's not going to just ... this is so serious, FOR FUCK'S SAKE!'

Kuiper's fist hit the painting but the noise seemed to trail far behind, cracking out eventually in a splinter-sound too sharp to be real. A thick rag of glass hung, pinned under Kuiper's knuckles, blood leaching into the cracks. The rest of the sheet sprawled in awkward shards on the sideboard. The painting remained steady in its frame. Above the brush-stroke of the mountains, the sky stung with a new blue. It appeared to Tarden more real than ever: a sky he'd first looked on, decades before, with guiltless, childhood eyes.

✑

Simon had spent all afternoon at the window, huddled up on the seat by its ledge. He found the view soothing; the sharp pain that had stabbed his mind like a pulse had now been worn down to a dull hum. He'd stirred once, half an hour ago, with literally no idea why he was feeling so sad. Then, the image, dusk-muted, of his parents walking away from him floated back, and he hated himself for forgetting it. He couldn't even picture their faces now. They must have been so familiar to him he had no need to keep them.

There was a gentle knock. 'Simon?' Ned's voice came through the bedroom door. Simon's legs flexed, ready to run, but he had nowhere to run to. Panicking, he looked for somewhere to hide.

Nowhere. The bed was too high off the ground. The cupboard was too full. Without really thinking he prised the edge of the seat and to his joy it rose up. The top was hinged, the seat was hollow. He climbed into it.

'Hello?' Ned knocked again.

Simon's heart thumped as he eased the lid of the chair down. He expected to be cloaked in darkness, but instead the light remained. He twisted his body around and realised the seat had no back: its edge jutted up right against the window pane; the glass went straight down into the floorboards. He crawled right to the edge of the glass, and suddenly he was hanging in mid-air, suspended out over the thin strip of garden below, the tufty expanse

163

of sand beyond. For a beautiful and terrifying moment, Simon thought he was floating.

Then his stomach rose in his throat, the familiar horror-flash of crawling to the top of his grandmother's roll-top desk where the beckon-curl of smoke rose from far-flung chimneys. A pink hand fat with world-trust, an explosion of paper-thin glass, a suffocating spin through all of innocence. And all the air there ever was not able to fill his lungs as he fell.

Simon realised he had stopped breathing, and sucked in a sudden chestful of dust-laden air. He coughed violently, tears surging to his eyes.

'Simon?' Ned's voice was right above him. Simon heard his weight creaking the floorboards. 'Are you ... under the seat?'

Simon coughed again, the dust was everywhere. But then, fresh air.

Ned peered down at him. 'What are you doing down there?'

Simon could see the crude hint of stitches at Ned's forehead. A yellowing bruise covered one cheek. 'Um,' said Simon, 'just looking ... out.'

Ned stuck out his hand. 'Why don't you come out,' he said. 'I wanted to have a little talk with you.'

Simon took Ned's hand and unfolded himself from the space under the seat. 'Okay.' He stepped out and brushed the dust off his knees and arms. It was dark grey, thick, and curled like fancy butter.

'Guess we never clean under there,' said Ned.

Simon stepped awkwardly out of the seat. It felt like he'd been caught doing something illegal. 'Are you ... okay?' he said.

164

'I'm fine,' said Ned. 'Don't worry about it. Shock, mostly.'

'I'm sorry.' Simon brushed down his trousers, a tiny charge of panic going through him as he felt a stone still in his pocket. 'Can I ... is there ... ?'

'Do you want to sit down?' Ned motioned to the bed, and Simon sat down on it. Ned sat down next to him. 'Listen,' he said, 'Simon. Don't feel bad about what happened at the lake. It was an accident, and they happen, and I'm fine.'

Simon twisted his hands in his lap. 'I really didn't mean to.' He desperately wanted to explain to Ned about his mother's voice, how it appeared in his head just as he was about to throw. But it sounded so stupid.

'I know you didn't mean to,' said Ned. 'But Audrey and Gin—especially Audrey—are still a bit upset about it. They're just being protective. I mean, you'd be the same if your—'

Simon gulped down a swallow, as if eating the air might make the silence go by faster.

Ned rubbed his head where the stitches were. 'Anyway it wasn't really the rock that did this to me, I hit my head on the ground when I fell. If I'd put my arms out to break my fall it would have been a different story.' Ned snuffed out a laugh. 'Just the old waiter coming out in me,' he said. 'Save the food and drink at all costs.'

'Were you a waiter?'

Ned nodded. 'That's how I started out, then I moved into the kitchen. Slowly worked my way up to owning my own business. It was great fun, really.'

'How big was your business?' said Simon. He shuffled his body further back on the bed. It was nice to hear an adult who sounded excited about what they did.

'Fairly big,' said Ned. 'I ended up doing events all over town. Brisbane, mainly. Gold Coast. Big dinners: launches, receptions, celebrations. Once I cooked breakfast for Neil Armstrong. You know, the first man on the moon?'

'Really? What did he eat?' Simon thought of the packets of Space Food he'd seen in the supermarket—sticks that were supposed to taste like whole meals. Roast dinner, pumpkin soup, Neapolitan ice cream.

'I can't remember,' said Ned. 'It was a business lunch he was speaking at. He had the same as everyone else.'

Simon looked down at the carpet. He had never met anyone famous, let alone made something for them. 'Why did you stop your job?' he said. 'Why did you come here?'

Ned rubbed his neck. 'It's sort of hard to explain.' He moved his tongue around in front of his teeth. 'Is there something you love doing, Simon?'

'What do you mean?'

'Is there something that you'd always rather be doing, rather than anything else?' Simon thought. 'I like reading,' he said. 'Reading books.'

'Well, that's what cooking was like for me. But imagine if someone told you where you had to read every day, which books you had to read, how fast you had to finish them—how wouldthat feel?'

'Not too good,' Simon said.

'Well cooking got to be like that for me. Once people knew I was good at it, they wanted more and more.'

Simon thought he understood. 'You mean, it wasn't fun anymore.'

'Exactly,' said Ned. 'My life wasn't just in a kitchen

166

any more. It was art galleries and racecourses and business meetings. No one was there to enjoy my food, they had other things on their mind.' Ned gripped his head suddenly, trying to hold it still. He closed his eyes, squeezing the lids tight. 'This place,' he said. 'Reception ... Stephanie—my wife—she was a local.' He smiled, but Simon thought he a glint of moisture at the edges of his eyes.

Simon turned his eyes to the floor.

'When she went ... when she—' Ned sighed. 'It was like the sun had gone.'

Simon sometimes had a competition with himself to track the darkness disappearing from the day. He would wait, concentrate, try and catch the moment when the light had completely gone away and afternoon became night, but he never could. Time would just stretch out and slow so much that he would always forget to watch and by the time he'd remember what he was doing, it would already be night.

'Anyway.' Ned shook his head and winced. 'Just wanted to check you were okay.' He got up and walked to the door. 'I'll probably make some lunch soon,' he said. 'If you're hungry.'

Simon went to fetch a jumper from the pile of clothes Ned had left for him the night before. He felt all the better for having talked to Ned; his mind had settled. It was strange the way this sick feeling came in waves, one moment he was panicked, the next, calm. He pulled the jumper over his head and decided that he would walk down to the ocean. Out the front door, around the house, through the garden and over the dunes. He ached to see the water up close.

As he walked out the bedroom door, he knew something strange was happening. It was a series of noises: slipping, straining sounds, and underneath a deep painful creak: Simon thought again of a ship. Coming out the door, he realised the sound was coming from a thick multicoloured rope tied to the banister on the landing, shifting and straining under a weight which Simon realised too slowly was Pony. The other end of the rope was wound around Pony's belt. He leant back into thin air, his feet planted firmly below the banister. He was wearing a battered felt hat, the kind they wore in the outback. Simon couldn't work out how the thin rope was holding him up.

'What are you doing?' Simon couldn't help the waver of panic in his voice. Pony whipped his head up; his body swayed on the rope.

'Standard safety tests,' he said.

'What for?' Simon pictured the entire banister giving way, Pony's body spinning to the ground.

'I'm seeing how much pressure it can take.'

'But—but what if it breaks?'

'Then I'll know it's not safe. Don't you listen to anything?'

Simon's leg itched. 'But won't it be weaker if you keep putting pressure on it? Won't it be less safe than if you did nothing at all?'

Pony gave him a dark stare. 'How's the search going?' he said.

'I'm not sure. Ned had ... you probably heard. The rock.'

'Yeah.' Pony's face fell. 'Help me back, can you?'

Simon took Pony's hand, and helped him clamber back onto the landing. Pony unwound the rope from his waist, loosening a series of complicated knots. 'Do you want a muesli bar?'

'Sure,' said Simon. 'Thanks.' He realised he was quite hungry.

Pony pulled out two muesli bars with faded wrappers and gave one to Simon. He sat down with his back against the banister and Simon did the same.

Simon had never really seen Pony's face close up. Most of the pores on his nose and down his cheeks were clogged with dirt. Simon had learnt all about pores from his mother. He'd seen diagrams in the brochures she had. Cleansers and toners penetrating deep into pores: little drawings of blue arrows driving out particles of dirt from the evil bulbous chasms.

'So,' said Pony, chewing a large mouthful, 'Why don't you ever talk?'

'What?'

'You don't seem to talk that much. You don't seem to be interested in other people.'

'Don't I?'

Pony shook his head. He finished his muesli bar in another giant mouthful and put the wrapper back into his pocket.

'I suppose I don't talk to anyone that much,' said Simon.

'You mean, not just here?'

Simon didn't say anything.

Pony stared at the floor. Then he said, 'Remember I told you both my parents died?'

Simon nodded.

'You never asked me how it happened.'

Simon fished in his mouth. A piece of nut from the muesli bar had lodged behind one of his teeth. 'I didn't know you then. It would have been rude.'

'I didn't know you,' said Pony, 'and I asked about your parents.'

'Sorry,' said Simon, not particularly meaning it.

Pony cracked his knuckles. 'That's okay.'

For a moment, Simon didn't know what to say. Why should he have spoken to Pony? His parents had gone missing: making friends wasn't the thing at the very front of his mind. Especially with someone who threw rocks at his door and made fun of his scars.

'We're not that different,' said Pony. 'That's all I'm saying. I know it can be ... not easy. When it's your parents, I mean.' His fingers twisted themselves into the rope.

'Is this why you came here?' said Simon. 'Did the Gales adopt you?'

Pony snorted, his laugh shooting out of him like a mistake too late to take back. 'Not exactly,' he said.

170

Simon took a deep breath. 'Do you think I'll have to be adopted,' he said, 'if my mum and dad don't come back?'

Pony shook his head. 'You've probably got other family to look after you.'

'Not really.' He thought. 'There's only Ir—my grandma. And she's ... not well.'

'Iris.' Pony rubbed his nose with the back of his hand. 'Not well indeed.'

Simon didn't know what this was supposed to mean.

'But your parents have got friends, or neighbours? People to look after you?'

Simon shrugged. 'We've moved around so much. My dad used to call his business his best friend.' Simon felt a fresh sadness rustle in his stomach.

'So it's just you.' Pony folded his mouth up. 'We're pretty much alike, then.'

'Are we? I thought you didn't like me.'

'Because I tackled you.'

'And made fun of my scars.'

'Oh,' said Pony. 'Sorry.' He poked his fingers at Simon's leg. 'How did you get them?'

'I fell out a window,' he said. 'When I was little. At my grandma's house. She was looking after me.'

'The window cut up your leg?'

'No, the window was open. I fell into a greenhouse. Broke both my legs.'

Pony winced. 'How on earth did you manage that?' Simon imagined him safety testing all the hotel's window frames.

'My grandma left me alone in my grandpa's old study. She was gone a long time, and I climbed up on a desk and was leaning against the window when it ... broke.'

171

'Did it hurt?'

'Not at first. I remember falling, but I can never really think about falling through the greenhouse. It was just a small one, where my grandma used to grow flowers. I broke ... I got cut up pretty badly, especially—' he pointed at his scars. 'I was knocked out and my grandma didn't find me for a while.'

'Why not? Wouldn't she have heard the crash?'

'She was ... taking some medicine. She was taking medicine then that wasn't really good for her.'

'Bloody hell,' said Pony. 'Iris.'

'It wasn't her fault,' said Simon, 'but my mum didn't let us talk to her after that.'

Pony suddenly stood up. 'What are you doing today Simon?'

'I was going to go to the beach,' said Simon. 'I wanted to see the water.'

'No you're not,' said Pony. 'I know somewhere even better.'

Sometimes, lying with his back to her, he would feel her fingers tracing down his back. She would smooth down his hunched shoulders, draw her hands over the old gouges of acne, over the deeper lesions: cigarette burns and unhealed bruises, cuts from forgotten blades. Her fingertips would sketch his spine as if tracing backwards through his life, making each wound disappear.

'I can't stay.' Tarden's voice rumbled in the quiet room. His feet moved up and down rhythmically against Iris's leg.

'You don't have to go,' she said. 'There's plenty of time.'

Tarden always reached a stage, when he was with Iris, when he would feel suddenly lost. Always a moment when he would find himself out of place in the ivory sheets and dappled seaside light. This was not where he belonged. He would never belong somewhere like here.

'I've got to go,' he said. 'It's kind of important.'

Iris rolled over, taking his face with her hands. 'You're a good man, Jack Tarden. You know that?'

'No,' he said. 'I don't.' Even her hands: softer and more tender than he ever deserved.

'You are. The way you're helping with Bill and Louise. The whole town is lucky to have you. And poor Simon.'

Tarden ran his hands over his face. He groaned and flopped back onto the pillows. His voice was muffled by his hands. He smelled seawater and wet plastic. Damp rust.

'What is it, Jack?'

For all the world, he wanted to tell her. For all the world, he wanted to take her away.

'You can tell me.' Iris stroked his arm.

Tarden knew this feeling too well, words roaring red in his mind, demons too big to exit his body. Then another thought, another layer. 'Simon told me you were sick.' These words came out lightly with no comprehension of their weight.

Iris shrank away from him and drew up the sheets. 'Did he.'

Tarden turned to face her. His arm ached, had ached for years. 'I'm sorry,' he said. But ... Jesus. I had no idea.'

Her eyelids fluttered and closed.

He said, 'You were the reason they came here.' It sounded cruel.

'Five years,' she said quietly. Do you know how long that actually is? Not to hear your daughter's voice, your grandson's?' A tear shivered at the inner corner of her eye.

Tarden reached out a hand, touched her temple. He was sure he could feel her blood, running just below the skin. 'I didn't know.'

'Of course not. It's not something you ask someone like me, is it. Any family? Any life outside these four walls?' She turned over, cocooning in the sheet, so all Tarden could see was her back: the soft white skin of her shoulders.

'You could have told me,' he said.

Iris started to cry, a sound that still gave Tarden chills

of whitehot guilt. 'You shouldn't feel like ... it's not your fault.'

Iris let out a wet laugh. 'You have no idea. I'm the reason I haven't seen them in so long. I'm the reason they came here. I'm the reason they went missing.' Her sobbing became a howl of lost breath.

Tarden drew her in close, holding her tightly. 'Don't say that. It's not true.' He pictured Bill and Louise's carparked inside his shed. He said, 'They'll turn up soon. We'll find them.' He moved his face closer to hers. 'What did you say?'

'This bloody town,' she whispered.

'This town?'

'It's a bolt-hole. All of us—we're not doing anything right.'

Tarden felt a prickle of heat. 'What's that supposed to mean?'

'Life isn't—' she paused. 'There's always something trailing you, and it'll always catch up. Like a ... a well that you're drawing up.'

'Well I sure as hell didn't come here to haul up my past.'

'Jack,' Iris turned back to him, 'I didn't mean that. I didn't mean you.'

Tarden looked away from her gaze. 'Nearly sixty years of my life, and this is all anyone thinks of me.'

'Jack—'

'No. You're right. This place is an escape. This town is for people who have apparently not done one worthwhile thing in their life. This is what you get for being honest with people.' Tarden stuck out his hand to an imaginary partner. 'Pleased to meet you. Name's Jack Tarden.

175

Recovering alcoholic. Recovering gambler. Fifteen years for accessory to murder.'

Iris held his gaze. 'This isn't you,' she said.

Tarden's head burned. 'Yes it is,' he said. 'And I'll be fucked if I'll do it anymore.'

'Jack. Stay with me. We'll talk some more.'

She was just a helpless old woman. Tarden saw this now. Her eyes spider-veined red, her mouth hinged with lines of sadness. He got out of the bed and started pulling on his trousers. 'If it's all the same with you,' he said, 'I'm pretty sick of talking. Time I actually did something.'

She reached out for him as he walked away. 'Jack, just—'

'Shall I send in whoever's next?' He watched Iris's face fall, and felt the sharp edge of satisfaction at having wounded her so deeply.

The afternoon sun was low and Pony adjusted his hat for shade. 'This is it.'

Simon could still see the Gales' house, a corner of it. They had taken a right turn at the bottom of the driveway and followed a short overgrown track. Pony was on his bike and Simon had borrowed an old one of Ned's, but it was such a short distance Simon wondered why they hadn't just walked. A tall chain-link fence was once a barrier to intruders, but now had either collapsed or rusted away. The iron gate had long ago come off its hinges and fallen onto the ground by the entrance.

'Yeah,' said Pony. 'Come on.'

He led Simon through the entrance; Simon followed Pony's footsteps exactly. Dry leaves and fern fronds covered the ground. By the entrance was the old ticket booth, an oblong sentry's box with a faded sign, a glittering carpet of broken glass on the ground around it.

'Ned told me they built it about fifteen years ago,' said Pony. 'Didn't stay open long because it was so close to the beach where you could swim for free. Stupid, really. Ned also told me to stay away because it's dangerous.' He grinned.

Simon saw horrible images of children running barefoot over the glass, blood running into cement cracks.

'I'm going to restore it,' said Pony.

'Restore it?'

'Yeah. No one uses it any more, so I've claimed it.' Pony stuck his thumbs under his armpits as if he was wearing braces. 'Squatter's rights.'

'But won't people still go to swim at the beach?'

Pony looked at Simon like he was slow. 'I'm not going to reopen it as a swimming pool,' he said. 'I'm going to reopen it into a restaurant.' He pointed to the ticket booth. 'That'll be the cloakroom. The front gate is where I'll be most of the time, greeting people, seeing who's arriving.' He walked away from Simon. 'This is the best bit, though.'

Simon followed him, gingerly stepping over broken glass and cracked pavers. They came to the pool itself, which was far bigger than Simon had imagined. At the near end—the shallow end—there was an angry mass of wrinkled canvas: an old pool cover, faded and desiccated by countless summer suns. Dirt and foliage caked the once-white pool floor, the black lane markers now only pale suggestions. At the deep end, someone had abandoned an old card table. It looked for all the world like some cumbersome animal that had lost its balance and toppled in.

'Up here!' Pony's voice cracked overhead. Simon looked up to see Pony strutting along the top tier of a wooden grandstand, the seats nothing more than long benches. One entire row had completely fallen away, and others were rotten and crumbling.

'Are you sure it's safe?' said Simon.

Pony turned around. 'I've tested it,' he said. 'I'll show you.' He scrambled down the rows, zigzagging back and forth, stuttering steps in places, loping full strides in others. 'Come on!'

Simon peered down the gap. He saw remnants of the bench below, pieces covered in moss. The grass was striped too, green and brown, where the rain and sun fell between the gaps.

'Here we go then,' said Pony, stretching across to place one foot either side of the gap. He held out his hands. Simon looked at him skeptically. 'Don't be a pussy,' said Pony, grabbing Simon under the armpits and swinging him effortlessly across the gap. Simon gasped at Pony's strength. 'There,' said Pony. 'Easy.' He swung his leg back past Simon and bustled past him.

'Wait,' said Simon. 'How old are you?'

'Fifteen.'

'Really?'

Pony spun around. 'What? Just because I'm short.'

'No,' said Simon, 'sorry. I didn't mean—it's just I didn't realise how strong you were.'

'Yeah, well. You have to be, don't you.'

Simon knew this was another question that didn't want to be answered. He followed Pony to the top of the grandstand, and Pony pulled two more muesli bars from his pockets. 'I don't know if I'll keep these seats,' he said. 'I want the best views to be from down there.' He pointed at the pool.

'How will the waiters get down carrying food?' said Simon. 'They won't be able to carry it down a ladder.'

'I'll put in steps, probably,' said Pony. 'Or a door in the side. But the people who come here to eat will have to climb down to get to the dining room floor.'

'What about the slope?' Simon remembered his own public swimming pool experiences, that sinister feeling of the water creeping up your body the further in you went.

'It doesn't matter. I'll put a grippy covering on the floor, and the tables and chairs will be specially made so it feels like you're sitting flat.' Pony pointed to the far end. 'Do you see down there?'

'The deep end?'

'Yeah. That's where the best seats will be.'

'Why's that?'

'Because you're in the deepest part of the pool. The best view's from the deep end table. That's where the famous people will sit.'

'Like Neil Armstrong?'

'The man on the moon?'

'Yes. Ned said he served him lunch once.'

'Neil Armstrong.' Pony smiled. 'Definitely. I'll make him something myself.'

'I thought you didn't like cooking, though.'

'What gave you that idea?'

'I don't know. I guess I've only ever seen you eat cereal.'

'Well, I help out in the kitchen sometimes. When it's busy.' Pony frowned. 'I'm not a freeloader you know.'

'How long have you lived here?' said Simon. 'At the Gales' house, I mean.'

'For a while.'

'Where did you live before here?'

Pony squinted up his eyes, as if trying to focus on some details at the pool's edge. 'Ned could help in the restaurant,' he said. 'He'd be very useful.'

Simon stared at the broken card table, and something

180

came to him. 'Did your parents go missing as well?'

Pony drew in a breath like he was going to say something. Then he shook his head and laughed. 'I was going to say yes,' he said. 'It was too good to miss. But that's not what happened to them.'

Simon's stomach lurched with anger and embarrassment. All his life's bullies howled in his head. 'That's not funny,' he said. 'You shouldn't laugh at me for that.'

Pony chuckled on. 'Admit it,' he said. 'It was pretty funny.'

Simon stood up and threw his half-finished muesli bar through the gap in the seats, even though he never littered. He started to walk back down the grandstand.

'Oh come on,' called Pony. 'I was only kidding.'

Simon made his footsteps rattle the wood.

'I'm sorry, okay?'

Simon kept walking. Sick of this, sick of stupid Pony, sick of everything.

'My dad shot my mum with a rifle, okay?' Pony's voice cut through. 'And then shot himself.'

Simon froze.

'That's how my parents died,' said Pony. 'If you wanted to know.'

Simon slowly climbed back up the grandstand. He sat down next to Pony. 'I didn't ... when?'

Pony took off his hat. He stared upwards. A threadbare awning was stretched above them, covered with the soft shadows of leaves and sticks. They twirled and danced: swishing fingers on the old fabric. 'I was ... maybe nine? Ten? We lived on this property, outside of Roma. Cattle farm. My mum worked in the doctor's surgery in town.

181

She was the receptionist, she'd organise everything for the doctors. She didn't like the farm, all that stuff. Neither did I. I spent a lot of time in the waiting room. I read a lot. National Geographics. Never thought I'd finish them all.'

Pony wedged his hat between his knees, and went on. 'Dad was just obsessed by the farm. Kept wanting to make it bigger. It wasn't making any money—the drought, you know—but he was always saying speculate to accumulate. We were getting poorer, and basically relying on Mum's wage and Dad couldn't believe that nothing was working. He'd get so angry.'

Pony was folding up his muesli bar wrapper, over and over on itself. 'We were just sitting down to breakfast, same as any morning. Walked in with a gun under his arm. Started shouting about living and dying on the land. I thought it was a joke, you know? Like he was overacting to make us laugh. But then—' Pony thrust his hands into his pockets. He pulled out a band-aid, flicked it against the palm of his hand. 'After he ... after Mum, he pointed it straight at me.' Pony put two fingers at the side of Simon's head, just above his eyebrow. 'Kept asking if I agreed with him, kept saying I'm right, aren't I, I'm right, I'm right?'

'What did you say?' Simon could barely get his voice to make a noise.

'I told him no. So he shot me.'

'He shot you?'

'Tried to, except the gun jammed. He kept pulling the trigger.' Pony tapped Simon's temple. 'Click. Click. Click.' Pony put the band-aid back in his pocket. 'I took my chance. Punched him in the guts and ran. I was out the

182

front door and I heard the gun go off again. I waited for the pain. I actually waited to feel the bullet. But it wasn't me he shot. They were there together, in the kitchen. I went back.'

Simon cleared his throat. 'That's horrible.'

Pony shrugged. 'It's not something I think too much about.' His voice was steady, but Simon saw his hands were shaking.

'Did you tell anyone?' said Simon. 'What happened ... after?'

'I just left,' said Pony. 'I knew where Dad kept all the money, so I took it. I dunno, maybe they think he buried me somewhere. Maybe they think I killed them.' He shook his head. 'I haven't told anyone that,' he added. 'Ever. And you can't tell anyone, okay?'

Simon nodded. 'You haven't even told Ned?'

'All they know is I ran away from home. Dad's money got me a bus fare and half a year's accommodation here. I just stayed. No one asks you much about what you did before.'

'Are the Gales your family now?' said Simon.

Pony didn't say anything for a long while. He studied the long wooden plank beneath his feet. Eventually, he said, 'You see these?' He pointed between his shoes. Simon peered over. A long line of light brown ants threaded a path over the wood. 'These are the same ants from this morning.'

'The ones stuck in the orange juice.'

Pony nodded.

'But they haven't got any wings.'

Pony raised his finger like a teacher. 'They haven't got any wings anymore.'

183

'You mean they fall off?'

Pony nodded. 'When they find somewhere they want to stay, they shed them.'

'But why? Why wouldn't you want to keep wings?'

'I guess,' said Pony, 'they know they won't need them any more.'

'Mr Tarden!'

Tarden jumped, physically jumped, as Audrey's face appeared at the bottom of the stairs. He always felt like a naughty child when he left Iris. Stupid, they were both adults.

'Jack,' he said. 'Audrey, you know you can call me Jack.' His heart hammered so thickly in his ribs he was sure Audrey could hear it. He tried to smile.

'Okay. Jack.'

It was a game they went through every time they talked. He disliked being called by his last name, a shorthand that reminded him too much of that long time in his past when his life was not his own.

'I'm glad I caught you,' said Audrey. She met him at the bottom of the stairs. Her outfit was strange, even by Audrey's standards: a tweed coat that crumpled at her feet and nearly obscured her head, her hands poking shapes halfway down the arms. She reminded

Tarden of the witch from that old movie, melting to the floor after getting splashed with water. She shuffled one hand out the end of the sleeve and held out an envelope. It was bright fluoro yellow and covered with red glitter. 'It's an invitation,' said Audrey, 'to Gin's birthday party.'

'Oh right,' said Tarden. 'It's his birthday, is it?'

Audrey looked at him like he was stupid. 'Yes,' she said. 'It's his actual birthday tomorrow. He told me he

185

was happy to have his birthday later, when things were less busy, but I told him that was silly. It's not the same if you don't celebrate on your actual birthday.'

'I suppose not.'

'Anyway, Dad said yes, just a small celebration, but he thought it might be nice to have a party. You know, after Simon's parents going missing and Dad going to hospital.'

'Yes,' said Tarden. 'Of course.' His ears burned at the mention of Simon's name.

'Say you'll come?' She pressed the envelope into Tarden's hand. 'You'll come, and Mr Kuiper? It'll only be for a few hours, and I'm getting proper party food. Dad wanted to make stuff, but it wasn't real things you eat at a party.'

Tarden smiled. 'We'll do our best,' he said.

Audrey put her hand on her hip. 'I need a definite RSVP.' She made a concerned face, a quizzical twist to her mouth. 'I need to confirm numbers.' Her face reminded Tarden so much of her mother that it shocked him.

'Of course we'll come,' he said. 'Wouldn't miss it for the world.' He knew exactly what Robbie would say, but—frankly—fuck him. He'd make him come along.

Audrey beamed. 'Excellent,' she said. 'Now, you don't have to bring a present tomorrow, but you'll probably need to give it to Gin soon after.' She sneezed, twice in a row.

'That coat a little dusty?' said Tarden.

Audrey wiped her nose. 'A little. It's been in storage.'

'Is that your mum's coat?'

Audrey's eyes opened, as if Tarden had unravelled a great mystery. 'Yes,' she said. 'Her opera coat. Look,'

Audrey dug into the other pocket and pulled out a piece of crumpled, yellowing paper. She handed it to Tarden. 'Be careful, though.'

Tarden took the piece of paper and peered at it. 'The ... Barber—'

'The Barber of Seville,' said Audrey. 'It's her favourite opera.'

'Was it, now.' Robbie listened to them sometimes, but to Tarden it just sounded like people hurting their voices.

'She took the train,' said Audrey, 'to see it in Sydney.'

'She must have loved it.'

'She does,' said Audrey, 'she does.'

Tarden looked up. 'Last of the true locals, your mum.'

'What do you mean?'

'Not many people left now who actually grew up here. This place has always been for people travelling through. Or people coming to work for a season, moving away. Now it's tourism,' Tarden said the word like it was sour on his tongue. 'People coming to spend time by the sea.'

'But we live here,' said Audrey. 'You and me.'

'Yeah, well we're the smart ones.' Tarden tapped the side of his head. 'We know how good this place is.' He remembered hearing stories about Audrey, about what she did to herself after Stephanie disappeared. It'd be enough to send anyone that young over the edge. 'Your mum, she was a good woman.'

'Is a good woman.'

The girl's eyes, Tarden thought, held something that would never soften.

'Right,' he said. 'She is a good woman.' He gave the opera ticket back. Audrey took it, but didn't put it back in her pocket. Instead, she reached back into the pocket and took out something else. A piece of glass, Tarden thought, bottle green, worn smooth.

'This is hers too,' said Audrey. 'This was in the pocket with the ticket.'

'What is it?'

'Sea-glass. Mum told me about how there used to be a city under the sea. This,' she held up the glass to the light, squinting at it, 'this was a part of the city once.'

Tarden nodded, wondering where that part of him had gone that would have once believed such things. He pictured a shard falling into the sea, tumbling, its edges eroding in a lifetime of saltwater. Currents and wind and the warmth of the earth carrying it to a random slice of coastline, where Stephanie Gale had found it.

'Don't worry,' said Audrey quietly. 'I know it's just a bit of a bottle.' She put the glass and the ticket back in her pocket. 'Anyway, you've probably got things to do, but I'll see you at the party?'

'See you there,' said Tarden, and turned to leave.

'Did you and Iris have a nice chat?'

Tarden froze. 'Yes,' he said. 'We did.'

'It's nice to have a friend to talk to.'

'Yes,' said Tarden, as Audrey skipped away down the hall. 'I suppose it is.'

≈

They spun off the sealed road and took a shortcut through a small patch of scrub. Simon hadn't ridden a bike in such a long time that it had taken him a moment to get used to the speed, the trust that momentum alone would hold you upright. Ned's bike was slightly too big for him, and he kept losing the pedals and having to stick his legs out for balance. Each time, he fell behind Pony, who pedalled furiously even down hills, arms locked straight, hat flapping from underneath his helmet, khaki rucksack swinging on his back. He kept swerving too, on straight roads, puffing the brakes to correct his angle. Simon guessed these were more safety tests.

When they sprang through some sandbanks and rejoined the main road, Simon could see the town centre at the bottom of a gentle hill. They passed a yard of abandoned cars, a decrepit garage, a small nursery ringed with terracotta pots. Pony came to a sudden stop by a large water tank at the top of the main street. It was set up on wooden struts and looked for all the world like a gallows. Simon went past him, had to turn around and pedal back. 'I usually go much faster,' said Pony. 'But I thought you might not be able to keep up.'

Simon had to tip the bike over to get off; his feet couldn't touch the ground otherwise. He tried to make it look like it was easy.

189

'Let's get a drink, anyway,' said Pony. 'Just lean the bike against the water tower. No one'll take it.'

'Are you sure?'

'Yeah. It's a rule. No one'll be around anyway.'

'Thought it would be busy on a Saturday afternoon.'

Pony shook his head. 'Everyone's done their shopping, now they're all at home. Trust me.' He strode away down the centre of the road, his shadow swinging behind him, lengthening up the hill. The street was as quiet as a painting. The only sound as Pony walked was the stones in his pockets.

Pony opened one of his trouser pockets with a Velcro rip and pulled out a fresh pink-brown band-aid. He peeled off the backing and placed the band-aid on the underside of his left wrist. Smoothed it down.

Simon was sure Pony didn't have a cut on his wrist, but he said nothing. After what Pony had told him about his dad, about the gun, Simon didn't think anything could be too strange. 'Are we going to ... what's it called, the cafe?'

'The Ottoman,' said Pony. 'Only it's not a cafe at this time of the day, not on the weekend.'

'Why is it not a cafe?'

'After two o'clock, that part closes, the other part opens up. For drinking.'

'Drinking beer?'

'Yeah, it's a pub in the afternoon.'

'What'll we drink?'

'Beer. Whatever.'

Simon's heart thrilled at the mention of something so adult. His dad had a separate fridge for beer in at home, or at least in the last home they'd been in. One bottle of each type, each with glass of different colours, different shaped lids and metal caps. Simon had never been allowed one. 'Beer,' he said. 'Yeah.'

Pony pulled at his bottom lip, puffed out a laugh. 'You're having a Coke.'

'Yeah,' said Simon. 'Whatever.'

Pony led them down the main street and through a door just up from the cafe entrance. Simon's stomach lurched as he recognised the entrance from the night before. Up the three steps. Inside, the sticky smell of stale beer. A darker room, a larger room. Behind the bar was the large man from the search at the dam, Nat, polishing a beer glass with a white cloth.

'Here.' Pony ushered Simon into a circular booth at the back of the pub.

Simon sat down. He realised he didn't have any money. 'Pony,' he said. 'The drinks—'

'Don't worry,' said Pony. 'I've got a tab.'

Simon nodded, impressed. He thought only famous people had tabs in bars.

Eventually, a waitress came over to their table, the same one that had served Simon and his parents the day before. She was wearing all black. Her T-shirt had a faded picture of a horse on it, a silhouette, upside down. 'Lads,' she said. 'What can I get you?' Simon noticed Pony pulling his shoulders back, sitting up straighter. His voice strained, even more than usual. 'Hi, Megan,' he said. 'Beer for me, Coke for Simon.'

'Pony,' she said, closing her eyes, making a wide smile. 'When have I ever pulled you a beer?'

'No, I meant—' Pony squirmed in his seat. 'I'll ... have a ginger beer.'

The waitress, Megan, chuckled. 'Wise choice.' She

191

cocked her head at Simon. 'Any news about your parents?'

'No.' Simon was sure he could see a tattoo peeking out from under the arm of Megan's T-shirt. The legs of a spider, maybe.

'Well,' she said. 'Fingers crossed, hey.'

Pony took off his hat. His hair was stuck down like moss to a rock. 'I'm helping Simon,' he said. 'No one else is, but I am.'

Megan looked at him strangely. 'Coke and a ginger beer, was it?'

Pony put his hat back on.

'Yes,' said Simon. 'Thank you.'

As soon as she was out of earshot, Pony leant into Simon and said, 'That's Megan.'

'Okay.'

'She works here sometimes. And when it's busy, up our place.' Pony kept tapping his hand on the table, his thumb and little finger vibrating.

'I know,' said Simon. 'You told me at breakfast.'

'She doesn't live in Reception. She stays over sometimes, or she drives back up the coast.'

'You two are friends?' Simon thought about the silver stud under Megan's lip. It would probably get in the way when you ate.

'What?' said Pony. 'Not really. Maybe. I don't really like her.' His cheeks tinged with red. He drummed the table more. 'How long does it take to pour two drinks?'

Simon knew Pony liked Megan, the way people sometimes liked other people.

'Won't be quiet for long,' said Pony. 'All the fishers'll wake up soon, looking for a drink.'

'What, they sleep in the day?'

'Yeah, that's how it works. They get up early, make their catch, ship it off, that's them done. Back to bed, sleep for a bit, wake up and head down the Ottoman. Course, they've got it easy. One day they'll all be working for me. I'll show them how to really work.'

'For your swimming pool restaurant?'

'Yeah.'

Megan came back with their drinks, in two giant glasses. 'Couple of pints,' she said, 'for thirsty men.'

Voices suddenly filled the bar and as Pony had said, a group of men walked in. Fishermen, Simon guessed, but they were all in jeans and jackets now instead of overalls. Tarden and Kuiper were there, laughing with the others. A younger man, just in his twenties Simon guessed, came over to Megan. He had a ruddy, flat face and hard grey eyes. He had on jeans, and a shirt with a logo on it, a truck, a semi-trailer, jumping through a hoop of flames.

'Babe.' He grabbed Megan around the waist, kissed her neck. His arms were covered in blonde hair like sawdust.

'Hey,' said Megan. She pulled away and squeezed his hand.

'Me and the boys are in the mood for a few brews,' he said. He winked at Simon, and Simon didn't know why.

'Put some money on the counter, Cody, and you'll get all the brews you want.'

'Awright.' Cody let go of her and went over to join the other men.

'You guys drink up now,' Megan said to Simon and Pony. 'It's about to get busy in here.' She went back to the bar.

'What an idiot,' said Pony.

'What?'

193

'That's Cody, her boyfriend. He drives trucks. Up and down the coast. Hardly ever here, really.' They didn't say anything for a while. Simon sipped his Coke. The glass was so big, he didn't think he could finish it. From time to time, he'd steal a glance at the group of fishers telling stories on the other side of the room. One grappled an imaginary fish, another cast out an invisible net. Megan came to collect the quickly empty glasses. The spider tattoo on her arm, just out of vision. A thought that had been circling came to rest in Simon's head.

'When we came into town,' he said, 'there was a shed, on the hill.'

'What?'

'Outside of Mr Tarden's house.'

'Him and Kuiper live out of town, yeah.' Pony shot a look at the fisher's table. Simon lowered his voice, though he wasn't sure quite why. 'There's a big shed near their house. Me and dad tried to open it. It's full of ... tin cans. It looked like tin cans. Like, hundreds of them.'

Pony frowned. 'Cans?'

'So you haven't seen it?'

'No,' he said. 'No one really goes that far out of town. Stupid to live that far out, if you ask me.'

'And there was something hiding there, too. A spider, or something.'

'A spider?'

'Yeah, I was the only one who saw inside. We only opened the door a little bit.'

'Well,' said Pony, 'We'd better go and check it out.' He upended his glass and gulped down the last of his ginger beer.

'We can't go there,' said Simon.

'Don't be a wimp,' said Pony, already getting up. 'Tarden and Kuiper'll be in here drinking for hours yet. Let's go.'

Simon had the hang of it now. That was what they said, wasn't it. It's like riding a bike. He and Pony rode together up the hill, back towards the highway. Simon wondered how long it would take to cycle back to the Gold Coast. He thought, he kept thinking, of the empty house waiting for him. He could live there, maybe. He could drag his bed down to the lounge room, watch TV whenever he liked. Eat cereal, like Pony did, at all times of the day. But then there would be the nights. Not even the nights—the knowing night was coming. The purple-streaked sky that would set over the canals. The dead glow of street lights outside the window. The buzz of lazy boats. The loneliness.

They passed only one car before they reached Tarden and Kuiper's house. A station wagon with wood panelled sides, a surfer car, Simon thought. A group of teenagers, shirtless boys, whooping out the windows. The tyres spat out a wave of sandy grit. Pony shot them a sideways glare, set his mouth. Simon tasted exhaust and the ocean.

When they came to a stop by the house, Pony wiped out his mouth with two fingers. 'Did you see those idiots?' he said. 'What's the godawful hurry?' He pulled out another band-aid, peeled it off its backing and attached it to his neck.

'Are you hurt?' said Simon.

'That's a stupid question.'

'Sorry, I—' Simon didn't know what he was really apologising for. A little fire of anger rose. 'Don't call me stupid, all right? It's not normal, doing that, and there's no reason I should act like it is.'

Pony shrugged.

'Putting band-aids on when you don't need to. And those safety tests. Nothing's really that dangerous.'

'Must be working then,' said Pony. He walked towards the house.

Simon followed him reluctantly, through the gate, through the maze of old cars. The boat was still there, blue netting hanging over the sides. Simon sighed loudly. What where they doing here?

The house was a fibro building in obvious disrepair. All along the bottom of one wall was a crack as thick as a pencil. By the back door was a pile of white plastic tubs, the kind Simon's mum made him keep his Lego in. A humming sound. A huge brown freezer, dented like the cars in the front yard, but with a shiny padlock. Pony kicked the side of the freezer and it clanged. There was a sound inside, only just noticeable above the hum. A scrabbling, scratching noise. Simon looked at Pony. They had both heard it.

'What's that?' Simon imagined a container full of spiders.

'One way to find out.'

'What do you—'

Pony spun around and grabbed Simon by the collar of his shirt. He threw him against the side of the freezer. Metal squeaked, and Simon felt a pain in his back, like a sudden, deep itch.

197

'Are you my friend,' said Pony, 'or not?' Pony's broken-up voice was now just a scratchy hiss.

'Get off,' said Simon, as calmly as he could, despite his pulse thumping in his ears. 'Of course we're friends.'

'Are. You. My. Friend.'

'Yes. All right. Yes.'

'And friends stick together.'

'Yes.'

Pony released his grip on Simon's arms, but kept him pinned. He nodded to himself. Simon thought suddenly that this, far from being hostile, was as close as Pony got to genuine affection. He wondered if Pony, like Simon himself, had not had a close friend his entire life.

'You can't tell anyone what I'm about to do. What we're about to do.'

Simon shook his head. 'Okay.'

Pony let Simon go. He took off his rucksack and reached inside it. He pulled out a black leather satchel, like a bag you'd keep marbles in.

'What's that?'

Pony put a finger to his lips. He crouched down and opened the satchel. It rolled out neatly, exposing four or five metal spikes, nestled in small leather clasps.

'What are they?'

Pony shot him a dirty look. 'You're supposed to be keeping watch.'

Simon scanned the house. He couldn't see the road, let alone if someone was coming along it. He watched the high leaves shiver in the eucalypts. The wind whistled loudly through the high wire fence encircling the yard. He turned back to Pony.

Pony had one of the metal spikes between his fingers.

198

Simon saw it was a tiny cylinder, with a sharp point at one end. Pony saw him looking. He said, 'I ordered them, okay? You can get anything mail order. Came with instructions and everything. Knew they'd come in handy one day.' Pony took another, larger tool from the satchel, and inserted them into the padlock.

'You're picking the lock.' Simon had seen it done in the movies, but never in real life.

'Well, yeah.' Pony jiggled the picks together in the lock. 'I need to ... listen,' he said. A knock came from inside the freezer again.

Simon had a sudden vision of his parents, folded up inside. A shiver travelled down his neck.

The padlock sprung open. Pony grinned. 'Help me with the lid.'

They each took an edge of the freezer's lid and heaved it upwards, Simon's heart pounding. It was dark inside, the light broken. His arms burning with the lid's weight, he willed his eyes to adjust and eventually they did. No bodies. He felt a wave of relief. Inside were just more white containers, stacked two abreast. The air inside wasn't as cold as it should have been.

'Hold on, can you?' Pony shifted his weight and shifted the lid onto his shoulder. 'I'll try and open one up.' He reached in, and Simon felt the lid dig further into his hands. He was sure he could see dark shapes inside the containers.

'You right?' said Pony.

'Yeah.' Simon's voice trembled. Pain shot all the way down his arm. Still, he wanted to see what was making the noise.

Pony's fingers scrabbled with the container's lid. 'Nearly—' He prised an edge free and lifted it. 'Jesus.'

A smell hit them: an awful sour fishy smell. Crabs. Dozens of them. Many floating motionless in water, a few still moving, grasping at the air with their claws. It was them making the noise. When Simon looked closer he saw the water was brown and foetid. It wasn't even cold inside the freezer. Then he saw crab legs rising to the surface of the water, parts of their bodies floating by themselves. He thought of Tarden biting his finger, the babies at the bottom of the lake.

'Man,' said Pony. 'That's crazy.'

Simon released his held breath and stood back from the freezer. At least his parents weren't in there. At least—

A car engine.

'Crap.' Pony pulled the lid back on the container. 'Shut it. Quick.'

Simon's heart hammered his chest as he shifted back away from the freezer. They let the lid fall with a deafening slam that sent a thin crack through the enamel.

'Crap crap crap.' Pony flicked the padlock shut and gathered up the satchel. 'What are they doing here?' He scanned around him. Beads of sweat crowned his eyebrows. 'They'll see us.'

Simon already knew the fence around the yard was too high to climb. The way they had come in was also the only way out. Why would they—'Oh no,' he said. 'The bikes!'

Pony grimaced. Two cars doors slammed. 'We left them in the yard. God damn.'

'What do we do?' Simon heard Kuiper's voice, his laughter, floating through from the front yard.

Pony scrunched up his face. 'The shed,' he said. 'That's all we've got.'

They sprinted across the yard. The roller door was on

200

the other side of the fence, but as Simon had hoped there was a narrow access door by the shed's back corner. The door was locked. As Pony scrambled to find the right picks to unlock it, Simon heard Kuiper and Tarden's voices, coming closer. Loud voices, shouting. Simon was sure they'd found the bikes. He pictured the two men running around the house, searching for intruders. 'Quick,' he said. 'Quick!'

'Shut up,' said Pony. 'Just give me a minute.' His hands shook. The metal picks ticked inside the lock.

'They're really close.'

'Simon. Shut. Up.'

Simon could almost hear footfalls behind him. He expected any minute for rough hands to grab him by the shoulders. He wanted desperately to look behind him, but knew as soon as he saw them, he would be done for. He hated his parents for bringing him here, hated his grandma for making them, hated the awful way his life had played out.

A hand grabbed his shirt, and all the air went out of him. He hit it with a blind panic, tried to fight it off, but it held fast. 'Simon,' hissed a voice. The hand wasn't behind him: it was Pony, dragging him inside the shed, slamming the door shut behind them.

All sound disappeared. Simon could hear only his own breath, his chest heaving. Way above him, strips of fluorescent lights droned out a thin constant flicker on piles of black and blue netting, bunched at the bottom of the near wall. And the big aluminium cans, far more than Simon remembered, stacked on long shelves. Rows and rows of shelves. Thousands of cans, it looked like.

Pony let out a low whistle. 'What the hell is this place?'

Simon swallowed. 'I don't know.' The whole space made him strangely, quietly, terrified. A shadow caught the corner of his eye. The same spiky sense of something he'd seen yesterday morning. He leant his head down and saw that it wasn't a spider: it was a crab, the same sort from the freezer. It scuttled away to a far corner.

Pony cocked his head. 'Quick.' He grabbed Simon's arm.

There was a noise of keys jangling. Two voices argued outside, the sound coming through walls as a thick whisper.

Simon froze.

'Come on!' hissed Pony. He flicked the lock closed just as the key went in, hauled Simon off his feet, dragged him away from the door. They ran to the other end of the shed, throwing themselves behind the end of a row that, luckily enough, was wide enough to cover them both from sight. In the corner nearest them was a large machine that looked like something from a history book, a steam-powered contraption, shelves of cans and lids sitting above it. Just beside it was something equally as big, covered with two bright blue tarpaulins. One of the tarpaulins didn't reach right to the floor and Simon could see a wheel; no, a tyre. The brand name was just visible. The same brand his father always went on about. Simon was about to say something but Pony put a hand over his mouth. Instead of sweat or dirt, there was a sweet, medicinal smell to Pony's fingers. Pony shook his head, and drew Simon down to a crouch.

The door opened at the other end of the room, and the two voices grew louder.

202

Kuiper clipped voice: 'You honestly can't be serious.'

The other voice, Tarden. 'Not as if you need me, anyway.'

The door closed. Simon turned his head, trying to peer past the row without being seen. The two men stood with their back to him. Kuiper's hand shook. He said, 'It's a bit late to be backing out, now. I think we've come a bit bloody far for that.'

'It's just getting too dangerous, Robbie. That's all I'm saying.'

Kuiper locked the door. He moved his body to block it. He was facing Simon now, but looking intently at Tarden. 'And who are we supposed to blame for that? The buck stops with us, Jack.'

'I came here to get clean,' said Tarden. 'All this,' he swung his arms out, 'I never agreed to this, it's getting too much. And I don't want to be a part of it.'

'The old Jack Tarden defence, I just happened to be there. That's going to wear thin pretty soon.'

'Fuck you.'

'Indeed.'

Tarden started pacing the floor. Moving down the rows and back again. 'I knew something like this would happen,' he said. 'It was just too easy.'

Simon swung his head back out of sight. He looked over at Pony, who was staring into his fists, clenching and unclenching them. At least, Simon thought, it didn't seem like Tarden and Kuiper had discovered their bikes.

'Jack,' said Kuiper, 'it'll be fine. Ned's little accident was a stroke of luck and—'

Tarden's shoes squeaked on the concrete floor. Simon

imagined him turning around abruptly. 'People haven't forgotten they're still missing!' he said. 'What are we supposed to do about that?'

Simon felt invisible hands tugging at his throat. His haunches burned. He wanted so badly to move his feet.

'People go missing,' said Kuiper. 'Things happen. Who's going to figure it out? Our police presence? I think we know them well enough not to be concerned. Or is it the dumb-fucks at the bar you're worried about?' He snorted. 'Remember the Gale woman? In a few weeks, everyone will have forgotten about all of this.'

'What about the boy? Simon?'

'Jesus, Jack. What's your preoccupation with that kid?'

Simon heard Tarden's feet shuffle. 'I just … I feel responsible. That's all. He doesn't deserve this.'

'I'll sort him out,' said Kuiper.

'Just like you sorted out the problem of his mum and dad? Their fucking car is sitting in our fucking production shed.'

Simon's breath left him completely. Pony's fingers dug into his leg.

A huge crash made them both jump. Then a series of deep, rolling sounds. Halting breaths.

Simon took a risk and peeked around the corner, Pony peering over his shoulder. Dozens of cans had fallen and rolled out in every direction. Tarden was pinned up against a shelf, Kuiper's forearm braced across his throat. 'Do not go soft on me now, Jack,' he hissed. I know more about you than you even do. You go running off anywhere, I will hunt you down.'

'Get the fuck off me.' Tarden's voice wheezed like a bellows.

Run. Simon's brain was screaming at him to run, telling him they were going to kill him and Pony too. But he was frozen to the spot.

Kuiper hitched his arm up further. 'We keep our heads down, we make a little profit, and we let the town go quiet again. Then you can get back in your little boat and keep fishing and everything will be fine. We just need to stay calm.'

'Put me the fuck down.'

'Are you with me Jack?'

Tarden was making horrific gurgling sounds. 'Yes, I'm fucking with you. Settle down.'

Kuiper's face softened. 'Everything will be fine, okay, Jack?' He removed his arm from Tarden's throat. 'I'm sorry,' he said. 'I just wanted to know that we're on the same side.'

Tarden rubbed his throat. 'Sure.' His voice was a weak croak. 'Let's not do anything stupid.'

Kuiper held out his palms, mock-apologetic. 'Jack,' he said. 'Darling, don't be mad at me.' He smiled his wide shark smile. Leant in and kissed Tarden on the mouth, his hand moving to cup the back of his head.

Simon exhaled with shock.

Tarden shrugged Kuiper away. 'No,' he said.

'Come on,' whispered Kuiper, 'let's seal this deal.' He fumbled at his belt.

'Not now.'

'Come on.' He walked around behind Tarden and put his arms around him.

'Robbie,' said Tarden. 'I said not now.' He tried to move away, but Kuiper held fast to him.

'You been seeing someone else?' said Kuiper. 'You

haven't been seeing some whore without telling me have you?'

Tarden whirled around, breaking Kuiper's grip with one arm, shoving Kuiper back against the shelving with the other. Kuiper came back at him, grappling for his throat, but Tarden was ready and felled him with a short sharp jab of his fist. Kuiper crumpled to the ground. He looked like Ned had when the rock hit him.

'Talk to me later,' said Tarden, 'when you're prepared to be more reasonable.' He slammed the shed door behind him.

Simon's pulse hammered in his temples. He put his hands over his ears. Tarden and Kuiper, what had they done to his mum and dad? They'd sorted them out. Just like they were going to sort out him. Why were they kissing?

A new noise between the pulsing. Kuiper crying, sitting up, his hands held to his mouth. A growth of blood seeping through his fingers as his shoulders heaved. He stood up, wiped his hands on the back of his jeans, his mouth was a wide red smear. Not crying, Simon realised; it was laughter. Still chuckling, he picked up all the fallen cans and put them back on the shelves. The last can he kept, weighing it in his palm. He left, eventually, locking the door behind him.

Simon's legs howled with pain, and he collapsed on the floor, stretching out.

Pony stood up and peered down. 'This is serious now,' he said. His voice was clearer, somehow. It had lost its strained quality.

Simon nodded, too much in shock to speak.

Pony chewed on his thumb, seemingly deep in thought. 'This is something big.'

'What were they doing?' said Simon. 'What did they do to my mum and dad?' He felt tears growing hot in his eyes.

'I don't know,' said Pony, 'but it's not good.'

Simon covered his face with his hands. He wanted desperately just to dissolve away, to be water gurgling down a plughole.

'Simon.'

He tried to make his mind blank, to slip into blackness.

'Simon,' repeated Pony.

When Simon opened his eyes, Pony was holding out a hanky. 'Don't worry,' he said.

'It's clean.' He unfolded it, showing starched white.

Simon blew his nose. 'Thank you.'

Pony knelt down next to him. 'I'm not going to let anything happen to you,' he said. 'You're my friend. We're going to work out what's going on, and you're going to be perfectly safe.'

And the way Pony said it—so sure, so clinically, triple-tested sure—Simon almost believed it.

It was well into the night by the time Simon and Pony cycled back up the path to Ned's house. They wheeled their bikes back through the garden, rolling them into a long tin shed that stood at the far corner of the garden. Simon felt the grass flicker against his ankles, wet in the night-time air: in the darkness it could have been water or blood.

Pony reached into the shed and flicked a switch, unpacking light from the door. Simon could see—along with mud-caked garden tools and cans of paint-thinner and petrol—a shiny red and blue BMX, with a ribbon attached to its handlebars.

'Gin's birthday,' said Pony. 'We got him a bike.'

'Oh,' said Simon. 'That's right. There's a party, isn't there.'

'Tomorrow.'

'Yes. Tomorrow.' Simon knew they were both avoiding talking about what they'd just seen. Their voices, echoing off the walls, the violence. The threat. 'Do you think—' Simon tailed off.

'What?'

'Do you think they'll go back to the lake tomorrow? Madaline, I mean. To keep searching.'

Pony blew out his cheeks. 'Simon,' he said, shaking his head. He wheeled his bike into the shed. 'You just don't get it, do you.'

Simon rolled his bike in too. 'Get what? I don't—' He stopped. The rest of the shed was a long wooden workbench, as big and thick as a car, scored with scars and nicks, clamped with coloured vices. To one side, all down the wall, was a row of hooks and shelves, locked behind glass, full of tools: hammers and chisels, knives and corkscrews. Ned's wife, Simon thought. Stephanie. Carving, creating.

Pony took the handlebars of Simon's bike and stared right into his eyes. The weak orange light turned Pony's skin to street maps. 'We can't trust them,' he whispered. His voice was a dripping drain. 'You heard what Kuiper said.'

Simon tried to remember the exact words he'd heard.

'The whole town?'

Pony scrunched up his face. He leant past Simon, pulling the shed's door closed, sealing them in near-silence. He went over to the bench, took off his rucksack. He pulled something out of it, clunking it down onto the wood. A tin can.

'Is that ... ?'

'Yep. Took it from the storeroom.'

Simon felt a fresh panic. 'What if they realise it's missing?'

'One can? They won't miss it. Kuiper took one himself.' Pony reached back into his rucksack and pulled out a thick pocketknife.

'You can't open it,' said Simon.

'Listen, I don't like this any more than you do, but if you want to find your parents, we're going to have to work out what's going on in this town.' Simon felt numb. He thought of a thousand empty houses, waiting for him to move through them. He nodded.

'Okay then.' Pony flicked open his pocket knife to reveal an old-fashioned can opener, with a hooked end, like you sometimes saw in Westerns and movies about soldiers. With an expert twistof his wrists, Pony made the can opener's edge bite its way around the rim of the can, peeling its top off bit by bit. Eventually Pony was able to lever off the lid off. His eyes narrowed. He turned the can over, and Simon heard a wet flop.

Peaches. Glistening orange. Juice swelling out to the bench's edge, dribbling over.

'What the hell?' Pony shook the can. A small rattle. He turned it back over. Reaching in, he pulled out a dripping sealed bag, made from thick black plastic. Pony grinned, the first time Simon had seen him smile. 'Bingo.'

'What is it?' Simon came closer.

Pony flipped shut the can opener and switched his pocketknife to a thin blade. He slid it carefully through the top of the bag. A handful of small coloured tablets fell onto the table, rattling like heavy rain. They were about the same size as a Panadol, Simon thought, but they were a different shape. He picked one up, brought it to his nose to sniff.

Pony suddenly lunged at him, grabbing his wrist.

'Ow! What's that for?'

Pony plucked the pill from between Simon's fingers. 'You can't just swallow these,' he said.

'I wasn't going to swallow it,' said Simon. 'I was just going to smell it.'

'Right,' said Pony, gathering the pills into a pile on the bench. 'You just shouldn't swallow them, that's all. They're drugs.'

'Drugs?' The word alone sent a cannon to Simon's

210

stomach. This was a word deep in the forest of the adult world. A secret word like sex, or insurance.

Pony switched on a lamp that was clamped to the bench. He bent down, picked up a single pill, held it in his palm under the light. 'Got to be,' he said. 'Amphetamines, maybe.'

'What are amphetamines?' Simon peered at Pony's hand.

'Big trouble is what they are.'

Simon looked over at Pony's face, reflected strangely in the under-glow of the lamp. It looked older, the wear of age sitting strangely on his features. 'How do you know about drugs?' Simon hated his voice then, how young it sounded.

'My mum,' he said, 'I told you. She worked in a doctor's surgery. I spent a lot of time with her there.' Pony picked, unconsciously, at the band-aid on his wrist. 'These things,' he weighed the pill, the amphetamine, in his hand, 'these tiny things do horrible things to people.'

Simon exhaled a breath he didn't realise he'd held in. He said, 'So Tarden and Kuiper are taking drugs.'

'They're doing more than just taking them,' said Pony. 'You saw how many cans were in that storeroom. That's a lot of drugs.'

'Why are there so many, then?'

'I don't know. They might be selling them, or holding them for someone else.'

'We've got to tell someone,' said Simon, 'the police.' He saw Madaline's face, heard her promising to find his parents. 'Madaline.'

Pony rubbed the side of his face. 'I'm not sure that's safe,' he said. 'Could be a risk.'

211

'You think Madaline could be ... involved somehow?' Simon thought he sounded like a police officer now. Words he'd heard on TV.

'Maybe not just Madaline.'

'Who else?'

'Who knows? But there's no way they could keep that many drugs just sitting there without someone in the town knowing.'

'What about the other policeman? Madaline's boss?'

'He's even worse,' said Pony. 'He's friends with them all already. He probably helps them.'

Simon's voice stammered. 'My ... mum and dad—' He felt dizzy. 'What have they got to do with all this? Tarden said they took care of them. What does that mean?'

Pony put his hand on Simon's shoulder. 'I don't know.'

'Well we can't do nothing!' Simon was surprised by the loudness of his voice. 'We can't just do nothing!'

Pony began putting the pills back into their bag. 'We're going to work this out,' he said. 'We're going to find out.' He fished a bulldog clip from his rucksack, and snapped it to the drug bag to seal it. 'Tomorrow, though. Nothing else we can do tonight.'

'But ... what if—' Simon could hardly bring himself to think it. What if Kuiper had killed his mum and dad? What if they weren't just missing, but dead? He tried to push the thought from his mind, but it was like trying to cram a snarling monster into a honey jar.

※

Madaline woke to the weight of sun-paled paper. She looked down. A whole ream of it, resting on her chest, had fanned out as she'd slept, spreading out from her chin to her waist. She shook blood into her arm, which had probably spent hours pressed up against the side of her chair. She felt her hair pasted to the side of her face, tasted stolen sleep. This graveyard of paper, she thought. This was her life.

When she was thirteen, Madaline had known exactly what her future would hold. She saw herself in a tall building, with a desk and a view through grey-tinted glass. Clocks showing three different time zones. One of those tiny swing-frames with silver balls clacking together. Her dream wasn't about importance or wealth. She wanted insularity, that intoxicating feeling of being truly inaccessible. Growing up, she was bracketed in by people who knew everything about her before she even did. Her home town was a bent speck on a map: hemmed in by canefields and seemingly endless horizons where all people could do once the sun went down was gossip and drink and sweat.

Her parents' house was central to the town's machine. A Queenslander stumped up on storey-high stilts, an enormous front deck her dad had extended, perfect for gathering under tin cover as afternoon storms churned in. Burnt steak and beer, big men with the same loud

213

mouths, the same tan lines where the sun stopped and their hat began. The women, squint-eyed, hungry and exceptionally bored. And at every get-together, the town trapped between bruised skies and fresh-burnt fields, there was Will Simpson, the son of her parents' best friends. Just a boy then, with a bowl-cut, a breaking voice and already muscled arms. They grew up together, comrades first, before they became friends. Childhood affinity turned inevitably to something else with adolescence. A ritual procession of night-time trips to the cane fields, awkward fumblings in barns and tool sheds. Sex, it seemed, was dust.

Will was two years her junior, and he was nice enough. But Madaline came to realise he was not a future she wanted. In her final years of school, she began to picture her and Will together. They had built a house the same as every other house in the town and Will worked the fields, the same as every other man in the town. Madaline saw herself as her mother, her desperate sense of happiness strapped to artistic dabbling.

When they caught her dad's cancer, she was in her final year of school. The stubborn bastard had let the pain spread through his stomach for nearly a year, grimacing through family meals and days and days of work. All the while letting that dark and threatening thing extinguish any hope his body had of surviving it.

When they were sure nothing more could be done, he convinced them to let him come home. This was his final day; like all the rest, it went too quickly. He left hair on the pillow, the tiny silver strands from above his ears and told her, over and over, Never settle, Madaline. Never. Not for anything. The words that eventually let her escape an expected life. Waiting at the airport, nineteen years old, the bright star of a marriage already burnt out.

Madaline blinked away tears and swung the chair upright, files spilling at her feet and the clunk of an empty wine bottle. Yes, a hangover. Not full-on, just a dull buzz she knew would take half the day to dissipate. She caught the stack of paper sliding down her chest. Stephanie Gale's case file, of course. Of course. She cursed the sun already thrumming behind her long living room curtains. She needed more time. More time to get her head together, to organise this case properly, to do it right.

Tommy was the one liaising with Regional Command. The missing car and the room key at the lake made it suspicious enough to notify them. Her case, Tommy doing nothing to help and still he wanted to be the one taking the credit. Which was fine, usually. She respected the privileges of hierarchy as much as the next person, but to be so removed from proper procedure felt insufferable. Floods down south, Tommy said; even if they wanted CID involved they wouldn't have been able to get over the river. She heard her mother's voice: They want to know how you are, Mads, and I can't tell them anything. She had to find the Sawyers today. This couldn't go on much longer.

There was something else today, too. Sunday, Sunday ... God—Gin's birthday. They'd all be there. All the fragments of her past. The two men, Tarden and Kuiper. Maybe they'd be there too.

Madaline showered, made coffee—still only instant—took the steaming mug out the back door, hoping to blast away her headache in a blaze of sun and caffeine.

215

The morning had brought with it a fierce wind; behind her back fence palm trunks creaked, sent their fronds shivering out like the innards of unwound cassettes. Not far off, Madaline knew, grey-green waves chewed at the coast, seagrass ruffled on the dunes, loose sand snaked along the foreshore. These things would never change.

She sat down in her plastic lounge chair, her single white chair, her matching white table. Even her own backyard, a simple concrete slab, had already succumbed to nature. Tough weeds in tiny cracks, pushing up tufted fingers, leaving little deposits of rubble. Nature would take over the house too, eventually: it would be consumed. Madaline ground the palms of her hands into her eyes. She had never managed to shake the belief that she was only an impermanent part of the landscape; she had never felt truly at home here. That constant foggy unease always there. She stared into her mug, at the scrabbly granules of undissolved coffee. Was it grief? Depression? She didn't know.

She went back into the house and on a whim decided to wear a dress; a birthday was a celebration after all. From the back of her cupboard it came, a vintage flower-dotted pinafore, a favourite from the collection she'd mostly left up north. She held it up, pinned it to her body with her chin. And she saw, of course, her mother. Missing only the shiny walnut skin, the darkness under the eyes. She removed her dressing gown, turning instinctively away from the mirror. One of a thousand unthought movements in a day but a habit that still shocked her when she caught herself doing it. She made herself turn back and run her eyes over her body. A punishment of sorts, even now noting a thickness to her

216

hips that she had never seen, shoulders sloping down more than they used to. Still strong, though. Still a strength. She exercised, she had no worn-in wrinkles, she was still only twenty-nine.

And Ned's face. His unshaven cheeks grazing her neck. His large hands circling her stomach. His touch like cold stones drawn across her, exciting every hair on her body. Madaline felt chills travel up from the small of her back, saw the goosebumps corkscrewing her arms. She had let herself slip. She had let Ned back in. Unprofessional: this was worst thing—she had been taught—you could be. Modern policing was a series of checks and balances, protocols and rules. That was the theory. But Madaline soon learned this was shorthand for paranoia, over-analysis and redundant bureaucracy. Policing, it seemed, had quickly slipped from doing good to not doing wrong.

Still. Whichever way she cut it, Madaline knew that falling for Ned was one of the most unprofessional things she could have done. Well, no: the most unprofessional thing was to let it affect the investigation of his wife's disappearance. She'd been distracted, made too many mistakes. This was the thought that kept her up every night. This was the reason she was so scared. This was why she was so sure she would never find Bill and Louise Sawyer.

But the kids, that was different. She didn't want to do to Simon what she'd done to Audrey and Gin. At least they still had Ned. Simon would have no one. Iris, maybe. This time the area was different, too. It was contained— the lake—and there were clues. The keys, the luggage. Stephanie had left nothing. Just a space in people's lives where she used to be.

Back then, like now, Madaline had waited too long to start the search properly; she had not followed protocol. The difference was, back then, at the start, anyway, she was still a police officer. She didn't feel like that now.

Audrey had gone all out. Streamers and balloons tied to nearly every tree, long trestles covered with tablecloths weighed down with cellophane bags filled with sand. Tied up with thin curled ribbons that whipped in the strong wind. From his window, Simon had watched her for nearly half an hour as she carefully curled each ribbon into a tight pig's tail with a pair of thin scissors.

He had hardly slept all night. He and Pony had come in late, eaten a dinner of cold pea and ham soup. Ned had not asked them where they'd been; he'd seemed distracted. Simon's sleep had been punctuated with nightmares, sudden lurches of anxiety. Pony showed him how to lock the door from the inside, showed him how the windows were extra secure. He told Simon not to worry, but of course he did.

Now the party was in full swing. Gin had his favourite silver spacesuit on and was running around the garden with friends from his school in a chaotic noisy game of their own making. Ned and Audrey had presented him with his new BMX that morning, which he was ecstatic about but refused to ride, for some reason, until the party had finished. He had taken his new bike helmet, however, and covered it immediately and completely in alfoil. He wore it now, the chinstrap framing his small oval face, the helmet transforming his head into a silver reflective mess with a crinkled, superhuman brain.

A smattering of adults Simon didn't know were sipping from disposable cups and eating the small pastries Ned had made that morning. Madaline was there, in a flowery summer dress, looking as far removed from a police officer as Simon thought was possible. The ever-present group of fishermen was inexplicably there, too, huddled under a tree, playing cards. Tarden and Kuiper were with them.

Simon kept hoping he'd imagined happened in Tarden and Kuiper's shed. What they said about his parents. About what they'd do to him. The car tyres showing underneath the tarps. The shock of the kiss. He didn't want to know. Especially, he didn't want to believe the whole town was part of some giant conspiracy to hide his parents. It didn't make sense. Nothing made sense.

Megan, the waitress from the Ottoman, sat alone sipping from a bottle of Fanta she must have brought herself.

'What's she doing here?' Pony came and stood beside Simon. His voice was muffled by the cupcake he was feeding himself, piece by ever-larger piece.

'I guess Audrey invited her.'

Pony shrugged. 'Right, whatever. What's in that?' He pointed at the toasted sandwich in Simon's hand.

'Banana and bacon. I just made it.'

'Ugh.' Pony screwed up his face. 'Budge up then.'

Simon shuffled over to let Pony sit down.

'How are you?' said Pony.

'What do you mean?'

'It's a simple question.' He fixed Simon with his unnerving gaze. Simon thought maybe this was his new friend's version of concern.

'I'm okay.' He looked up. He watched the gauzy grey clouds that seemed to materialise in the air. 'It's just ... I want to tell someone.'

'Trust me,' said Pony. 'We have to tread carefully.'

Simon felt a fresh wave of anxiety. 'I can't believe they're here,' said Simon, nodding his head to the group of fishers. Tarden and Kuiper, playing cards on the lawn.

'Why wouldn't they come?' said Pony. 'They don't know we heard them.'

'But they ... did something to my mum and dad!' Simon dropped his voice to a whisper. 'We've got to tell someone.'

Pony took off his felt hat and scratched his head. 'Look around you,' he whispered back. 'All these people might already know. They might be keeping it quiet. Might be in on it too.'

'But how? Even Madaline? Even Ned?'

Pony nodded solemnly. 'There's always been something wrong with this town,' he said. 'I've always thought so.'

'Are you saying the whole town's bad?' The word sounded so tiny, inadequate.

'What I'm saying is I don't trust anyone here. Only you, because you're the only one who doesn't know what's going on.'

'But Ned? Surely we could tell Ned?'

'Do you want to know what happened to your parents or not?' Pony slapped his hand on the grass. 'This is the only advantage we've got.'

'But the whole town? That's crazy.'

'That's what I used to think,' said Pony. 'But I've seen things.'

'Like what?'

221

'Like what? Like the dru—' Pony lowered his voice further. 'Like the storeroom with the cans. Like what Iris does in her room.'

'My grandma? What do you mean?'

Pony put his hat back on. 'Sorry, I shouldn't have said that.'

'No, tell me.'

Pony ran his tongue over his teeth. 'She has a lot of . . . visitors.'

'Visitors? What's—' A tennis ball whirred by Simon's head and smacked into the fence.

'Sorry!' Audrey came jogging over, red-faced and smiling. 'We're playing French cricket.' She waggled the ball in one hand. 'Want to play?'

'No,' said Simon. 'I'm fine.'

'Are you sure? I can teach you the rules.'

Pony's voice came out coldly. 'Simon said he's fine, Audrey.'

'Well Pony, I know you won't play. You never play anything you know you can't win.'

Pony's face set still. 'Bullshit.'

'Yeah right. Catch!' Audrey threw the ball into Pony's chest. He grappled at the ball and it spilled to the ground.

Audrey laughed. 'Round one to me!'

Pony silently stood up again, the ball in his hand. 'Let's play,' he said, stalking off to the centre of the lawn.

Audrey smirked. 'You know where are, Simon, if you want to join in.' She ran off, racing Pony back to the game.

Simon went about finishing off his sandwich. The wind blew back into his eyes. He felt more alone than ever. All the kids in one group, all the adults in another. The fishers under the tree. Simon looked over to where Megan sat, in

222

the full sun, by herself, her white-blonde hair whipping in the wind. She swivelled her gaze to stare at him. Her weird eyes—one blue, one green, shocked him somehow. She got up without using her hands, pushing herself up off crossed legs. Simon stared at the ground. He didn't want her coming over. There was something about her he didn't like.

'Hey.'

Simon saw a pair of black boots in front of him. He looked up.

'What's happening?' said Megan. 'Mind if I join you? Simon, isn't it?' She stood right in front of the sun, so her face was hidden in shadow.

'Yeah, it's Simon,' he said. She sat down. Simon smelled bergamot on her—his mum and dad had a hand cream that was bergamot—and something else, pungent and thick.

'How're you holding up?'

'Okay.'

Megan sniffed. 'Man of few words. Yeah, I get it. What you eating there?'

Simon held up the uneaten wedge of his sandwich. 'Banana and bacon.'

'Wicked. How old are you, anyway?'

'How old are you?'

Megan laughed. 'Twenty in a couple of months.'

'I'm eleven.'

'Fucken heavy. Oh.' Megan clamped her hand over her mouth. 'Sorry. Pardon my French. But . . . man. All by yourself. Here.'

'So what?'

'No offence. Just that it's horrible. What's happened, I mean. I'm sorry.'

'It's not your fault.'

'Nah, but I mean I saw you at the Ottoman, with your folks, just before. You must be really missing them.'

'Yeah,' said Simon. 'I really am.' It was strange to put it so simply. If anyone had asked him only a few days ago whether he'd be better off without his parents, he would have said yes without hesitation.

Megan scratched at her arm with purple-tipped nails. 'Bloody awful,' she said. 'Just like Stephanie Gale. You heard about that, right?'

'Ned's wife.'

'Yeah. Saddest thing. Really screwed up the kids, you know?' Megan shuffled closer to Simon. Her perfume was too much. Simon could see flakes of mascara falling from her eyes when she blinked. 'Gin's like a permanent Superman, right, and Audrey? Tried to top herself. I mean, fuck. Shit—sorry. Sorry.'

'Audrey tried to kill herself?'

'In the bath, apparently, with scissors, you know? Hardcore.'

Simon's chest tightened. Poor Audrey.

Megan blew air from her cheeks. 'Shouldn't be bringing all this up. I mean, Stephanie—it was in the ocean, which is like—' she swung her arms wide. 'But your folks, at the lake, they'll turn up in no time.'

Breath caught in Simon's throat, hot and ragged. Something else, think about something else—'You don't live here,' said Simon, 'do you.'

'Nah, live with my folks up the coast. Stay down here sometimes.' She rearranged her legs. Her black jeans had perfectly round holes all down one leg. 'Stay here when it's busy, otherwise help at the Ottoman.' She drummed her fingers. 'Fucking Reception. Sorry. I mean, it's pretty good, but I never really, you know, belong.' She made quotation marks with her fingers.

'Like you're being left out.'

Megan closed her eyes, leant her head back against the fence. 'I've got Cody down here, I guess, but he's ... a bit of a fucking idiot, actually. This is like my other life, in a way. People back home don't know what I'm like here. And vice versa I guess.'

Simon smiled. Vice versa was one of his dad's favourite expressions. Simon didn't quite know what it meant; he wasn't sure his dad did either. Suddenly, Simon wanted to tell Megan everything. About the drugs, about Kuiper and Tarden, about everyone in Reception colluding, keeping something from him. He thought maybe—

'Enjoying yourself?' Kuiper's voice slid down Simon's back like cold water. He was standing about a metre away, feeding himself corn chips from a pile in his hand.

Simon didn't say anything.

'Asked you a question,' said Kuiper, coming closer. 'Are you having a good time?'

Kuiper kissing Tarden. Simon shook his head. 'I'm fine,' he said.

Megan sat up. 'How are ya, Robbie?'

'Tip-top, Megan,' he said. 'Tip-top.' He finished off his chips, brushed his hands together. 'You've got to love this weather, don't you?'

Simon fixed his gaze on the ground.

'Did I see you and that dirty kid in town yesterday?'

Simon froze. 'What?'

'Pony, is it? Saw you and him skulking around town yesterday.'

225

'I ... we were just having a drink. At the pub.'

'A drink at the pub. Priceless. You and Nat serving underage patrons, Megan? Going to have to report you, am I?'

Megan scowled. 'Soft drinks.'

Kuiper laughed. 'Don't worry love, not giving you the third degree. Word of warning though Simon, that Pony kid. He's a compulsive liar. Wouldn't listen to a thing he says.'

'He's not a liar,' said Simon boldly, inwardly spinning with his courage. 'He's the best friend I've got in this ... this place.'

'This place? Gratitude, hey?' He produced a cigarette and lighter. 'A lot of other towns wouldn't have bothered.'

'Jeez, leave him alone,' said Megan.

'Stay out of this,' hissed Kuiper. 'Boy needs to learn some manners.' He went to light up.

'A lot of other towns,' said Simon, wondering where the confidence had come from, 'would've looked harder for my parents.'

Kuiper dropped his hands from the front of his face, cigarette unlit. 'And what does that mean, exactly?'

'It means,' Simon stood up, 'that as far as I can see, no one in this town wants to find my parents. I've been fed and ... given clothes and somewhere to sleep, but I'd much rather be hungry and naked and have no home as long as my parents came back.' Simon's hands shook. He had never been this brave in his life. This was the man who had killed his parents, but he hardly cared what Kuiper did to him.

Kuiper moved his jaw around like it was out of place.

Megan stood up too. 'How about we calm it down.' She smiled strangely at Kuiper.

226

'Shut the hell up,' he said, without looking at her. 'I'll deal with you later.'

Simon got ready to run. He had overstepped the line; Kuiper was about to drag him away and murder him. He would have run if he hadn't noticed everyone else running. Ned came first, puffing with effort and flushed.

'It's Gin,' he said, putting a hand on Kuiper's shoulder. 'He's gone.'

❧

As Simon followed Ned back across the lawn, an unease rippled through the party guests; you could see it. Parents corralled their children, some of the other guests had formed a barefoot search party. They walked around peering uselessly, holding sodden paper plates and going no further than the garden's edge.

Simon thought he caught sight of Audrey's white skirt. He followed her around the corner of the house, and found her by a cardboard cubby-house. 'Audrey—'

She turned to look at him. Her eyes fat with tears, her mouth a red, sad line. She had ripped off the cubby-house door, held it in her hand. Simon could see the interior held no more clues than a used dinner plate, some comics and a plastic sword.

'He's gone,' said Audrey. 'Gin's gone.' She handed Simon the door.

'He can't be far.' Simon set the piece of cardboard down. 'Have you checked the house, places he likes to hide?'

She nodded. 'He wouldn't just run away on his birthday. He's been talking about it for months. And we haven't even had the cake.' She started to sob.

Simon thought about what Megan had said about Audrey. After her mother ... The sadness. 'Wait,' he said.

'What.' Audrey tried to dry her face with her sleeves.

'Audrey, when ... your mum—'

'No!' She slapped Simon on the arm so it stung. 'Shut up about my mum! She's got nothing to do with this!'

'No,' Simon tried to brush away her flailing arms. 'No, where did she go?'

'How the hell am I supposed to know? If I knew—'

Simon tried to gather his thoughts. 'I mean, where did she go missing? Whereabouts?'

Audrey went to hit him again but at the last second held her hand. 'You think—' and then she was off. Her feet exploding from the grass as she half-ducked half-slid under a low hanging tree at the edge of the garden and was gone. Simon ran after her. He crawled under the same tree and realised it covered a gap in the fence that led to a faint track through the scrub. Audrey was some way ahead, weaving through branches, legs pistoning, her canvas shoes pounding through the tussocky grass.

'Audrey!' With a grunt of frustration, Simon set off behind her, the whip-thin branches lashing his cheeks as he ran. His bare feet laboured in the soft sand and his breath soon spun in ragged spirals, but he kept his eyes on Audrey, never letting her out of his sight.

Just as she crested the top of a dune, her left foot caught an exposed tree root and she fell in a flash of white, tumbling onto her arms, her shoe flipping off behind her. Simon caught up to her as she struggled up.

'Are you okay?' he said.

'Fine. Just my ankle. We've got to get—ow!' She winced as she stood on her left leg. 'The beach. By the bluff.'

'That's where Gin is?'

She nodded. 'That's where Mum went missing.'

Simon looked up. Beyond the dune was simply blue-grey sky, the death-drop of air that meant the end of land.

He retrieved Audrey's shoe and she slipped it back on.

'This way,' she said, limping to the top of the dune.

Simon joined her. The beach opened out below them, shimmering away in both directions. Ahead, the water was unsettled iron all the way to a storm-smudged horizon. The white glint of a ship way out to sea caught Simon's eye, a crisp human detail. The bluff sat to their left, waves roiling at its base. It was sheer, scooped from the sand like a wave itself, a huge dark rock caught in an elemental wedge.

'There!' Audrey pointed to the bluff's base, and Simon made out the flash of tinfoil. Gin's helmet. The boy was a tiny speck on the sand.

'Gin!' Audrey shouted, but her voice was carried away. 'Gin!' Hands cupped at her mouth. Gin didn't move. He was sitting among a collection of driftwood, swinging his legs back and forth. 'Come on,' said Audrey, grasping Simon's hand. She led them carefully down the other side of he dune, stepping down sideways with careful steps.

Simon thought of Pony and the grandstand, stepping over the rotten seats. Audrey grimaced with every step as they halfslid to the bottom of the dune then began to jog towards her brother, dragging her left leg along with her. When they were close enough, she shouted again, and Gin lifted his head. Beneath his helmet, his cheeks had been stung pink by the wind. The piece of driftwood he was sitting on was enormous, and Simon realised it was part of a ship, eroded slices of hooped wood from a hull.

Audrey let out a loud sigh. She flopped down on her knees next to Gin and looked into his eyes. 'Are you okay?' she said. 'Is everything all right?'

'Yes,' he said. 'I just came to the beach, Audrey.'

'I know you did. But you should have told me.'

Gin nodded solemnly. 'I wanted to come alone.'

'But it's your birthday. There's going to be cake soon. Don't you want all your friends around you? And your family?' She smoothed down creases on her brother's shirt.

'I came to see Mum,' he said.

Audrey's eyes sprang with fresh tears. 'Yes,' she said. 'You did, didn't you.' She struggled to her feet and sat next to Gin on the wood.

Simon stood a little distance away, unsure.

Gin waved at him. 'Do you want to sit down, Simon? This is a ship, but you can sit on it.'

'Okay,' said Simon. 'If that's okay.'

'It's for everyone,' said Gin. 'It was my mum's favourite spot, but everyone's allowed to use it.'

Simon walked over and sat down next to Gin. Audrey stayed silent, staring out across the water.

'My mum liked birthdays,' said Gin. 'She would make us something. From wood. Animals.' Gin's crinoline space-suit crackled as he moved.

'Do you still have the animals?' said Simon.

Gin nodded. 'I keep them in my room, side by side.'

Audrey sniffed. Her voice came out quietly. 'She'd tell us the sea made them. She'd say she'd found them on the shore.' Simon looked over to see her smiling. 'The same way the water washes rocks smooth. Million-to-ones, that's what she'd say. The only pieces of wood in the world to have travelled just the right distance and touched just the right amount of water and salt and tumbled and turned in just the right way to come out looking like an animal.'

'She made me a shark,' said Gin, 'last time. With teeth and everything. I told her sharks don't come to the beach, because of the nets.' He pointed out at the ocean, counted out the buoys with a bouncing finger. 'She said baby sharks swim through the nets when they're little and then they grow up and can't get back out to sea. So she gave me it to look after.'

'That's sad,' said Simon. He pictured sharks biting at the nets, trying to get back home. 'It must be sad, coming here. To your mum's favourite spot.'

'We haven't come back in a while,' said Audrey. 'Anyway, it's not the saddest thing I know.'

'What's the saddest?'

'The G minor chord.'

'Like in music?'

Audrey nodded.

They both turned their heads: movement back down the beach. A pair of people were coming towards them, flickering shapes in the distance. Simon picked out the yellow flutter of a summer dress. Madaline and Ned, breaking into a run across the sand.

Tarden had seen her, standing in the shade of the marquee regarding the day, the collection of people, with her cool detached gaze. Iris. From above the buzz of a poker game— the good- and bad-natured taunts and provocations of the other fishers, the lazy mental arithmetic of points and betting, the crazy hum of his own mind—there she was. With all the knowledge of the world contained in her almond eyes.

He wondered again what illness ate her from the inside, what affliction was removing her from life, piece by piece. Cancer, probably. One of the world's great unfairnesses: the indiscriminate art of death. A concept he was intricately, and forever, entangled with.

He paused his hand in mid-air, steadying it to knock. The back of his hand was a mountain range, kinked with veins and scattered with sunspots, fingers long since buckled into permanent zigzags. He wasn't naive enough to think himself still young: rather, his body still surprised him, the way an empty room surprises someone thinking it full. All those children at the party, all that energy— this would happen to all of them, if they got this far.

He knocked on the door, and the sound was as familiar as a voice. He always rapped on the same section of wood, just above a dark whorl in the timber that looked like an elephant's eye. He knew other hands knocked on this door; he hoped they knocked lower or higher, that this square inch was his very own. He pictured Iris, inside, touching makeup to her face, getting ready for him. Did every man feel the same way, so protective? Did every man think, She puts up with the rest, but the one she wants is me? The others ... the others took more from her. Tarden felt that he added something; had the thought, then dismissed it as ridiculous.

'Come in.'

Her voice from the other side of the door meant something good expanding inside him.

Iris sat on the cushioned seat by the window, knees drawn up to her chin. A small crack in the curtains lent a thin strip of light to her profile. Her face was coated in makeup, her skin shimmering unnaturally in the dim light, purple eyeshadow falling back sadly to her face. She rubbed her thumb against one eyebrow, sending tiny hairs spinning through the shaft of light and back into darkness.

'Jack,' she said. 'I'm so tired.' A change in her voice, like an accent, lapped from her lungs.

'I can come back.' Tarden hung in the doorway, aware of the creases the length of his untucked shirt, the stiffness of new jeans.

'No. Stay.' She sniffed, shifted something in her lap. She closed it—a book. A photo album.

'Are you all right?'

'Yes. Just ... nostalgia. You know how it is at our age, Jack.' She drew the curtain back and Tarden saw the album more clearly. It was wrapped in thick green leather, embossed with gold.

'Looks nice.'

She patted the album. 'I used to ... we used to take so many pictures. Karl was the photographer, of course, but I caught the bug. After.'

234

Iris's dead husband. Tarden did not want to imagine her as she was, her previous life. 'You didn't stay at the party,' he said. 'I saw you standing at the house, then you went.'

'Yes, well, not really my place. Not really my family.'

'The boy, Gin, disappeared.'

Iris raised a hand to her mouth. 'Is he—'

'Turned up soon enough. Just ran off to where Stephanie swum out.'

'That swim,' she said. 'Well, as long as he's safe. Is the party still going?'

'No, everyone's headed home.'

'But not you.' Iris raised a smile, spreading out her wide mouth. She put the album down. 'Is today the day, then? Are you finally going to make an old lady very happy?' She slipped her dressing gown off one shoulder, laughed gently.

Their ongoing joke. Tarden unbuckled his belt, leant his weight on the bed. Beneath the humour, somewhere in her voice, Tarden could tell something was wrong. 'I guess we'll find out.' He took off his shirt and jeans, climbed beneath the covers.

Iris removed her dressing gown, revealing an ivory camisole. 'Where's the good lady wife today?'

'Said I'd meet him at the Ottoman. Said I'd stay and help clean up the party.'

'So he's not home baking cookies for you?'

Tarden groaned. 'Can we not do this?' he said quietly. 'Not today.' As soon as he'd said it he hoped she hadn't heard it.

She sat down on the bed. 'What happened?'

'Nothing.'

Iris eased back onto the bed, staying above the covers. 'Come on, Jack. You know you can't just leave it at that.'

Tarden felt guilt burning in his forehead. He had never liked unloading his problems.; it felt like cheating yourself of your own responsibilities. Enough people had told him to open up though. The psychologist, once a week in his tiny metal office, a soundtrack of barbells and shoe-squeaks coming through the thin walls; the skinny girl, drunk and stoned, as they sat and smoked on the roof of the first hostel he'd lived at; his own mother, sitting in the courtroom with her blue hat, her only good dress.

But Iris, she was the only person he could come close to sharing with. Not even Robbie, who ... Well that, he supposed, was the problem.

'He's ... gone further.' Tarden rubbed his face. He couldn't even begin to explain it. 'I feel he's ... drifting away from who I know.'

Iris reached out and stroked his hair. 'He's changing?'

'He's not the same. I keep feeling like I'm waiting for him to change back into the person I knew, but—'

'But you love him.'

'Of course. I mean, that's not the problem.'

'Well,' said Iris, 'what if it is?'

'I don't—' He let her fingers stroke his head, feeling their electric paths.

'I mean, what if love is the problem? What if your feelings are getting in the way of seeing what's really going on?'

Tarden thought of Robbie's hands wrapped around his throat in the storeroom, how easily and instantly he could have broken the grip, knocked Robbie to the

236

ground. He felt anger rising. He felt stupid that Iris could see through him so easily. 'That doesn't come into it,' he said. All the times he'd stood up for Robbie. All the times he'd forgiven him. He rolled over, removed himself from Iris's reach. A deep shame burned its way into him. He said, 'Is it cancer?'

Tarden felt her body turn still. There was a long silence. She sighed. 'Look at me, Jack.'

Tarden didn't move.

'Turn your damn body over and bloody look at me!' Her voice was loud, the crack of shattered confidence.

Tarden rolled over. Blood thundered through his ears. He saw, before anything else, that Iris was crying, her hands held rigid at her sides. Her breath turned to a single, short laugh. 'Do you think what I do is right?'

'What do you mean?' Tarden's voice came out wavering, weak.

'This, Jack. Being a whore.' She raised up her knees, stretched one foot in the air.

'Iris, I—'

'No, Jack. I asked you a question.'

'I don't know,' he said. 'I don't know what you want me to say.'

'For Pete's sake, it's simple enough.' She held up her other foot. Her camisole rucked up her thighs. Tiny veins were there, a secret blue like spider's legs.

Tarden reached out a hand, but she brushed it away.

'It's smoke and mirrors,' she said. 'All concealment and polish. I just don't know—' she let her legs fall back to the bed. 'Underneath all this,' she gestured down her body. 'Whatever I am,' she said, 'is not real. And it doesn't inspire me that the only people who think they

237

know me are a few fishermen killing time between the ocean and the pub.'

Tarden winced. Men he drank with, joked with, talked with. They never discussed Iris, but he knew. 'Your family,' he said.

She nodded. She had closed her eyes, cheeks slick with tears.

Tarden felt a wave of affection. 'Come here.' He propped up so she could move in next to him and closed his arms around her. Held her as she shook with sadness. 'I just wanted to see my daughter,' she said. 'I wanted to show her I'd changed.'

Yes. A thought he'd buried as fanciful, as impossible. 'You're not sick,' he said, 'are you?'

Iris buried her face deeper in Tarden's shirt. She said, 'I couldn't think of any other way.'

Tarden yanked his arm out from under her. 'So you made these poor people come all this way,' he said, 'you caused all this ... trouble? For what?'

'Jack, I didn't mean for it to be like this.'

'How did you mean it, then?'

'I had—a month ago, I caught that cough. You remember?'

Tarden exhaled. 'You had a cough.'

'It was pneumonia. And I was fine, but there was a day when I couldn't breathe properly. And I thought, what happens when I do die? What if I never get to see my family? I had to try.'

'Oh my God,' Tarden held his head, thoughts unravelling.

Iris's stared at him. 'Why do you care so much? It's not your family, it's hardly your business at all.'

'The boy, though. Your grandson, you've completely fucked his life up. You—' Tarden reached for his shirt on the ground but couldn't find it. He was sure he had put it on the floor.

'Right,' said Iris, 'yes. Well actually I am sick. I'm sick in the same way you're a fisherman, Jack.'

Tarden leapt from the bed. 'What is that supposed to mean?' His thoughts were turning red. Where was his goddamned shirt?

'Your friends,' she said. 'The real fishermen, the ones who actually come here to fuck me, they tell me about you. About how you hold yourself so high and mighty, last of the true craftsmen, when in fact you haven't sold a catch in years. The ones you catch aren't nearly good enough to sell.'

She was sitting up in bed now, bedclothes gathered around her, her back straight. All the rage in Tarden's head screamed at him to hit her, to keep hitting her until she shut up. Strike her until the shame went away, and she felt for herself what it was like. His breath came white-hot from his nostrils as he fought desperately to quell his anger.

Think it out. Think it out. Think about what comes after. The repetition, as he was taught. His mantra. He saw his shirt draped over the back of a chair. She had folded it up.

She kept rubbing her arms, as if trying to warm them up. 'Jack,' she said, 'I didn't mean that.'

Tarden picked up his shirt. 'I have to go,' was all he could let himself say.

'Jack, no. I—'

He strode across the room, pulling on his shirt, slamming the door behind him.

Of course. Of course it would be the bluff. The hulking black shape cast a permanent shadow in her mind.

Madaline shivered as the wind went through her. The dress had been an awful idea; the wind made it cling to the side of her body like something attacking her. The three children sat together on the old shipwreck, that wooden shape, that collision of curved lines. Madaline had not been back to this place in years. In her mind, this portion of landscape was a static tableau, it almost hurt her physically to see it as a living, moving thing. Gin was safe: that was what was important. She had feared the worst.

She remembered Gin on the day after Stephanie vanished. Younger, smaller, still the same face, the wide eyes the colour of rich soil. Playing on a plastic trike in the living room of Ned's house, wearing down the carpet as he swivelled the tiny wheels back and forth. Back and forth, watching the window, sunlight streaming across him. Waiting for his mother to come home.

They reached the children, and Gin ran out to hug his father's legs. 'Hi, Dad,' he said.

Ned hugged Gin back. 'You're okay,' he said. 'You had us worried, mate.'

'I just came here—' Gin looked guiltily up at Madaline.

'I know,' said Ned.

240

'I thought maybe she could hear me,' Gin buried his face in Ned's jacket, 'if I came here.'

'That's okay, Gin.' Ned's voice caught in his throat. 'We can come here any time you want. You just have to let me know where you are. All the time. That's our agreement.'

'I know,' said Gin's muffled voice. 'I just ... I wanted to tell her about my bike.'

Audrey wiped her eyes with the back of her sleeve. 'I knew he'd be here,' she said. 'I'll always know.'

Madaline felt intensely warm, even in the cold. Shame, she thought, or maybe just the heat of memory. Audrey stood and put her arm around her brother. Side by side, Madaline could see their similarities. Ned, too, with a softer face, drawing his children in, protecting them. The three Gales standing close together, the wind buffeting them, ruffling their clothes.

'And Simon,' said Audrey. 'He helped me.'

Simon blushed and shifted his weight on his shipwreck seat.

'Did he?' said Ned. 'He's a good friend, isn't he.' He released his grip on his children. He looked down at Gin. 'Julian,' he said. 'Are you okay to go back to the party? We can have it another time if you want. We can just have the day to ourselves.' Gin shook his head. 'No,' he said. 'I want to go back.' He was smiling, his face shining from tears no one had seen him shed. 'I want cake.'

'Are you sure?' said Ned. 'I can make another cake on another day.'

Gin frowned. 'You can't have a birthday cake not on your birthday. It doesn't taste the same.'

'Well,' said Ned, 'that's true.'

241

'Can Audrey take me back?' said Gin, taking his sister's hand. 'And Simon?'

'If they want to,' said Ned.

'Of course we do,' said Audrey. 'Don't we, Simon.'

Simon stood up, nodding.

'Okay,' Madaline said, rubbing her hands together. 'Let's go and find that cake, shall we?'

'No,' said Gin seriously. 'We have to walk back by ourselves. We're growing up now.'

'Fair enough,' said Ned. 'I guess we'll just wait here, Madaline. Give the grown-ups a head start.'

The three children departed, and Madaline felt the chill return. She tried to push back thoughts of what would happen to them, walking off alone. 'Will they be all right?' she said. 'They know the way back, don't they.'

Ned smiled. 'Of course. They used to come down all the time with their mum. They haven't been in a while, but—'

Madaline followed Ned's gaze to the edge of the ocean where a white-top burnt white for an instant like a camera flash.

'I used to worry,' he said. 'When I first came here. The danger of the unknown, all that. It was all just too. ...' He gestured at the expanse of water. 'Too much like one big question. I was a city boy, wasn't I?' He chuckled. 'You'd be used to it, cane fields and train tracks. All that.'

'I guess. But Reception—' she swallowed a slivered flame of indigestion, cast an eye up to the bluff. 'Do you ever get the feeling this place is something all of its own? Feels like those dreams where you're running as fast as you can, but you're going nowhere. Like a ... slowing down.' She sat down next to Ned. Her weight shifted the wood like a see-saw, lowering then lifting. 'It's stupid.'

'No,' said Ned, sinking his hands into his pockets. 'It's not stupid. I—' He stopped himself, as if turning over words in his head. 'When Julian was born, it was different. Audrey was excitement, our first child, and the town was still vibrant I suppose. Industry still going, tourism taking off. But Julian—little Gin ... It really felt like a change of generations. Stephanie's parents had passed away, only a few months apart, and they were true locals, born and bred. It was like our little world was growing, but also getting smaller.'

Madaline saw police tape. The tiny section of beach glaring with sunlight, crawling with people. A marquee, borrowed from Ned himself, the search centre. Her idea, of course. Her notion of what a missing-persons case looked like.

'He came four weeks early,' Ned went on, 'this tiny thing, a little pink animal. All you can think about is how he's not ready for the world. How you think he'll never be ready for the world.' Ned fixed his eyes to the ground.

Madaline focused on the patch of skin they'd shaved on his head. The red and black stitched flesh.

'And I couldn't even hold him for a week, I just had to watch him through plastic. When all I wanted to do was protect him, keep him safe.'

Madaline wanted to reach out then, to run her hands through Ned's hair. To trace her finger down the stitches.

'His eyes,' said Ned. 'Like ... like thumbprints, sunken rightdown. And I kept thinking he's sleeping, even when I knew he was awake. I never thought—it's horrible—but I never thought he'd get this far. His fifth birthday,

I mean—' Ned scrunched up his mouth, wiped at his eyes. 'It's just, you just think, I'm all they've got. And that's the scariest thing you can ever think. In a way, I can understand those people—' He coughed. 'Sorry. You don't want to hear all this.'

'It's okay,' said Madaline. 'Don't apologise. You've—' She wanted to say you've been through a lot, some trite phrase that ought to mean something. She wanted to place her hand on his, feel his skin against hers. She wanted to say she loved him, that she was sorry, that she wished they'd never met.

'Well,' he said after a time, 'I just ... I just wanted to tell you that things get easier.'

Madaline stood up, smoothing down her skirt. 'We'd better get some of that cake before it's gone,' she said, smiling like any sentiment could rescue her.

Tarden parked in a back street a few blocks from the pub. He didn't want the temptation of his car there waiting, knew what would happen. It was bad enough he was about to hurl himself off the wagon.

His body still stung from Iris's words, as if she had physically hit him. How did everyone know he hadn't sold a catch in so long? He had certainly never mentioned it, just went along and exaggerated his stories like they all did, tales of bigger hauls and quicker bits and the usual bullshit.

A thought hit him as he hustled down the empty Sunday street: how much else did everybody know? If they knew his money didn't come from fishing, did they guess where it did come from? Did Madaline know? Did Tommy? But if they did, what was taking them so long? Only a week from now, a semi-trailer would roll in, pull up outside the shed, and roll out with a few hundred cans of 'Assorted Tinned Fruit' on board. And if they weren't caught then, there was always the next load of raw product dropped off for storage, always the next pick-up. Any time the cops could burst in, guns drawn. Any time they could catch him and Kuiper sitting by the canning machine. What would that be worth? Another twenty years? Thirty?

He stopped to control his breathing. Equal breaths in and out. First a drink, he thought. Some hot chips and a few schooners. Already he felt the shameful buzz. Already he knew a few drinks would become more, and more still. But what the fuck, no one could put up with all this and stay clean. He entered the pub from the side, enjoying the way you had to give a little push against the swinging door and there was that moment when the warm, comforting smell washed over you—not even a smell, but a feeling—and you immediately relaxed. It was these tiny moments he knew he would miss most of all if he went back inside.

And those familiar sights and sounds: the gentle clink of glasses, the hum of conversation. Rhythms, thought Tarden. Things you didn't have to worry about because they'd always be the same. He couldn't see Robbie anywhere. Probably better that way. He took a seat by the bar, watching Nat fiddling with the cash register, pushing buttons and whacking its side. Eventually— and as always—Nat hefted it up and tipped it forwards, yanking out the drawer to deposit some change.

'Should replace that thing,' said Tarden.

Nat smiled. 'Gonna replace it for me are you, Jack?'

Tarden chuckled. He always enjoyed Nat's company, one of the rare locals who took things with a grain of salt. Born pessimists, the rest of them, happy to wallow in their own misery and, especially, that of others. He knew now, of course, how much they enjoyed his misery. But they could wait. He raised his hand to Nat. 'Schooner, thanks.'

'Not a Coke, mate?' Nat tilted his head. 'Sure?'

Tarden shook his head. 'Schooner.'

Nat shrugged. 'You're the boss.' He pulled a beer.

Tarden's mouth watered. Nat was all right. He wished

Robbie wasn't so constantly rude to him. He'd called Nat coon to his face more than once, and worse behind his back. Not that Tarden much to say about those things one way or another. But there were some things you said and some things you just thought. And offending the owner of the only pub in town was just stupid.

'Plans for the evening?' said Nat.

'You're looking at it.' Tarden tipped his head back and downed half the schooner. There were some feelings in life that were hard to beat. 'Another of those, thanks.' He raised the glass again, drained it.

'Might want to slow down, mate,' said Nat. 'At this rate, we'll be empty by eight.'

Tarden spread his hands on the bar and nodded. 'Just had to get that first one down.' He slapped a twenty on the bar, turned to the TV fixed high on the opposite wall. End of a league match, or the start of another: the static on the screen made it hard to tell. He felt the barman's eyes still on him. He turned back around. 'You right, Nat?'

Nat scratched the side of his nose. 'You know,' he said. 'I could really use another old head behind here some nights.' He pulled another schooner, placed it on the bar.

Tarden sighed. 'This again? You know I'm more comfortable on this side of the counter. Where's Megan?'

'Took the night off. Sick, she said.'

'Well, good help's hard to find. As is a good drink.' Tarden sipped his beer. 'So my position remains.'

'Really, Jack.' Nat leant his considerable weight forward on the counter. 'Decent hours, plus you know the regulars.'

247

The regulars, Tarden thought. Back-stabbing pricks. He said, 'I'm pretty happy where I am thanks.'

'No offence,' said Nat, 'but it doesn't look like it.'

'Listen.' Tarden put down his glass, harder than he meant to. 'I just want a couple of quiet drinks, maybe watch a bit of the game, get a bucket of chips.' Equal breaths: in, out. He pushed the twenty across the beermat and turned back to the TV. Everyone wanted in on his fucking personal business.

He peered down the bar at the two old bastards teetering on their stools, middies gripped death-tight in crusty fingers. This was his future, he supposed: hunched over and calcified, a smalltown gargoyle. Where the hell else would he go?

A spike in noise. One voice, above the others. Tarden spun around and Robbie was right behind him, his arm around somebody. A girl, a woman. Dressed in black, chlorine-blonde hair hanging in front of her face. Fucking kidding—Megan. A fresh wave of anger rose in him. It wasn't allowed to get to him, he knew. Him and Robbie, nobody in town was supposed to know. But of course, he realised now, everybody fucking did. Everything hidden, nothing a secret.

Robbie and Megan collapsed into a round booth at the back of the bar with tallies, both nearly empty. There was his too fast laugh. There was the shake of his head. Tarden's anger was shot through with a vein of fear. When you knew someone well enough, you knew their warning signs. Robbie drew his fingers down Megan's cheek and kissed her. She ran her hands through his hair; Tarden could feel the hair in his own hands. He got off the barstool and made his way towards them. He felt

248

moisture on his fingers, realised he'd tipped his glass too far over. He stood by their table, wondering why he the one lost for words.

Kuiper pulled himself away from Megan. His eyes were wide. 'Jacky boy,' he said. 'Jacky boy. What a pleasant surprise.' He made a sit-down motion.

Tarden didn't move.

'This is Megan,' said Kuiper, his arm wrapped securely around her shoulder. 'My new friend.'

Megan eyed Tarden with distaste. Her mouth hung open. It was clear she was ripped on something. Tarden hoped to hell it wasn't their product.

'She's from Mudgee,' said Kuiper. 'Originally. That near where you grew up?' He gestured to Tarden with a grand hand movement. 'You probably fucked her once, Jack.' He laughed, and Megan joined in. He slid his hand along her leg. 'But you'd have been long gone from those country towns. You were the Sydney Strangler by then. Is that the right name?'

'Robbie,' said Tarden. 'Leave it out.'

'Too late for that,' he said. 'I've already put it in.' A fresh round of sniggers. 'Isn't that right?'

Megan nodded, her head swinging alarmingly from her neck.

'What?'

'This girl,' he poked his finger at her, 'can suck cock like it's what she was born to do. Bookends, Jack. That's what we are. You fucked her then and I fucked her now.'

Tarden felt the floor shift under his feet. 'Shut the hell up.' Fingers flexing, trying to keep his weight even.

'Best I've had in ages.' Kuiper groped Megan's breasts through her T-shirt.

249

She pushed his hand away. 'Fuck off,' she said. 'You said I'd get another sample.

Tarden watched her trying to focus. 'How much have you two had?' he said, trying hard to keep his voice a whisper. He put his schooner down on the table. His hands were shaking. How the fuck could Robbie be so stupid?

Kuiper rolled his eyes. 'See what I have to put up with? Jack here did not go to business school. He has no idea about supply and demand.' He laughed. 'He's got twelve years on me, and treats me like I'm the old bastard losing my mind.'

Megan let her chewed fingernails play at her mouth. 'I want another one,' she said. 'Just need one more. You promised.'

'Jesus give me strength.' Kuiper held his hands in the air. 'These little cunts are never satisfied.'

Tarden stole a glance at the bar. Nat was somehow oblivious, restocking bottles with his back to them.

'You got anything on you, Jack?' Kuiper stood up. 'Jacky-boy, you got something for my fuck-buddy?'

Tarden breathed in deep and let his anger bloom. Smaller evils for the greater good, he thought, aiming his first punch straight at Robbie's mouth.

Simon watched Pony's rucksack jiggling on his back as they passed over a rough section of road. He would swear he could hear the tin can, the drugs rattling inside. It was Pony who'd insisted they bring them along. Evidence, he said. A bargaining chip. Simon hoped to God Madaline would not be home. Or maybe he hoped she'd would be home. Maybe Pony would lose his nerve and they could forget the whole thing. After Gin's disappearance, Pony had decided it was time to begin investigations in earnest. After they'd eaten the cake, he'd taken Simon aside and told him. Pony already had his rucksack packed and the bikes ready to go at the side of the house. Simon couldn't help thinking that maybe Pony was too preoccupied with the adventure, and that two boys on bikes with a handful of pills had very little chance of making anything happen. As Simon's mind wandered, he'd fall behind Pony, who kept on looping back, turning his bike around to flash past Simon and appear behind him again.

'Come on. You're riding like a girl.' The wind punched holes in Pony's voice.

'What if she's home?' said Simon. He let his feet coast the pedals. 'She only just left the party.'

'Then we wait. Anyway, she should be out trying to find your mum and dad.'

'I just think—what will we do when we get there? What are we looking for?'

Pony lifted his fingers from the handlebars, stretched them out. 'Simon,' he said, 'I don't know. Okay? I don't know what we'll find. But we have to try something. Name me one other person in this town who is lifting a finger to help you.'

Simon's cheeks fired with shame. 'Pony, I'm sorry,' he said. 'Thanks—thank you for helping me. I don't know what I'd—'

'Save it,' said Pony. 'Let's just go.' He began to accelerate away.

Simon rose up in his seat and pushed into the pedals, his legs already burning with the effort. They swung from sealed roads to dirt paths, Pony following a tiny white track just off the verge. Simon wondered how many times Pony had cycled these paths. At a set of crossroads they turned left and huffed up a short sharp hill. Simon's breath felt sour and jagged by the time they reached the top. He sighed with relief when Pony skidded his bike to a stop.

'This is it,' he said, clipping his helmet to the handlebars.

Simon couldn't see a house anywhere, but then realised they were at the bottom of her driveway. The entrance was guarded by thick rainforest foliage; Simon remembered the ferns slapping the windscreen of Madaline's car in the dark. Pony wheeled his bike into the undergrowth. 'Just in case someone comes looking for us,' he said.

'But if someone's looking, shouldn't we let them know where we are?'

Pony shook his head. 'You're still thinking like a kid, Simon. Like everyone wants to look after you. That's not how the world works.'

Simon rolled his bike off the road in silence and set

it next to Pony's. What was the point of the world, he thought, if no one cared about anyone else?

They made their way up the steep driveway on foot, gravel crunching with each step. The overhanging plants made the day darker, thick as they were with shadow and moisture. Simon remembered a trip to a plant nursery with his mother where he had become lost among the dark hearts of ferns and rubber plants. The same smell. The sense made him calm, now as it did then, despite being alone, out of his parents' reach.

They got to the end of the driveway. Pony slowed his steps to slow-motion, drew himself back into the leaves. Madaline's car was clearly visible, parked in front of the house.

'She's still here,' said Simon. 'What do we do?'

'You keep your voice down for a start,' whispered Pony.

Simon joined Pony at the edge of the driveway. He sunk back into the foliage, feeling the wet tips of leaves on his back. Above Madaline's roof, the sky was leaching colour. Behind the house were tall palm trees. He heard the creak of their trunks, watched the fronds shimmer with life. 'Weird,' he said.

'What?'

'It's like a desert island.'

Pony screwed up his face. 'You're weird.'

They stood in silence for a few minutes. The wet leaves seemed to grow in around them. Simon's back was freezing. Whenever he went to say something, Pony would shush him. Just as Simon was ready to turn around and walk back to their bikes, the front door to Madaline's house banged opened and she ran out, not in her dress now but jeans and a jumper, holding a thick black belt and a black leather case. As she drew closer, Simon saw it was a gun in a holster. Pony had seen it too: he mimed a pistol with his finger, shot it with his thumb.

Madaline jumped in her car and fired the engine. Pony set his arm across Simon's chest to force him back further into the leaves. The smell of earth was overpowering. Madaline's car drove past them. Simon held his breath, but Madaline's eyes were fixed dead ahead.

'Where's she going?' said Simon, after the car had gone.

Pony stepped back onto the driveway, brushing wet leaves from his shirt, and shrugged. 'Somewhere she needs a gun.'

'Should we follow her?'

'On our bikes?' Pony shook his head. 'Come on, let's find a way in.'

'What if she comes back?'

Pony ignored him and bounded up the driveway, up the stairs. He tried the front door, which was locked. He tried to get his fingers under a window frame. Peered up at the roof, as if it were possible to climb in through the chimney.

'Don't break anything,' said Simon.

'God,' said Pony, 'you are a girl.' He set his rucksack down on the porch, unzipped it and pulled out the leather wallet of lock picks. He was in the middle of choosing the right ones when his eye seemed to catch something at the bottom of the door. He clucked his tongue. 'Dead bolt.'

'You can't pick a deadbolt?'

'Not with these things.' He drummed his fingers on his leg.

254

'Maybe there's a back way in,' said Simon.

The two boys went back down the steps and made their way around the side of the house, down the narrow space between wall and fence, their feet treading carefully over uneven pavers. Eventually the path led them to a wooden gate. It wasn't locked, but when Pony pushed on it, a whoosh of leaves suggested it was hemmed in by a thick thatch of plants. Simon leant his weight on the door as well, and it gave in with a creak, dark green leaves springing from the gap. They squeezed through, fighting through the ferns to get to open space.

Madaline's backyard was a large concrete slab, surprising in its plainness against all the greenery around it. There was a tiny dead garden at the back of the lot, a washing line near it, but everything else was bare. A chain-link fence ringed the property. A collection of spindly potplants sat by the back door, a white plastic table underneath a window. One plastic chair. One mug.

'We've got to get inside.' Pony walked over to the door, eyeing it up. He held his palm to his forehead. 'Oh, come on.'

The door was bracketed with two deadbolts.

Pony tried lifting the window. 'We're going to have to break the glass,' he said.

'No,' said Simon. 'You can't.' He knew they would already be in trouble, but breaking in to a police officer's house?

Pony looked at him. 'Got a better idea?'

'Just wait. Just wait.' Simon tried desperately to think. 'Hold on.' He went over to the door and crouched down. He put his fingers into the dirt around one of the potplants.

255

'What the hell?' said Pony.

Simon dug into another plant. 'I just thought that maybe ... hey!' He pulled out a set of keys, stuck with clods of dirt.

Pony slowly clapped his hands. 'Fair play, Simon Sawyer. Let's get in there.'

The door opened into Madaline's kitchen, a dingy room with a burnt-orange countertop and dirty wooden cupboards. There was a baked-on smell from something that had been cooked long before and had never really left. The only signs of life were strange little plants in clay pots under the unboarded window: cacti, Simon guessed, some with spikes and bumps, others with wispy hair, spindled fingers. One had a wide ceramic hat and sunglasses painted on. Simon led them through the kitchen. Pony traced his fingers over benches and chairs as they went. The lounge room was as Simon remembered it. Perhaps even messier in natural light. Piles of paper that had been hidden in the shadows were now exposed. A slice of full light that fell on a pile of plastic folders had fallen there more than once; the sun had faded their covers from black to light grey. On the arm of Madaline's chair, the brown leather recliner, a half-eaten sandwich sat, its dry edges curling.

'Man,' said Pony. 'You were right about all the paperwork.' He peered at a blue folder on the floor. 'Expense reports,' he said. 'Cool.'

Simon couldn't see anything cool about expense reports, but he had to admit that all the information potentially held in the room was exciting. Surely something here would tell them about his parents, or about the drugs, or about ...

Pony let out a low whistle. He was examining the large bookcase on the opposite wall, the shelves crammed with an odd mix of normal books and coloured ring-binders, the sort Simon had used once for school. Pony ran his fingers the rows, tilting his head to read each binder. 'This is crazy.'

'What is?'

'It's ... this isn't the police station. That's Tommy Parker's house. But there's all these reports here.'

Simon came over and peered at the ring-binders. Some had small, cramped writing on their spines, the others were labelled ina larger, looped hand. Most of the titles were boring, but they all had one thing in common: a date written at the bottom. 'How do we even know where to start?'

Pony rubbed his cheek. 'I dunno.' He took a binder off the shelf and started flipping through it.

Simon felt a flutter of panic. 'What about fingerprints?'

Pony held up his hand. On the top pad of each finger was a small round band-aid. 'You think I haven't done this before? You've got so much to learn, Simon Sawyer.'

Simon shook his head. Pony was the strangest person he'd ever met.

They spent a few more minutes looking through the bookshelves, not finding anything of interest, until Simon spied something on the very bottom shelf. A folder bound in red leather, standing out from the vinyl covers around it. 'What's that?' said Simon.

Pony pulled it out with his band-aid fingers. He flippd it open, scanned it. 'Holy shit!'

'What?'

'Holy shit!' Pony smacked his palm against his forehead.

'What?' Simon could only make out a plain page of writing. 'Show me.'

Pony slowly turned his head. 'You're going to want to sit down.'

They went over to the couch and sat side by side.

'This,' said Pony dramatically, handing over the leather folder. 'This is Madaline's resignation letter.'

'What?'

'She quit the police force. Two years ago. Look!' He pointed at the page. It was a letter, with official police letterhead. It was dated two years before. 'And look why.'

Simon scanned the words. Owing to my unprofessional mismanagement in the disappearance of Stephanie Gale, it is with great regret ... Simon looked up. 'It's because of Audrey and Gin's mum.' The thought settled on him.

Pony tipped his head back. 'This is wild.' He was grinning. 'This is absolutely wild.' Simon's head spun. If she wasn't even still a police officer, then why was she pretending to be? Why hadn't she been replaced? Why was she in charge of the search for his parents? Who else even knew about it? 'She's not going to find my parents, is she?'

'I knew it,' said Pony. 'I mean, I knew it, but this is wild. We've found this out, you and me. No one else has figured this out.' He rubbed his hands together. 'We've got to find out what happened,' he said. 'We've got to work out why she quit.'

Simon stared at the abandoned sandwich on the coffee table. He felt the taste of sour mustard and curdled cheese. He felt his stomach giving way. He smelled mothballs

258

and old ink, dust and hand cream. This was the feeling of all hope disintegrating. He lowered his head between his knees, willing away the dark thoughts that were piling up like wet fish flapping on a trawler's deck. He grabbed his ankles tightly, fighting the heat-fermented bubble of vomit rising at his throat. Just before he was sick, in one clear-eyed moment, he saw the other binder, bigger than the others, hiding under the couch, held together with rubber bands. And the name, printed sideways on its spine. Case File: Stephanie Rhelma Gale.

❧

Madaline could already feel blisters beginning on her ankles. Her canvas shoes, still wet from yesterday's rain, rubbed viciously against her skin and she ached to take them off. The last thing she needed was a bloody public disturbance, and usually she would have pleaded with Nat to deal with it himself, but the panic in his voice had convinced her. She'd already bothered Tommy once on his sacred nights off: she was on her own. She wiggled her foot deeper into her shoe, pressing down the accelerator, making the pain sharpen her senses. She brushed back her hair as she reversed down the driveway. Her police belt sat on the passenger seat. It looked like a child's toy. She had put her gun in its holster on the floor below it.

Another day spent frozen by indecision, trapped by inaction. The sun already so low in the sky, and no more progress on the missing visitors. Going to Gin's party had been a mistake in so many ways. That ridiculous dress, trying to impress a man she had no right to even talk to. This town was full of traps she'd set for herself. It felt sometimes like she spent most of her time not quite awake, in an uncertain mid-conscious state, isolated and confused in equal measure.

She was past the pub before she knew it, the broad grey façade of the Ottoman flashing by her window. She slowed the car and U-turned in the middle of the street.

Pulled into a parallel space, gathered her belt and stepped from the car. She wished dearly she'd taken the time to change into her uniform. She felt like a cranky mother, roused from the warmth of her home to sort out errant children. Usually it was nothing more serious than that: a taxi service, pretty much, for some local with a skinful in him.

This time, though, there was no local slumped down on the kerb outside the pub; Madaline heard breaking glass even before she stepped through the door. The place was a mess, upturned tables and glass everywhere. Leaning unsteadily on a wall in the corner was Jack Tarden, using one hand to stanch a clot of blood at his shoulder. Madaline recognised Nat's broad back bent over a blonde girl who was on the floor, sobbing. Megan, she realised. What the hell had happened?

A flash of movement at her side and Madaline instinctively sprang out of the way just as a dark shard of glass came at her. She wheeled around, catching her attacker with a swift pointed elbow. Kuiper. He stumbled back and the first thing she noticed was his nose, ringed with red like a child had drawn it. She thought for a moment she'd done it, then realised she had caught him in the chest; the blood on his face was too dark, already dry from an earlier attack. He lunged for her again, but she had whipped out her baton. She raised it quickly to deflect the glass then swung it around before he could react, catching him straight in the armpit, just above his ribs. He fell to the floor with an animal grunt.

She already had her knee in the small of his back, snapping the handcuffs from her belt and around his wrists in one fluid movement. She ratcheted the cuffs to bite hard. 'Nat,' she called over her shoulder. 'Is everyone okay?'

'We're fine,' he called back. 'We're fine now.'

Kuiper groaned. 'Get the fuck off me.'

Madaline ignored him. 'Is anybody hurt?' She scanned the room, noticing only a few old regulars standing by the pool table, unconcerned. Tarden remained motionless against the wall.

Nat was helping Megan to her feet. 'We're all alive,' said Nat. 'That's the main thing. This one though,' he nodded his head at Tarden, who stared sheepishly at the floor. 'This one started it all.'

'Jack?' said Madaline. 'You started this?'

Tarden shrugged.

'What the hell happened?'

'He just came up and punched me,' wheezed Kuiper.

'Can't think why,' said Madaline, pressing harder with her knee. Kuiper cried out. Fresh blood from his nose was soaking into the carpet.

Suddenly, Megan made a break from Nat. He grabbed her quickly.

Madaline shook her head. 'What's going on, Megan?'

She struggled in Nat's grip. 'Lemme go, you cunts!' she yelled.

High as a kite, thought Madaline. 'Nat, what's her story?'

'No idea,' he said. 'Supposed to be off work tonight. Not that she'll be coming back to work after this.' His face was filled with frustration. Madaline knew how hard he worked to keep the place in business, how hard it was to get staff.

'Oh God,' Megan's shoulders slumped, and Madaline thought she could almost see the spirit pass out of her. She'd seen it often enough: the moment of realisation. When bravado, adrenaline, whatever it is that's keeping you from crashing, runs out. When it all comes true.

'What happened, Megan?' Madaline said. 'No one's in trouble. I just want to hear it from you.'

She shook her head, over and over, tears flowing. 'So stupid,' she said, 'so bloody stupid.' Nat released his grip, let her wipe her eyes. 'I let him fuck me for ... he promised me more.'

'Who's he,' said Madaline. 'What did he promise you?'

'Product,' she choked. Her eyes leaking black claws of mascara.

'What product? Who?'

'Yabbies.' Tarden spoke up. 'Crabs. Her boyfriend drives a freeze-truck. Wanted to take hauls back up the coast. Sell themstraight to retailers.'

'What?' Madaline's mind spun for a moment. 'Jack, that's—' she turned to Megan, 'is this right?'

Megan sobbed in a breath and shrugged.

'Nat?'

'Yeah,' he said. 'She goes around with this guy, Cody. Works for a trucking company. Look, I don't want to get into this. Just want someone to clean up this mess and let me get on with things.'

'It's true,' said Megan. Madaline could see her features firm up, see her start to think of damage control.

'Amazing,' said Kuiper, 'what lengths people go to for fresh seafood,'. Even though Madaline couldn't see his face, she knew it was plastered with a mangled version

263

of his usual irritating grin. It was all bullshit, of course. They were on speed probably, or meth, but unless they were carrying or one of them said something there wasn't much she could do.

She moved her knee further up Kuiper's back and went through his pockets, patting him down. Nothing. 'Get your kicks, Constable? Not much action for a single lady in a small town.' She let him stand up, but tightened the cuffs another notch.

She went over to Tarden, searched him too, came up with nothing. 'Why'd you start the fight then, Jack?' she said.

'Just a disagreement,' he said. 'A misunderstanding. I'll—we'll pay for the damage.'

A tired, bitter part of Madaline wanted to make a snide remark about lovers' tiffs, but she held her tongue. She pieced together a night of frustrations and jealousy.

There were fresh boot-steps at the door. Madaline swung her head around, ready to dissuade whoever it was from entering then saw it was Ned, strands of hair frazzling from his head, skinny arms sticking out from an old Midnight Oil T-shirt. 'Jesus,' he said, taking in the scene. 'Is everyone okay?'

'Ned,' she said. 'What are you doing here?'

'Nat called me. Fight?' His eyes scanned the room nervously.

More steps at the door. Tommy huffing into the pub wearing stubbies and a huge short-sleeved shirt. 'What the hell?' He drew his hand over his face. 'Nat,' he said. 'You shoulda told me it was a full-on brawl. Woulda dressed up.' He grinned at Kuiper in cuffs. 'You been a naughty boy, Roberto?'

Kuiper piped up. 'We had a misunderstanding,' he

said. 'Jack hit me, as friends sometimes do. And the good constable decided to handcuff me.'

'That may have more to do with you trying to attack me,' said Madaline. She shot Tommy a dirty glare.

Kuiper said, meekly, 'Yeah, well.'

'What are we doing, Nat?' she said. 'You want any of these idiots charged?'

'Not worth it,' he said. 'If they want to reimburse me for the damage and lost custom we'll call it quits.'

Madaline felt a deep exhaustion overtake her. She knew—as Kuiper did—that she couldn't really arrest him if Nat wasn't pressing charges.

'And you?' Madaline turned to Megan. 'Any complaints? The sex consensual?'

The girl nodded, the gravity of the situation slipping over her face like a mask.

'Perhaps you'd better get back home then.'

'You need to stay somewhere tonight, Megan?' Ned's voice was calm. He flung on the kick-out lights and the pub was filled with harsh yellow.

'Maybe,' said Megan.

'She can stay here,' said Nat. 'Stuff's here anyway. We can talk everything out tomorrow.'

Kuiper chuckled. 'No harm done, really.'

'As for you,' Madaline said, walking back to Kuiper, turning him roughly around to get to the handcuffs, 'I can assume you won't be taking action against Jack for assault, can I? Much in the same way I'm taking no action against you?'

'Yeah.' Kuiper nodded.

'And I don't have to tell you what will happen if I

catch you doing anything—anything—remotely illegal again, do I.' Madaline pinched the cuffs in tighter before she released them.

'Fuck you,' Kuiper yelped. 'Tight-arsed fucking frustrated bitch!'

'Right.' Madaline's eyes narrowed. 'Tommy, would you mind escorting Mr Kuiper to the lock-up for the rest of the evening?'

Tommy clucked his tongue. 'My night off I believe,' he said. 'And you seem to have this all wrapped up.'

Madaline blew out a long breath. 'Or maybe you'd prefer to stay and help clean up.'

Tommy shot her a venomous look, but it quickly dissolved. 'This fucking town,' he said. 'Few more years and I'm on pension. You jokers can fight amongst yourselves while I'm out fishing. Finally get a decent night's sleep.' Tommy put his hand on Kuiper's shoulder. 'Let's go.' He gestured to the door like a gameshow host.

'And Jack,' the thought occurred to Madaline, 'be home tomorrow. I want to interview you both. Properly.'

Tarden followed Tommy and Kuiper out the door, and Madaline felt a shiver run through her entire body. Like the weight of everything had finally landed.

Simon hardly felt like he pedalled any of the way back to the hotel. It felt like flying, as he coasted through the darkness, following Pony, tracing his well-worn paths. He could tell Pony was as troubled as he was. Pleased at first, of course, as anyone whose suspicions had been validated would be, but on a deeper level, Simon could see Pony was troubled. The town's deception was as much a betrayal to him as anyone: Reception was the place that had welcomed him in, that had sheltered him from his past. The drugs were just the tip of the iceberg, it seemed: there were deeper problems: disappearances, cover-ups, even murder.

Back at Madaline's house, they had scoured the file on Stephanie's disappearance, and learnt that the case had been plagued by mistakes. Page after page—emails and letters printed, reports logged: a trail of correspondence between Madaline, Tommy, and their superiors. The further they'd read, the less detailed the reports became. Statements they hadn't taken, evidence they hadn't collected. By the time detectives from Sydney had made their way to the town, the trail had gone cold, although they had gone through the motions.

They'd learnt, too, that Ned had been a suspect in his wife's disappearance. For what reason Simon could not imagine, except he was the last person to see her. Even

Madaline's involvement had been brought into question. But when they came down to it, it was nothing more than this: Stephanie Gale got up one morning, presumably went swimming as she did most mornings, and simply did not come back. There were no witnesses—at least none who came forward—no reason, it seemed, for her to disappear from the face of the earth. This was what had begun to nag at Simon's mind: that something so inexplicable could happen. He wondered if any other police officer could have uncovered the truth. What if his parents had suffered the same fate? A disappearance, for no reason at all. And what about Pony, whose parents had suffered the most definite of endings?

Simon and Pony skated their bikes up the path towards the Ned's house. They cycled over the grass and left the bikes at the back door.

'Do you want anything to eat?' said Pony.

'Maybe,' said Simon. 'Sure.'

Pony led him through the door and into the kitchen, flicking on the lights. The dishes were half done. A tall stack of glasses sat on the kitchen table.

'Thought there'd be dinner up,' said Pony. He huffed as he opened the fridge. Simon caught a glimpse of plentiful party leftovers, but Pony slammed the door shut. 'Where is everybody?' He put his hand into his pocket, and Simon knew he was searching for a stone. 'Gone to bed, probably.'

Simon wasn't convinced of this, and he could see Pony wasn't either. A deep unease filled his thoughts.

'Well,' said Pony, 'I'm having a hot chocolate. Do you want one?'

Pony filled the kettle and put it on the stove. The gas

hissed and the water boiled, but silence settled over the two of them like a flung sheet coming to rest.

'What are we going to do?' said Simon eventually. He held out his hands flat against the table, palms turned upwards.

Pony took off his hat and pushed his hands through his hair. 'We have to tell someone,' he said. The kettle simmered, rolling upwards towards a boil. He turned away to pour milk into a small saucepan.

'And we still don't know,' said Simon, 'how much Madaline knows about the drugs.'

'She must know about Tarden and Kuiper though,' said Pony. 'The files were right there in her house.'

Simon nodded. In Stephanie's folder, among all its various documents they'd found files on Jack Tarden and Robert Kuiper: Kuiper gaoled on fraud charges; Tarden's story more sinister. Gambling, debt, favours owed to a succession of dangerous criminals. Ending up as an accessory to a botched gangland hit, the wife and daughter of the target killed while the target got away. According to his file, Tarden had not been found guilty of the murders themselves, but was given fifteen years anyway. The two men had met in Long Bay.

The milk steamed. Pony took it off the stove and got two large mugs from the cupboard. Two teaspoons of cocoa in each, dissolved with hot water and warm milk poured carefully over the top. He sat down opposite Simon and pushed a mug across the table. Simon accepted it with a weak smile, wrapping his hands around it.

'I think we should tell Ned,' said Pony. 'He's the only person I think we can tell.'

'Tell him what?' said a voice from the doorway.

They turned around to see Audrey, wrapped in a large brown coat. It was so big that its hem skirted the floor. Her hands werehidden deep in the sleeves. 'Tell him what?'

Pony froze. His mouth gaped open, and he couldn't seem to close it. Audrey regarded him with passive eyes.

'Where is everyone?' said Simon.

'Dad went out,' said Audrey. 'Gin's playing upstairs. What's going on?'

'You'd better sit down,' said Simon. 'There's quite a lot.'

Kuiper swore and pushed past Tarden to the house, swinging the flyscreen back so it clashed and hissed against the brickwork. Tarden walked in after him, leaving a safe distance, pondering on the irony of two convicted criminals living in a town where you could always leave your front door open. The same town, he thought, in which police officers fucked off home to bed instead of doing their job. And others left their car doors open with a handgun lying on the floor. Tommy had uncuffed Kuiper outside the Ottoman, saying he had better things to do than babysit grown men; Tarden had given him scout's honour they would go straight home.

He went into the house. Could hear Robbie rattling open the fridge in the kitchen. He heard him, still muttering: 'Fucking bitch,' over and over, like he had in the car. Then a clattering sound. Tarden was almost past caring. He came into the kitchen and saw Robbie had swept everything from the table: newspapers, magazines and plates and pens lay on the floor. He had a bottle of beer open already, hand closed tight around it. 'Jack,' he said. 'We've got to think quick here.'

Tarden said nothing. He crossed his arms. The quiet, the calm, in Robbie's voice worried him. When he was in the middle of a hit, when he was raving and screaming, at least Tarden knew what he had to deal with. 'You're using,' he said flatly.

'You know what, Sherlock? I need you to shut the fuck up for a moment and let me think.'

'It's our stuff,' said Tarden, 'isn't it? Taking it from storage. Giving samples. Samples, Robbie?' He threw up his hands. 'You keep telling me I don't understand. You keep telling me we have to keep our heads down, and you're fucking barmaids—no, you're fucking the girlfriend of one of our delivery guys? Oh, and trying to glass the town copper. Fucking outstanding.'

Kuiper rubbed his hands on his face. 'Let me. Think. I just need a release sometimes. This motherfucking backwater gives me anxiety. I just need to let off some steam. Just like you and that whore at Ned's place. The grandmother. Jesus. At least mine's a way off the pension.' He laughed, scratching at his neck.

Tarden stole a glance at Madaline's gun, which Kuiper cradled in his left hand, the holster swinging from his finger. He'd begged Robbie not to take it, but couldn't argue with him once he had it in his hand. 'Iris,' he said. 'I just talk to her. That's it. You know that.'

'Whatever.' Kuiper took a swig of beer. 'Whatever makes you happy, mate.' Tarden sat down at the table, tried to push down his anger. He had to keep his head clear. They had to move the stuff. Somehow. But Robbie's attitude—Jesus. Something bubbled up, spinning his breath ragged. He said, 'Do you know what used to make me happy? Being with you. This—all this—you know, it really wasn't what I had in mind.'

'This again.' Kuiper leant back in his chair, widening his redrimmed eyes.

Tarden sighed. He was sad and he was frustrated and he was tired, and all he had left was anger. And a thought he had been trying, desperately, not to think. The thought that this man, sitting across the table from him—this face that he knew so well—was someone he no longer cared about. Robbie, who had made everything make sense. The man who had managed to convince him that good days could be strung together, that good days became good weeks. That there was something worth living for after those years in Sydney where every day meant waking up with your nightmares so close behind you. Where every day you expected, you accepted, that you wouldn't make it to the next. The moment they fell into step with each other's lives was perhaps his happiest moment. Were a few good years better than none at all?

He went to the fridge and took out a beer. Cap off and already halfway through it, already thinking of how good the next one would taste. He took another, leaving the fridge door open. This life they led now: Tarden knew he had gone along with it. He hadn't objected to it, not forcefully enough, anyway. Even with Robbie's habit, with his indiscriminate fucking, Tarden had stuck around. He had—or told himself he had—conquered his own vices, exciting his brain with the crisp sting of early morning air, gambling only his own skill against the sea, replacing the dick-led confusion of his youth with something like monogamy, something approaching a stable life. Even his time with Iris, he had never once had sex with her: had never wanted to, which surprised him perhaps more than it did her.

He threw back his third beer, felt the softness creep across the edge of his mind. He no longer loved Robbie. He just didn't. Not this Robbie, anyhow. And he also knew he never, ever wanted to go back inside. Anywhere, he thought, anywhere but back there. He put down the empty bottle. 'Let's get the boat hooked up,' he said. A plan coming together in his head. 'If we move it all tonight ... move it offshore. Won't have to worry about that at least if Madaline comes sniffing around tomorrow. Or tonight more likely. Get rid of that fucking car, drive it somewhere and torch it. Going to have to ditch the gun, too.'

Kuiper clutched the holster at his hip protectively. 'Fuck that.'

'Listen.' Tarden used his last ounce of calm to keep Robbie's attention. 'If we don't get this right, we're both going back inside. The merchandise, the missing couple—shit, it's going to be a long rest of our lives with other people telling us what to do.' He watched his words settle in Robbie's head, hoped they could reach that part of it where intelligence was still alive.

Kuiper pushed back from the table. 'The boat,' he said. 'Right.'

꘍

It was one of those uncertain winter nights. Mist appeared on the windscreen like ghostly breath, appearing from nowhere and fading out in random patterns. Ned's headlights picked out only a small space of road. Madaline focused her eyes on the narrow stretch of light, nothing else. They had come out of the Ottoman together and evening had already slipped into night. Ned had invited her to dinner and of course she had agreed. She was too exhausted to say no, too full of adrenaline to imagine driving herself.

'Thanks,' she said. She drew herself up in her seat. Rain began to appear and dark slashes through the mist. 'Thanks for coming to help tonight.'

'I didn't really do anything.'

'Well, you came anyway.'

He looked over at her and smiled.

Silence, and Madaline counted the Morse code of bumps making their way through the car's suspension. She ran her fingers over the fine whorls of hair at the hinge of her jaw. She watched Ned, in profile, surreptitiously, not able to push the thought from her mind of what his lips would feel like. Only the lightest of touches, she told herself. A graze, a delicate moment like two magnets passing.

Madaline tipped her head back, closing her eyes. 'I roped you into all this, and I had no right to.'

Ned said nothing, steered the car into a right turn. Madaline let her body crush up against the passenger door. The seconds stretched; they were at the bottom of Ned's driveway, heading up to his house. Madaline's heart thrummed.

'You—' Ned began, just as she blurted, 'What's for dinner?' He broke off. 'Dinner. I don't know.' He stopped the car halfway up the driveway. Pulled up the handbrake and cut the engine. The rain returned as a static hiss on the roof.

The headlights cut out and it felt to Madaline like the end of a thousand awkward dates. All the misspoken words she had ever uttered collecting in her head.

Ned's breath fogged up the inside of the window. 'If you're worried that all this makes me think about Stephanie, then yes. It does.'

Madaline clenched her fists at her sides. She had to leave. She'd have to walk back to town, pick up her car.

'But that's not ... I mean it's something that we ... that the kids and I never talk about.' He stared through the driver's window, at the house lit up in yellow squares among the rainy haze. 'It's always there—she's always there, with us all, but we never acknowledge her. Did you know we never had a funeral?'

'No, I didn't.'

He nodded. 'She was pronounced ... but I mean how can you can you say goodbye to someone without—'

Madaline pictured the case file hidden under the couch. Full of so much information, none of it useful. None of it had helped.

'Audrey, she still thinks her mum's out there somewhere. She thinks Stephanie abandoned her. She

used to be so utterly devoted to her mum. But now—'
He gestured helplessness. 'She's got this habit of picking
up the phone and slamming it down. Every time she goes
past it. She says she can feel Stephanie picking up another
phone somewhere in the world. But she still keeps things,
things she's found that belonged to Stephanie. There's
a coat she took from storage. She thinks I don't know
about it. She's left-handed like her mum but she tries to
do everything right-handed now.'

Both he and Madaline kept their gazes dead ahead, as
if the car was still moving. She imagined shapes in the
shifting rain. 'Audrey,' she said. 'Is she better than she ...
than she was?'

'Yeah.' Ned scrunched up his mouth. 'She's better than
then.'

Madaline shook her head. The image of Audrey in the
bath would not leave her. She couldn't imagine what it
was like for Ned.

'And Gin.' Ned turned to her and sketched a weak
smile. 'I guess it's not so bad, being a superhero but I
wish he was himself again.' His mouth wavered for a
moment. 'I can't even remember what that was like.' He
bowed his head, leaning over to touch his forehead on
the crest of the steering wheel.

Madaline reached over and rested her fingers on his
back. She smoothed down the fabric of his jacket and
imagined, despite herself, the feeling of his skin. 'You've
done your best,' she said. 'You've done everything you
could.'

His breaths shuffled together. Madaline realised she
had never seen him cry. He was the resilient one. Always
calm.

'I've gotten used to Stephanie not being here,' he said softly. 'But when my kids disappear as well—'

'Oh, Ned, don't—' She stroked the base of his neck as he drew his arms up around his face. 'Gin and Audrey, they're still so young. They've got a loving dad who'd do anything for them.' She held him tightly as his shoulders shook. The rain came down harder, a roar on the car roof. It felt like it enfolded them.

Eventually, Ned's breathing calmed and Madaline withdrew her arms. 'Do you know what it feels like?' he said. His eyes stared at his feet.

'What what feels like?'

'To have someone missing from your life.'

Madaline stayed silent.

'It's like those divers, who go down into those trenches in the sea, and come back up too fast. That pressure squeezing your whole body. They always talk about the heart, don't they? But it's the base of your throat that tightens up, it's your guts that get the vice.'

Madaline was unprepared for the match-strike of her own tears. 'I know,' she said. 'I do know.' This was the sensation that grabbed her in every unguarded moment. The constriction of guilt. The asphyxiating struggle of what could have been. And before she knew it: 'Ned, I'm sorry.'

He looked at her. His eyes swollen. 'For what?'

'For the way I handled the case. Stephanie.'

'What did you do? You did your job.'

'I didn't find her.'

'You—'

'I made mistakes.' Madaline dug her fingernails into her palms. 'I feel like I let my ... feelings for you affect the way I behaved.' Madaline wanted to open her door and run out into the night. What the hell had she just said? She shivered. She felt the pressure drawing in around her. 'Sorry, forget I said anything.'

Ned gripped the steering wheel, his knuckles whitening. 'Your—'

'Just forget it. I don't—'

Ned was perfectly still.

'No, actually.' Madaline tensed her shoulders, then let go. 'I'm ... For most of the time I've known you, Ned. I know there's nothing I can do about it. I know the timing was horrible, but that's the story of my life, really. Every ... day I feel guilty that it happened. I tried my best to find your wife anyway, but the best wasn't good enough and now I'm fucking up another case and I knew I would and I got you involved because you're the only good person left in this town and I'm sorry. I'm sorry—'

Ned clasped her hands between his. 'Please,' he said. 'Don't. It wasn't you that made it happen. She made her decision.'

'What, you think—'

Ned moved his fingers on her hand, seemingly oblivious. 'It was pretty clear Stephanie didn't want to be found. No matter what anyone else thinks. I knew her. You were ... you were nothing but professional. I don't know what we all would have done without you.'

'Ned, that's—'

His touch was not what Madaline had expected. It was a weight, somehow.

'I think it myself sometimes,' he went on. 'What it would be like to just disappear. Remove yourself from what—from who—you know. Start somewhere new. I

279

hate myself for thinking it and then ... then I hate her for doing it. It's me thinking maybe she just wanted something else.'

Madaline thought of her own departure. Leaving her husband, her three-week marriage, her mother. She had somersaulted beneath a wave and reality was the inverted world above. Nothing would ever be like it was.

She looked past Ned, to the mist shifting at his window. Diffuse lines shot suddenly into a face. Madaline cried out. A white shape hit the glass, the flat pink map of a palm slamming, over and over.

Tarden fumbled the keys, jangling them so loudly that he imagined someone hearing them all the way across town. It wasn't just the darkness making him clumsy. His head buzzed from beer, pissed off a few drinks. They'd dragged all his crab pots from the back of the house and Tarden cursed himself for not investing in better, lighter traps. Not that they ever had the money to spend on them. His back ached from the lifting.

'Let me do it,' Kuiper told him, a rare strain of warmth inflecting his annoyance. Robbie placed his hands over Tarden's and together they guided the key into the lock. They hauled the first pots through the door. The metal frames shuddered over the concrete, clashing out hideous echoes. The next pot Tarden dragged in had a crab's carcass stuck to its inner edge. The acrid smell of stale sea life, the smell that haunted him. The smell of the midnight trips along the dirt track to Magpie Lake. The rotten stench of his failures.

Kuiper hit the lights and the fluorescent strips stuttered on. 'God,' said Kuiper, hands on his hips. He had attached Madaline's holster to his belt, but it didn't fit and the gun stuck out at an alarming angle. He surveyed the room. 'So many of the damn things.'

There it was, Tarden saw, the only doubt he'd ever seen in Robbie's eyes. The thought that maybe they'd taken things too far. It was Robbie's endless confidence rupturing, finally. Robbie, who was always ahead.

They'd been released from prison two months apart. That was always the problem, Tarden saw this now. The ever-present imbalance. Robbie getting out first, a head start, a precious few weeks out of Tarden's watch in which he had already set up their new life. Robbie had met him at the train station. He already owned a car, already looked impossibly different. His face and body had filled out; he seemed so comfortable in a world Tarden was only just remembering. In the following weeks, Tarden saw their roles reversed: Robbie was the protector now, showing him how to live. By the time he realised he'd fallen into someone's debt, it was too late.

'Are you sure these'll keep the cans together?' said Kuiper. 'They won't float away?'

Tarden smiled. 'Crabs never float away.'

'Don't see what you're grinning at. This is our livelihood. This is our future.'

Tarden wanted to kiss him. He wanted to taste Robbie one more time. 'Let's just get this done,' he said. 'Sooner the better.'

Kuiper held a can in his hand, weighing it up before placing it with the others in the pot. 'There's two boats,' he said. 'Right?'

Tarden nodded. He had explained it three times already. The pills, he knew, were spreading their chemical confusion through Robbie's system. 'My tinny'll be there,' Tarden said. 'And I'll hotwire the motor on someone else's. We each take a tinny out, drop the pots from one, anchor it and take the other tinny back. Safe as houses.'

'What if someone finds the boat?'

There it was: a definite tremour of anxiety. 'We'll anchor it in the cove. No one's going to go looking there. If they do—which they won't—they'll just see a boat, nothing attached to it. We'll only need a few days I reckon, just wait for it all to blow over.'

'Yeah,' said Kuiper, smoothing down his hair. 'Safe as houses.'

They made their way to the end of the row. The Sawyers' car was still there, hardly hidden under the tarpaulins. 'One of us is going to have to drive that out of here.'

Kuiper nodded. 'Have to dump it.'

'Have to burn it.' Tarden flexed his fingers. 'Jesus. The last thing we need when we're trying not to attract attention.'

Kuiper made his way back to the door for another crab pot. 'I said I'm sorry. I was just—'

'Forget about it,' said Tarden. 'We'll deal with it.' He rubbed his cheek. 'Supposed to be a pickup next week though.'

'I'll make some calls,' said Kuiper. 'They'll understand.' He flashed an empty smile. They both knew the people they dealt with weren't the understanding type.

Tarden knew they'd been incredibly lucky up until now, with a constant stream of work and a small town where nothing ever happened. Perfect until something did happen. Tarden had got on the wrong side of these people before. Groups of paranoid men drunk on power and shit-scared of losing it. No resolutions, no compromises, only high-stakes battles that always ended in bloodshed.

It was the reason he was here, after all. The two battered bodies he could see every time he closed his eyes.

The sun beating on their naked backs and the two other guys, fucking animals, sniggering, wiping their hands on the front of their pants. Adjusting identical trucker caps, spreading their legs, posturing like it was a fucking Clint Eastwood movie. And Jack—himself, still just Jack, still just a young man with his hands shaking, soft-baked bile in his mouth, the stench of soil his only connection to anything he recognised.

'Robbie,' he said, 'if we get out of this, we're going to make changes. Scale all this back. We don't need this.'

Kuiper turned around. 'How do you propose we do that,' he said, 'when it barely works now?'

'Shut up for one sec. We've got to get you clean. You've been skimming off the top, handing out samples.'

'That's fucking—'

'No, I know you have. And you wonder why nothing ever adds up. I won't even ask how long you and Megan—' Tarden waved away his thoughts.

Kuiper stared at him. 'Like you say, Jack. If we get out of this.' He hitched a knot tight at the top of a pot.

Tarden wiped a slick of sweat from his brow. A pain shot up his side as he collected a can from the lowest shelf. Just get through it, he thought. Was this the best he could hope for now?

Audrey had taken it well, Simon thought. Dredging up her mother's disappearance, telling her Madaline's secret, what Kuiper and Tarden were doing under the noses of the town.

She had just sat at the table, a calm look on her face, even when Simon admitted he and Pony had broken into Madaline's house. Pony let Simon do the talking. He got up and boiled the kettle again, heated the milk, made Audrey a hot chocolate. She seemed surprised by Pony's generosity. Simon wasn't. He knew Pony was a decent person beneath his bluster. Audrey seemed to relax as Simon finished telling her what he knew; perhaps she was just as glad of the revelations.

But then a car's headlights swept across the wall, its engine rumbling to a stop, and her face grew suddenly serious. She got up from the table and went over to the window.

'Dad's home.' She clambered up onto the bench, tweed coat and all, pushing aside the plumes of Ned's herbs to get a better look. Suddenly, she slammed her hand against the glass. She dropped down off the bench and made for the doorway.

'Where are you going?' said Simon.

'I've got to talk to Dad.'

'Are you sure you're okay?'

She turned around. 'I'm fine, Simon,' she said. 'My life's just fine.' She stamped off down the hall.

Pony didn't move from the table. He looked down into his mug of hot chocolate as Simon got up quickly and followed her.

Simon had reached the front door just in time to see Audrey fling herself at Ned's car, hammering her palm at the driver's window. She looked like a spectre in the darkness: just a white head and hand in her dark coat. Simon could see Madaline in the passenger seat. Then Ned got out of the car and put his arm around Audrey, trying to calm her down. Madaline stayed where she was.

'She's not real!' shouted Audrey, pointing into the car. 'She couldn't find Mum because she's not real!'

'Audrey, hold on,' Ned began.

'There are criminals in the town and—and she doesn't do anything about it!'

Simon saw Madaline's face through the drizzle, inside the car, frozen in horror. He felt the first trickle of remorse at the base of his throat.

'I think we're all a bit tired,' said Ned. 'Why don't we get out of the rain and I'll make us some dinner and—'

'You don't even care about your own family! You can't even tell us the truth!' Audrey's body collapsed. She crumpled into Ned's arms, retreating from angry ghost to sobbing child in a matter of moments.

Ned held her, rubbed her back. 'I don't know what's happened,' he said. 'I don't know where you've got this from, but it sounds like you've got things a bit mixed up.' Ned raised his eyes, picked out Simon in the light of the front door. 'Simon,' he said. 'Do you know what's going on here?'

Simon nodded, despite himself. 'Pony and I went to Madaline's house.' He shot a quick look at Madaline, who was getting out of the car. 'We ... we went into her house. But we didn't break anything. She keeps the keys in the same place as you.' Ned looked at him quizzically. 'We went through some of the files.'

Madaline looked pale. She put one hand on the car roof. 'The files?' There seemed no anger in her voice, just a deep resignation.

'Yes,' Simon said, 'but we wee only trying to find out about my ... my parents.' Simon knew he couldn't mention the drugs. He hear Pony's croaky voice in his head.

'You went through Madaline's house?' said Ned. 'Without her knowing?' He sounded far more indignant than Madaline had.

'Just in the living room. We just looked at the files. Nowhere else.' He turned to Madaline. 'We're not robbers.'

'What on earth where you thinking?' said Ned. 'Breaking into someone's ... ? I thought better of you quite frankly Simon.'

Heat rose in Simon's chest. His scars prickled. He was sick of being blamed for what he did, what he didn't do. 'I want to find my mum and dad!' he shouted. 'No one else except Pony is doing anything to help me. They could be out there, waiting for someone to rescue them, and nothing's being done. If there were real police here, then—' Simon let his words trail off.

Ned turned to Madaline. 'What's he talking about?'

Madaline blew a lungful of air through her lips and shook her head.

'She resigned,' said Simon. 'We saw her letter. She's not a real police officer.'

'You saw—' Ned removed his hands from Audrey's shoulders.

Simon sensed someone at his side. Pony, holding something in his hands. It took Simon a moment to realise it was the can. The drugs. Simon shot him a wide-eyed look, but Pony dropped his gaze.

Madaline shook her head. 'I did write a letter,' she said, 'but I never sent it.' She bit her lip. 'I wanted to. Ned, I wanted to. I didn't think I deserved to keep my job after—'

Pony walked forward. 'This,' he held up the can for everyone to see. 'This was why me and Simon broke into Madaline's house.'

Madaline regarded Pony flatly. 'A can of fruit?'

'It's not just fruit, actually.' Pony passed the can to her, across the bonnet of the car. With a frown, she reached inside. 'Ugh!' She pulled her hand out, examining her sticky fingers.

Pony shook his head. 'There's a bag.'

Madaline reached back in and pulled out the bag. It was still covered in syrup but she managed to tear it open. 'What the hell?' She took a s

'A storeroom,' Pony said. 'Belonging to Jack Tarden and Robert Kuiper. We saw them.'

'A storeroom?'

'At their house. A big shed. There's hundreds of cans like this.'

'What is it?' said Ned.

Madaline swallowed. She held out the bag. 'High-grade amphetamine by the looks.' She stared straight at Pony. 'You are telling me there are more of these cans?'

'Yes,' he said. 'Lots more.'

'And you're saying you saw Mr Tarden and Mr Kuiper with the cans? You're telling me these cans belong to them?'

'Yes,' said Simon. 'They have a key for the storeroom, and there's machinery and everything.'

'I told you, Dad,' said Audrey. 'I told you there were criminals.'

'They've got—' Simon couldn't find his voice. Everyone looked at him. 'In the shed. I think … they have my parents' car.'

'What?' Pony spoke first. 'Where?'

'At the end of the shed. It was covered with sheets, but I recognised the tyres.'

'Simon,' said Madaline. 'Are you sure it was your parents' car?'

'It had the same tyres. I couldn't see the rest of it because we were hiding.'

'Christ.' Madaline stared at the ground for a moment. She looked back up, an anger in her eyes. 'All right,' she said. 'Ned, I'll need you to drive me back to the Ottoman. I'll get my car and head out to Tarden and Kuiper's place.' She looked at the drugs again. 'I've got to get back to my car and get my radio.'

Ned turned around. 'I'm going to need you guys to stay here, okay? I'll be back in a minute, but I want you all to go into the house and stay there.'

Audrey nodded. 'Come on boys,' she said, ushering Simon and Pony indoors with her wide black sleeves. 'We've got to get inside.'

There was a look in Audrey's eyes that Simon had not seen before. A fire, perhaps. An impossible spark.

Madaline knew as soon as she walked back in the car. A habit returning she thought she had lost. Reaching to her hip for the cold comfort of her pistol's grip. 'Shit.'

'What?' Ned picked at the pocket of his coat.

'My gun. My fucking bastard gun. I left it in my car at the Ottoman.' She turned around. 'I'm going to drive.' They got in the car and Madaline gunned the engine. 'You're going to want to use that seatbelt, Ned.' She hit the accelerator and Ned's station wagon hared down the driveway. She hooked the steering wheel and they swung out onto the main road.

'Jesus,' said Ned, his arm reaching for the handhold above the passenger door.

'Defensive driving course,' she said as the car rounded a bend and just missed a tree.

'Madaline,' said Ned, 'the resignation letter. I still mean what I said. You shouldn't blame—'

'Forget about it,' she said. 'We just need to get—'

A dark shape veered in front of them. A dark blue new fourwheel-drive shot quickly from a side road, roaring past. The tinted windows gave no clue as to who was inside. Madaline wrenched her head to catch the licence plate, but she already knew. 'That's the Sawyers' car,' she shouted.

Another car sped past, the tell-tale yellow of Tarden's

ute, a rust-streaked trailer rocking behind it. Madaline saw Kuiper's shark-face in momentary profile. 'The fuck?' She noticed both the ute's tray and the trailer were stacked with blue and orange mesh, and inside the mesh were shapes that glinted silver.

'That's the cans,' said Ned, but Madaline was already turning, yanking up the handbrake and wrenching the steering wheel to the right.

'Hold on!' she called. The car slammed itself in a tight circle, tyres screaming. They both shunted roughly to the left and Madaline felt the painful bite of her seatbelt. The car slewed to a precarious tilt before righting itself, fishtailing back onto the road. Madaline floored the accelerator and the car lunged, engine whining before the tyres caught purchase on the bitumen and they hurtled forward.

The cars had made a couple of hundred metres on them but Madaline did her best to keep up. She focused on the dim beacons of the trailer's tail light; tried to coax what she could from the wagon's motor, but she couldn't get them closer. The gearstick felt caught in honey. The engine complained with angry growls. She struck her hand on the steering wheel. 'Come on!'

'This beast isn't used to going much further than the shops,' said Ned.

'Bloody hell.' She should have gone back to get her own car. If she had, she would have lost them anyway. 'Shit.' The tail-lights were gone.

'Where would they be taking the cans?'

Madaline racked her brain. They were heading the wrong way for the highway. Almost as if—

'The wharf,' she said. 'They're taking the drugs offshore.'

They sped through town in silence. It was only as they approached the wharf that Madaline realised they had almost doubled back on themselves. They were near enough to Ned's house to have walked. Madaline slowed the car and cut the lights. 'Hopefully they didn't recognise your car,' she said. 'If we're lucky, they won't think they're being followed. Better safe than sorry, though.' They approached the wharf, where the bluff provided a natural shelter for the large collection of fishing boats. Most of them were tiny things, fishing vessels made of aluminium with canvas strips for roofs. All around were heaped nets, the bright punctuation of buoys; a few were full-sized trawlers, with outriggers that looked like giant feelers. Madaline parked the car a little distance away and unsnapped her seatbelt. 'Ned, you don't have to … I mean, you can drive back into town and get Tommy. I don't need you here with me.' She rubbed her forehead. It was all coming out wrong.

Ned said nothing, just opened his door and stepped out.

Madaline let out a noise of frustration. Was there a time in Ned's life when he didn't want to please everyone? She got out of the car. 'Just stay behind me,' she said. 'Just stay quiet.'

They crept down the slope, picking out Tarden's ute among a handful of other parked cars. The trailer was empty. Kuiper had left the engine running and the headlights shone out over the wharf. Madaline edged up to the car, motioning for Ned to stay where he was. She withdrew her baton, snapping it out with a flick of her wrist. Cringed at the metallic crack it made. She carefully approached the left back passenger window, squinting her eyes at the car, trying to make out any movement inside. It was empty.

She caught movement on the wharf and ducked down behind the car. Peering up, watching through the windscreen, she made out two figures dragging a flatbed trolley. It looked like they were hauling the crab pots down towards the boats. A mist had come up on the water, shrouding them further. She turned back to Ned, beckoning him closer.

'They're down there,' she whispered. 'I can surprise them.'

'We can surprise them.'

'Ned, I'll be fine. You need to get back to the kids.'

'Like hell.'

'Ned—'

'Come on.' He got up and started down the hill.

By the time they reached the wharf Tarden and Kuiper had started loading the pots into a boat, the metal cans clicking and squeaking as they fell together. Madaline and Ned hid behind a heap of fishing nets. Poking her head over, peering through the swirling mist, Madaline could see they had stopped loading the pots in. They stood beside what looked like a bollard, arguing. The darkness ate their words but Madaline could make out their movements. Hands on hips. Angry hand gestures. Kuiper twisted his body around and a dark shape appeared in his hand. The familiar shadow of a gun. Madaline's stomach lurched, her mind racing ahead to dozens of possible scenarios. Her mind flashed back to training: disarmament techniques, siege psychology ... it was too long ago. Her mind had been dulled by paperwork and inaction. Kuiper put the gun back into a holster that stuck out oddly from his hip. Oh, Christ. It was her gun.

The bollard moved and suddenly there were three figures. The third was too small, it couldn't—

'Gin!' Ned sprang up leapt over the netting and sprinted towards for Kuiper; Madaline's lunging hand just grazed his shoulder as he jumped away. She gritted her teeth.

Kuiper swung around, coolly removing Madaline's gun from its holster. 'Easy there, Ned,' he said. Tarden put his arms around Gin to stop him moving.

'Dad!' Gin was in his Superman outfit. His hair was thatched, slept-on.

Ned slowed, but didn't stop. 'Get the hell away from my son!' he shouted, his voice cracking out across the water.

Madaline had never heard him sound like this.

'I don't think we will,' said Kuiper. He flicked off the safety, steadied the gun with his other hand, pointed it at Ned. 'You're going to have to stay right where you are.'

Ned stopped. He clenched his fists.

'I'm going to assume that your friend the police bitch is with you,' said Kuiper. 'And I'm going to ask her to show herself, unless she wants two dead Gale males on her hands.' He giggled.

Madaline rose slowly from behind the netting, carefully stepping around it and out onto the jetty. She took in the scene, assessed the angles. Kuiper was a write-off. 'You don't have to be stupid here,' she said, looking past him, talking directly to Tarden. 'You don't want to throw away the rest of your life.' She focused on Tarden's hands, his grip around Gin's chest. She willed his fingers to loosen.

'Hello, Senior Constable,' said Kuiper. 'I think you're forgetting who has the gun and the hostage here.' His face held a half-grin. 'Thanks awfully for that, by the way. I'll need the baton, too. In fact, give me that whole belt. Shame not to collect the whole set.'

Madaline slipped her baton back into her belt, unbuckled it and lowered it to the ground. 'Where's Tommy?'

Kuiper laughed. 'Probably asleep at home. Left me outside the pub. What a trusting gentleman. Slide that belt over.'

Madaline kicked the belt across the jetty. The one thing she needed Tommy to do for her the fat bastard had shirked out of. She had to put him out of her head. 'You okay, Gin?' she shouted. 'Are you hurt?'

Gin shook his head. His eyes were huge with fear.

Kuiper picked up Madaline's belt. 'Shut the fuck up. Not our fault if the boy's wandering around the wharf in the middle of the night. Can't say that's good parenting, hey Jack?'

Tarden said nothing.

'I was looking for her,' said Gin. 'I was Superman. I went looking for her.'

'It'll be okay, Gin,' said Ned. His voice had lost its strength.

Madaline stepped slowly over to Ned. 'What are you trying to achieve here, Kuiper?' she said. 'The evidence in that storage shed of yours'll already put you both away for what, five years? Eight? This is just off the top of my head.' She was pleased to see the confusion that momentarily crossed Kuiper's face. 'Backup's on the way,' she went on. 'Give up now, score yourself some points. Or you could wait until this place is swarming with cops.'

Kuiper barked another laugh. 'Backup?' He turned to Tarden, keeping the gun pointed at Ned. 'Hear that?' he said. 'There's backup coming. Would that be your boss, snoring on the couch? Give me some credit.'

'Believe what you want,' said Madaline, 'but they won't want to negotiate. We can resolve this first.'

Kuiper backed away, and Madaline knew. She had taken the wrong tack. Kuiper moved towards Tarden and lowered the gun until it was pointing at Gin's head. 'I appreciate the effort,' he said. 'Highly entertaining, but it's probably time we stopped fucking around.' He pressed the gun into Gin's temple. Gin started to cry, and Tarden tightened his grip around the boy. 'The way I see it,' said Kuiper, 'the only way this is going to resolve is for you three to disappear. How many bullets in here Madaline? We got enough?'

'Touch him and you're dead,' said Ned.

Kuiper laughed.

'You'll make us disappear?' said Madaline. 'Just like you made Bill and Louise Sawyer disappear?'

Kuiper cocked his head. 'Detective work, is it?' he said. 'Lovely. But I'm afraid we didn't touch them.'

Madaline's body shivered with exhaustion. 'If you're going to kill us, you can at least be straight with us.'

Gin's voice: 'I don't want them to kill—' Tarden put his hand over the boy's mouth.

'I'm not saying I wouldn't have liked to do away with them,' said Kuiper. 'Amount of trouble they've fucking caused. But I've never even met the damn people.'

'Why do you have their car, then?'

296

Kuiper cleared his throat. 'A souvenir,' he said. 'Couldn't resist. Nice car like that?'

'So you admit you were at the lake?'

'Jesus. Shall I remind you again who has the gun? I told you I've never even met them. Jack saw them last. Maybe you should interrogate him?'

Madaline was positive she saw doubt in Tarden's eyes.

'So I'll ask you again,' said Kuiper. 'How many bullets?'

Madaline turned to Tarden. Her final throw of the dice. 'There doesn't have to be any more trouble,' she said. 'You know what's right and wrong Jack, I'm sure of it. You can't let him ruin your life. Let him get the help he needs.'

Kuiper let his head fall back. 'For fuck's sake!' he shouted. 'Can't answer one simple question! Can't even count a couple of bullets! I guess I'll have to find out for myself.' He shoved the gun back into Gin's head. Gin whimpered and shut his eyes. 'You all had your chance to keep things quiet.' Kuiper's arm trembled. He took a deep breath and his finger moved on the trigger.

A bright flash ambushed Madaline's senses, freezing a scene before her eyes. She saw Kuiper, lit for an instant in a crisp, perfect portrait. In the next moment his shadow grew out, not around him but somehow through him, enveloping his body in a monstrous dark mass. She heard Ned cry out, saw him running towards the men who had his son. Madaline sprinted forward, knocking Ned aside from harm's way, her instincts taking over. She saw the gun and went for it, felt a weight hit her and went to strike back but connected only with air as the heat began in her knee and she knew she'd been shot, the sound following the thought. She

297

saw Gin in her periphery and grabbed for him, driving her shoulder to into the ground to protect his body. She felt a deadweight hit her: another body landing on her and slamming her into the wooden boards, her vision jagging sideways in time to see Kuiper's face next to hers. She saw the zigzag cartilage of his nose. His eyes had rolled up, leaving red webs of blood. When she looked down, she saw his shirt soaked with the dark stain of blood.

She tried to get up from under the weight of Kuiper's body, but a piercing pain shot through her shoulder and exploded in her skull. She cried out and collapsed back down to quell the pain. Her knee was molten hot. It was then she noticed Tarden standing above them. He was holding the gun out in front of him. His eyes were completely blank, his head moving slowly from side to side. Madaline tried to call out to him but could make no sound.

Ned's voice came; close by. 'Jack, it's over.'

Tarden just shook his head.

'Jack,' Ned repeated. 'Just put the gun down. Gin's okay, and—'

Tarden turned the gun around and slipped his thumb over the trigger. Madaline squeezed her eyes shut as the shot rang out.

It was slower, this time, the flash of white more like a wave, the sound more like a sail's snap, the feeling more like the heat of the sun as you passed between two shadows.

When Madaline opened her eyes, all she saw were the stars, perfect white dots against the winter sky. She wondered for a moment at the patterns people saw in them. Faith, she thought, and meaning, drawn from such heavenly but ordinary things, whose existence had long since passed, whose light was only ever a reminder of the impermanence of everything.

Simon had not been in a hospital since his fall, all that time ago. He was too young then to remember much except the room he lived in for two weeks while his broken legs set. There was a tree just outside his window that scratched when the wind picked up. A nice nurse who brought him in a pack of cards. He remembered the colour of the band they made him wear on his wrist. He remembered the light, too, he realised now. Even here—a different hospital in a different state—the light was the same sickly yellow white that felt like it stuck to you.

It was morning now, early, the sun nothing but a suggestion below the horizon. The emergency waiting room was in the heart of the hospital, in an alcove where four paths met. It was painfully cold. One of the nurses had given Simon a blanket, and he shared it with Audrey, who was asleep in the chair next to him. She tucked the blanket to her chin, holding it there with two bare arms. With no coat to cover her, Simon saw long sleek lines of scar tissue hatched into Audrey's wrists. He tried not to look, but he had to. He wanted to wake her up, to tell her it was okay. He wanted to tell her that he had scars too.

Audrey had wanted to stay with Gin, but they had to wait for Ned to say it was okay. They hadn't seen Gin, Ned or Madaline since they got to the hospital, but people kept saying they were fine. The doctor told them that Gin was okay, that nothing bad had happened to him. Ned had hurt his ribs, they said, and they had to keep an eye on him because of the concussion. Something had happened to Madaline, something that meant she was having an operation. Tarden was in another part of the hospital, and no one would tell them anything about him. The doctor hadn't even heard of Kuiper.

Simon saw his grandmother coming down the hall from reception. She looked, now, more like Simon had remembered her. No makeup, her hair pulled back to a loose ponytail. Dressed in a jumper and light brown trousers, plain sandals on her feet. She walked with short deliberate steps. She had a bunch of flowers in her hand, held out in front of her like a firecracker. Simon wondered where she got flowers so early in the day. They were bright and loud, great rainbow tassels, like hats and gloves and shoved into wrapping. The cellophane hissed as she walked, past the other people in the waiting room: a young couple asleep with an empty pram beside them; an old man with a suitcase, his head in his hands.

'Simon,' she whispered. 'Everything okay?'

'Fine,' he whispered back. 'Did you find anything to drink?'

She shook her head. She held out the flowers. 'I want to take these up to Jack. Will you be all right here?'

'Why do you want to see him?'

'I just do.'

'Will they let you? We don't even know what's wrong with him.'

She shrugged. 'I'm going to see.'

She shot a glance at the policeman by the nurse's station. He was a big guy, middle-aged, his grey hair buzzed short. He held his hands awkwardly behind his

301

back and seemed to have trouble deciding which leg to stand on.

Simon liked the other policeman better, the one he gave his statement to a few hours ago. They'd done it at Tommy's house, although Tommy wasn't there. In a proper office, with a proper police notebook, using a proper tape recorder. The other policeman told him that Tommy would be 'taking a break'.

It was his grandma who had called the police—the proper police. After Madaline and Ned left in Ned's car, Simon knew he had to tell her what was going on. It seemed like—after he told her—that she'd lost her breath. She kept asking him to repeat himself, as if she sort of believed him, but couldn't quite. Then her face seemed to get longer, and she made the phone call. Whilethey waited, she showed Simon her photo album. Pictures of him as a baby, and pictures of his mum growing up, then with a young guy without a beard who was his dad. His Grandpa Karl took most of the photos, but now and again he'd appear in front of the camera. His grandma had told Simon that he looked like Karl, but he couldn't see it. He thought about the pictures his parents took, their portraits for the calendar every year. He wondered if there would still be a calendar to make.

'Can I go and look for something to drink?' said Simon. He thought he'd seen a vending machine in the hall.

'Maybe soon,' said Iris. Her eyes looked glassy. 'Just stay here a moment.' She walked over to the policeman by the nurse's station and started talking to him.

Simon couldn't hear what she was saying. All he heard was the cellophane rustling from the flowers in her hand. She and the police man talked for what seemed like five

302

minutes. His grandma's hand movement got bigger and bigger the more they talked. Eventually, the policeman bent down his head. He put his hand on Iris's shoulder.

Simon thought his grandmother's body seemed to change. Her shoulders dropped, her arms fell to her sides. It was as if the whole shape of her had deflated. The policeman stroked her shoulder, shifted his weight again. His grandmother sniffed. Her legs began to shake.

When she finally turned her head to look at Simon, her eyes were the colour of a slow, sad ocean.

Simon stepped back out of the glare that struck off the surface of Magpie Lake, returning to the shade afforded by one of three giant marquees set up below the carpark. The scene before him was hard to believe. Three police vans parked beside the marquees, teams of searchers in orange and white jumpsuits combing the landscape. A police boat out in the lake, the black heads of divers dotting the water around it.

Audrey came over to him with a can of Coke. She handed it to him. The police had even brought food and drink for the searchers: there was a fridge on a trailer with a loud motor keeping it cool.

Simon took the can. 'Thanks.'

Audrey had on her mother's tweed coat, but she'd cut the arms and hem so she more or less fitted it.

'Look, they're using gridlines,' said Simon. He pointed at a screen to their left. A large map of the lake was pinned to a corkboard. It was a satellite picture, turning the lake into opal blue. Thick yellow lines hatched through it, dividing the map into equal squares.

'I always thought of battleships,' said Audrey. 'Trying to sink each other.'

They heard a sloshing sound and turned to see four men in fishing overalls hauling in a net at the shore. They dragged it onto a line of yellow tarpaulins and upturned their catch. A fresh loadof carcasses spread out, tumbling off each other.

'More of them,' said Simon.

Audrey scrunched up her face. The stink wafted over them. 'How many are there?'

Simon shrugged. This was Jack Tarden's legacy to the town. Magpie Lake was a graveyard for his mistakes. Simon couldn't imagine how many times he had travelled out here to dump his catches. Or why he'd done it. He was gone now so they would never know. His life had slipped away in the hospital room with two policemen guarding his door.

Kuiper never got to the hospital at all; not the bit for people who were still alive, anyway.

'What do they do with all the bodies?' said Audrey.

'What? Oh, the crabs. I don't know.'

'Think about all their families,' she said. 'All those crabs and yabbies. All the babies that won't be born.'

Simon pictured a funeral for all the creatures. It would be pretty strange. Maybe the news crews waiting up on the road, behind the police cordon, would want to cover it. Those vans with satellite dishes perched on their roofs. He'd seen them camped outside Tarden and Kuiper's shed, too, filming and snapping photographs as dozens of police officers filed in and out.

'Anyway,' said Audrey. 'We'll keep waiting. Do you want anything else?'

Simon shook his head and she touched his hand. She was about to say something, but decided not to. She walked off, back to where Gin was waiting patiently for her to play her hand in some complicated card game. Gin clearly hadn't enjoyed his first taste of real adventure.

Today he had abandoned his superhero costumes and instead wore a T-shirt and shorts. He'd kept on his gumboots, the same ones he'd had on when Simon first saw him, that morning at the Ottoman.

Simon peered over at the next marquee along. A score of police officers in reflective vests stood in a semi-circle around Madaline, who was pointing to a poster on another corkboard. She had on her full uniform, one trouser leg cut open to accommodate an impressive cast, her arm in a sling. She'd come out of hospital to take charge of the search, although Simon could see that the leg still hurt her when she put weight on it. As Madaline said her piece and the other officers nodded, Ned appeared with a tray full of steaming coffee cups. He handed Madaline a drink and said something, smiling through the dark plum bruise that covered one side of his face.

Simon wished Pony was here. He wanted to be alone, he wanted to watch the search by himself, but really he wanted Pony next to him. Without Pony, nothing might have happened. Away at the far shore Simon saw his grandmother. She had asked to join the search. She looked strange in the orange jumpsuit though. Simon wondered again why she had been so upset by the news of Jack Tarden's death.

Simon finished his drink and put the can down on the ground next to him. He looked out past the tarpaulins, to the place where he and Audrey had thrown the rocks. The sky was like a grey sheet hung between the trees. The sun had probably just tipped over its highest point, hidden as it was behind cloud. His sadness, his grief pressed into its permanent place, a thick thatch in the air, a warm compress over his heart.

The sound of whistles cut through the air. Simon couldn't tell where it came from, but he saw people go still, the searchers stopping where they were and looking towards the head of the lake. He heard a buzz pass through the marquee. Simon felt it too, a shiver of excitement and dread. He wanted to run out to see what was happening but he couldn't. His feet were stuck. It was the same feeling he got in dreams, when he knew he was in a dream, and knew knew that if he put one foot wrong everything would disappear.

He closed his eyes and stayed where he was for a long time. At last he heard a walkie-talkie hissing beside him. He turned to see the policeman, the same one from the hospital, with the short grey hair and a giant's unsure steps.

'Simon?' the policeman said.

Simon nodded. He searched the man's face for clues, trying to guess what he was about to say.

The policeman's eyes kept straying to the water, flicking sideways as if tugged by an invisible line.

Simon saw the police boat, lying still near a point along the left side of the lake. The heads of divers left a short black trail to the shore. A join-the-dots.

'Simon,' said the policeman at last, 'I'm very sorry—' He reached out a hand, and Simon saw that it was shaking. 'It's your parents, Simon,' he said. 'Your mum and dad.'

By the afternoon, the sun had swung around behind the grandstand, pulsing strips of light through the wooden seats. The warmth of late-day softened the harshness of the corners and the edges, lent a certain elegance to the shapes the concrete took. Simon couldn't see Pony anywhere. He had hoped he'd find him lying in the grandstand, sleeping perhaps under his felt hat. Or doing a safety test on the seats, pulling on a rope, weighing stones in his hand, peeling band-aids apart, letting the plastic strips flutter to the ground.

Simon wandered past the ticket booth, peering inside. Still nothing there but glittering pieces of glass. Monster's eyes in their artificial darkness. The pool cover there, too, still unmoved from when he'd seen it last. As he got closer, he noticed a new shape at the far end of the pool. Pony was in the deep end, sitting on a chair he'd dragged in from God knows where. He had pulled it up to the broken card table, now fixed with gaffer tape and string so it stood up by itself. He rested his elbows on it carefully, hands bunched under his chin.

Simon called his name and Pony looked up.

'Simon,' he said. 'Simon Sawyer. I was just thinking.'

'Okay.'

'What's that?'

'What?'

'That bag.'

Simon had been carrying it with him all day—he hadn't put it down since it was given to him—and almost forgot he had it. 'It's a camera,' he said. 'It's my parents' camera.'

'Oh,' said Pony. 'Right. Well.'

'I hadn't seen you in a while, Pony. I was worried something had happened.'

'Happened? No, I'm fine. Not going anywhere, me. Do you want to sit down here too?'

'Okay.' Simon climbed down into the pool. The handles on the ladder were rough with rust, but his feet found easy purchase on the rungs. It felt kind of good to walk on the bottom of an empty pool. It was something not many people got to do, he supposed. Little segments of the surface view disappeared the further down he walked until all he could see was the top tiers of the grandstand, the tips of trees and the sky. The sun receded too, the temperature dropping as the pool fell into shadow. Simon hadn't noticed it before, but a set of tiles ran in a thin stripe around the inner edge of the pool. They were covered in an intricate design, a complicated pattern of deep blue and ivory that reminded Simon of the surface of rippling water.

Pony saw him looking. 'Byzantine,' he said.

'What?'

'Byzantine. That's the design of the tiles. They're amazing, aren't they. That colour is Byzantine blue. I want to find more tiles like that, and cover the walls completely.' He got up and ran both arms through the air with his imaginary tiles. 'Here,' he said, pulling out the chair. 'Try the seat.'

Simon put the camera bag on the table and sat down.

309

He pictured the whole pool covered in the tiles. He imagined them lit by rows of soft blue lights, the feeling of being inside all that colour. Enjoying a meal. It would feel like eating underwater.

Pony stood beside Simon. 'Why are you carrying that camera?' He zipped open the bag and peered inside.

'There's pictures of us there. Together. I'll show you.' Simon took the camera out and turned it on. It was surprisingly small, covered in buttons and switches.

He found the pictures he wanted. In the first photo, Simon and his mother were sitting at a wooden picnic bench. She had her arm around him, squashing him into her shoulder. He was making a face. It was the place they'd stopped for morning tea. The next photo was Simon and his dad, standing by the car, ready to set off again. Simon's dad had his hands on his hips, one leg on the car's running board, like a noble explorer. Simon copied him, aping his pose, smiling. All three of them in the next picture; Simon's dad had asked a stranger to take their photograph. His parents each had an arm around Simon's shoulders. Simon remembered the weight of their arms.

'Where's that?' said Pony, leaning over the chair.

'On the drive down.'

'Never understood why people take so many photos,' Pony straightened up, hands in his back like an old man. 'People spend too much time trying to remember what was fun and ?don't have any fun.'

There was silence for a minute.

'What was it like?' Simon said eventually.

'What was what like?'

'Losing your parents. To know that they were gone. Does it stay ... I mean—'

Pony shrugged. 'I guess. It gets less bad I suppose, with time. But it never really goes away. There's always—' He tapped his fingers against his chin, at the place where acne ended its journey along his jaw. 'Something, though,' he laid his hand across the middle of his chest. 'You start to think it never actually happened.'

Simon thought about it. It made no difference really. Pony had landed here, that was all. They both had.

'It's weird,' Pony went on, 'you start to think I could hug Mum with these arms. You think I could reach up, easily, and find Dad's hand.' He shut his eyes, rubbed them with his fingers. 'Are you going to stay?'

'Maybe,' said Simon. 'Depends.'

'Yeah, well. Won't be the same without you here.'

Simon smiled, and wiped his hand across his nose.

'You know what's great?' Pony stretched his arms.

'What?'

Pony sat down on the bottom of the pool. 'This.'

'What?'

'You lie down here.'

'Then what?'

'Jeez. You watch the stars come out, idiot.'

'Really?'

'Yeah. There's nothing else like it.' Pony lay down on the pool's floor, his head towards the ladder, his feet pointing to the deep end.

After a moment, Simon lay down next to him.

For those minutes, as the sky darkened, as they waited for the stars to show through, Simon pretended that there was no world outside the pool's walls, that all that existed was the sky. He closed his eyes and in his mind brought a beach to life. In the distance, he saw two figures walking,

311

side by side, hand in hand, the day's dying light falling across their shoulders. He let them walk on for as long as they wanted. Because he knew even in winter the horizon shimmered, made mirages from ordinary things, made the world only real for as far as you could see it.

SCOTTISH BORDERS COUNCIL
LIBRARY &
INFORMATION SERVICES